The Vale of Mysteries

The Vale of Mysteries

Energematrice6

THE EPIMYTH - BOOK 2

JARED N. MICHAUD

The Vale of Mysteries

Energematrice6—The Epimyth, Book 2

ISBN: 978-1-965598-12-2 ebook
ISBN: 978-1-965598-11-5 paperback
ISBN: 978-1-965598-14-6 audiobook

Cover Art
Sarah Michaud Illustration and Design
sarahlynnmichaud.wixsite.com/my-site

Interior Design
Jared N. Michaud
jarednmichaud.com

Other Works
by Jared N. Michaud

Energematrice6
Brightstar
From the Void
The Vale of Mysteries

Mythologia
Winternight
Il Alka E'Talania (Forthcoming)

Free Ebooks!
(And Value4Value)

The entire Energematrice6 library is available for free in ebook form at https://www.e6universe.com.

I offer this to you primarily because as a young person I wasn't able to afford to buy books, and was limited to what I could find at the library or, as I grew into my teens, online.

Please take advantage of it! Read everything!

If you enjoy my writing, I would appreciate it if you can return some value to me by buying something (like a physical book) to say "thank you" when you're able.

I hope you enjoy the Energematrice6 Universe!

For Christ, who will always be my hero.

Acknowledgments

This book is a sort of literary chimera. It was originally written as the second half of Brightstar (a fact that some of my beta readers still grumble over). In the end, I think both halves have come out of the ordeal better for it, and I hope to incorporate what I learned in this process into future works.

Despite my beta readers' unhappiness, in hindsight I find myself fairly sanguine about the whole thing. It does put me in a strange place when it comes to the acknowledgments, because it was actually edited and beta read twice over (...and, okay, that part of things I'd rather not do again). That said, I'm in the position now to thank some people twice for the same job, which, yes, makes me doubly grateful.

In addition, I know there are those to whom I owe thanks who haven't been named herein. I appreciate everyone who helped with this process in even the smallest way. If you're one of those I've forgotten, thank you.

To Mary—Thank you for the bad days and the hard days. I value the ones with the highest cost by far the most. Thank you for sixteen years, seven kids and innumerable troubles. You are the only one I've ever chosen.

Greg—My friend and alpha reader. You told me God put it on your heart to be a part of this project, and I wouldn't have gotten this far without you. Thank you.

My beta-reader-in-chief, Nick—I'll avoid asking you to re-read in future, but you STILL managed to catch a critical flaw on your second go-round. Also, I do agree: the ending to Vale of Mysteries is better than Brightstar's. Thank you.

My lore collector, Multaan—You always look at things so differently from me. It's both an education and a joy to see my work through your eyes. Thank you.

Luke—You're picky, you know that? It's really helpful, even when I grumble about it as I'm reading your comments. Love ya, brother. Thanks for staying up wayyyy too late for me.

Natalie—You made a great gamma reader. You make an even better beta reader. I treasure your contributions that have become a part of my world. Thank you.

Uncle Greg—Your original contributions to my manuscript are still paying dividends today. Nobody else caught what you did, and this book is still more readable because of it. Thank you.

My parents—I'm never quite sure how clearly you see what I'm trying to do, but I've never doubted that you're behind me in it. Thank you.

My original beta readers, in no particular order—Zack, Luke, Kymberly, Adam, Justin, Aunt Susan, and Uncle Bob. Thank you. I hope the second half is worth the wait!

My cover artist, Sarah—I keep asking and you keep delivering. Not only that, somehow you keep outdoing yourself. Thank you, Sarah. You are a gem!

My editor, Tim McKay—Working with you is actually fun. I take a surprising amount of pleasure in saying, over and over again, "Nope. He's right." You made the story flow at least twice as well as before. You're a good editor and a good friend.

Finally, as ever, to the father of the heavenly lights, to whom I trust my everything. I AM the little drummer boy. Thank you.

The vessel called "Hope" hung in the void. Once, she had been Earth's greatest achievement, created during the most difficult time in man's history to carry a few thousand brave souls to the stars. She was conceived as a modern-day Ark—built to save humanity from a world consumed by a deluge of madness.

Her builders were the most accomplished geniuses of their generation, men driven to their absolute best by a world bent on their destruction. Their sole aim was the salvation of those they loved. They invented completely new scientific disciplines in their pursuit, and did it all in complete secrecy.

All the while, their opponent, the most powerful tyrant in the history of their world, hunted them relentlessly with the most advanced tools his age had to offer. Hope's construction concluded with the most desperate first-flight in the history of astronautics, proving once and for all her inventors' competence and dedication. She escaped, the sole survivor of their small fleet.

That battle had left its marks upon her hull, but by the Lightmaker's grace she prevailed, carrying her precious cargo to a new home in what they thought was an entirely different universe from their own.

The ages since had passed with an unrelenting, metronome pace, while Hope languished. The light of the remote sun around which she orbited shone with unwavering brilliance upon the impossible dust cloud that protected the entire star system. Three thousand years had come and gone as her creators would have reckoned it. Still she circled, all-but-forgotten, through the least frequented solar system in her new galaxy.

In the time that followed the Escape, Hope's name once again gained new meaning, even as she aged into senescence, for she had become home to the Guardian of the Remnant, the universe's most powerful Energematrist. Hope was the guardian's sanctum, and when he disappeared, he left within her objects so powerful the galaxy would have braved even the Vale of Mysteries that protected her to gain them, had they known.

They had not known, however, and the departed master's gift remained undisturbed...as did Hope's other passenger—the passenger that even the master had not understood, when he found it. He had been far too powerful then, too well-disciplined, for it to show its true nature. He, after all, might have found a way to destroy it, or hide it away forever, so it had remained quiescent, waiting.

If Hope had truly been as alive and intelligent as her once-passengers fondly imagined, she might have felt the darkness at her heart, but she didn't. Heedless of the passage of time, she carried her cargo through the void, waiting for the one called Brightstar.

Prologue

It felt like being stuck in sucking mud inside his own mind. Every time he tried to shift his attention, to pull free, he was wrenched back into dull blankness. He swam in a lake of soft, heavy darkness—drowning in it, and he couldn't get his head above water no matter how hard he tried. He fought it as best he could, pulling himself toward clarity over and over as the weight of his own consciousness sucked him back. It took hours, he thought, or maybe it was days...or only seconds. Whatever the vision's timescale might have been, his mind slowly, ever so slowly, began to clear.

Even from the beginning, he knew somehow that he wasn't awake. It was like a dream that wouldn't release him, but at the same time it was too real. He was thinking clearly enough to know he wasn't awake. That was something.

It had taken what felt like an age for him to remember his name. Or that he had a name. It was still dreamlike enough that the next thought came very slowly.

He was Nate, but where was he? Why was he here?

The darkness pressed in upon him, and at first he was afraid. He knew somehow, instinctively, that pain was waiting for him. At first he shied away. Hadn't he had enough pain? But his resolve strengthened. This wouldn't be like before. He could barely remember what before was, but he would not run away. Never again.

He focused, pushed himself forward. After a time, when he focused as hard as he could, he saw something. The view came in pulses, and there was blinding pain with each wave. If he could have gritted his teeth he would have, but this dream wouldn't allow it.

Through the pain, he saw a boy, beating his head relentlessly against a wall, hands clenched over his ears. Each smack of the boy's head assaulted Nate with a new wave of pain. The familiarity of the scene was eerie. He didn't know what it meant, but he should. He should KNOW. The feeling was so deep that he couldn't doubt or question. It left him with a sinking sensation in the pit of his stomach, and in that moment he didn't know why.

As he watched, bewildered, the boy stopped hammering his head against the wall and looked up, eyes pleading. Those eyes were familiar. Who was this poor, wretched boy? What was he doing here?

Then he remembered, and the sick feeling in the pit of his belly blossomed into full life. He remembered who he was, and seeing himself from the outside, he felt pity. Not self-pity, exactly, but the pity he would have felt for another in his own place. He was truly a wretched human being.

He reached out to offer succor. Anything had to be better than this. As he reached, what he saw was almost like a reflection on water. The boy's arm came up, reaching out toward him. It was like looking at himself.

Then it dawned on him. There was no one there but him.

It was then the duality of his current state cleared and he remembered what it was like to sit on the floor, rocking, unable to focus, thoughts jumbled. He found himself weeping helplessly, hopelessly. There was nothing but tragedy here. He was seeing himself as others must, and it was unbearable. What was a wreck like him good for? There was no question that it was his own memory, but now that he remembered he wished he hadn't.

The pain and despair almost drove him away again, into the darkness.

Almost.

In that, his moment of greatest despair, he was buoyed up by a strength greater than his own. It was peace and certainty, and as the boy before him—the vision of himself—came clearer, Nate did not shrink from it. Then he saw something new. He was on a beach, and there were footprints in the sand. The footprints led away, far away into the distance, and for the first time he felt a stirring of hope. Those footprints marked the path he must follow, and so he rose and stepped out into a new world.

Part 1:
Sanctuary

Interval

Elder Neil Eden, Journal Entry, 6-4-1033 NST

I am not an evil man.

...Am I?

I don't know who Rebus is getting his instructions from. He won't tell me.

At first, I would never have thought an elder of Sanctuary capable of what he's doing, and now I'm in too deep to back out.

If only I'd seen this coming before I took his credits. In my defense, I was going to vote yes on his motion even without the bribe. It just made life easier. My father would be ashamed. Grandad would space me.

...If the others ever find out, our reputation will never recover. We might as well be Raddinks.

Of course, I might have gotten free of him if I had the sense to confess to the rest of the council... before the second time.

Voids. Right out the airlock. And I'd deserve it, too.

I don't know what he's going to do to this boy, the one they call Brightstar, but I saw the look in his eye. Whatever he does, I want no part of it. None.

I'd run, I think, if not for the Vale. Who would ever have thought I could look at our great protection as a curse?

Chapter 1

"Hah. You could be wandering around in that soup until the
heat death of the universe...or until you die,
whichever comes first. Suppose that has to happen
someday even to a freak like you."

**- Trevor Gorman to Siver Radding,
Attributed before Radding
pierced the Vale of Mysteries Year 653 NST**

The gyrating mass of interstellar dust and gas was beautiful in an otherworldly sort of way. The cloud's dim, ruddy color made the slow swirling of the surface seem like a mirage. The murky, billowing nebula was so vast that it should have taken millennia for the surface of the cloud to move at all. Still, as they watched, the surface seemed to shift ever so slightly, and the whorls and wisps that made up its texture were subtly different. It was mesmerizing in a subtle way, and Nate, called Brightstar, found himself lost in its patterns, wondering what caused them. He contemplated the cloud calmly, studying the dimly visible stars toward the edge of the mass and the deeper darkness directly in front of Adamant, the tiny vessel in which Nate was a passenger.

Tyler "Tye" Wrighten stuck his head through the bridge hatchway, breaking Nate's reverie with an awed question. "What's THAT?"

From his seat across the bridge, Keevan Raddink chuckled merrily. "It's the Vale of Mysteries, o'course."

Tye snorted, giving Keevan an irritated look. "I thought you said it was like a rainbow."

Keevan groaned. "That's Sanctuary. Inside!"

Shannon Logan, one of the three siblings to whom Adamant belonged and their current pilot, cleared her throat noisily, interrupting the byplay. "We still don't have a way in. Unless you've thought of something new?" She eyed Keevan balefully, as if they were stuck there, staring at the incomprehensibly-large, impossibly-dense mass of dust and gas, because of something he was holding back.

Keevan raised his hands to fend off her scowl. "I told yeh, we haf'ta find the Keeper fer that. Unless you wanna warp straight into a gravity well. I did warn yeh didn' I?"

He *had* warned them. Nate could still picture Keevan's dubious frown when Nate told the little group where he wanted to go. Keevan had been the only member of their party who actually knew how to reach the Vale of Mysteries, having been born in the hidden star system at its core, but as he told Nate, getting through the Vale was impossible without Teron Galton, the Keeper of the Mysteries.

Nate had met the Keeper briefly a month before, shortly after he first appeared in the Aurora Galaxy. The Keeper had imprinted Nate with the Great Schemic to guide his use of Energematrice6 and gave him the Sigil of the Mysteries, a powerful Energematrice6 artifact laid aside for Nate by Paul Casisia nearly a thousand years before. The Keeper was practically family to Jon and Rachel Casisia, Nate's first friends in the Aurora galaxy, who had accompanied the Keeper back to the Vale of Mysteries while Nate went with Drake Loriden to the Telestry. Unfortunately, the only way Keevan knew to contact the Keeper was through agents in star systems near the Vale. It could be months before he responded.

They would still have been in Casisia City arguing about what to do, except that their pre-departure argument had been cut short by Shawna Logan insisting, with a haunted look in her eye, that it was time to go.

As her brother Andrew explained after ordering everyone to strap in, "When Shawna gets one of her feelings and we ignore it, somebody dies." Keevan rapidly provided confirmation by means of a terse report from one of his contacts. Dominion 'guests' were expected at the Telestry in short order.

Adamant left immediately, without even taking time to sell the bulk of the salvage they'd gathered from Resolute, Adamant's sister ship. Dubiously, Keevan had pointed them in the direction of the Vale of Mysteries with repeated warnings that it was "completely impenetrable." That left them, a day later, staring at the massive, impossibly-dense nebula, arguing among themselves once again.

After they activated Adamant's Retton drive and the inertial sump's gravity stabilized, allowing them to walk around, Tye and Keevan both expressed their relief that the ship actually had artificial gravity, which drew a snort from Shannon along with a sardonic, "Oh you think we're savages?"

Her terse instruction to go sleep while they traveled evoked a shocked stare from Tye along with Keevan's assurance that it would take at least a week to reach their destination and it might give them a chance to figure out how to get in. Shannon had laughed at them, claiming the trip would take a maximum of fifteen hours if she didn't cut through the edge of the Abyss.

Now, with the cloud before them, Keevan returned Shannon's stinkeye with an annoyed look of his own.

A tense moment passed before Shannon sighed peevishly, "I'm going to sleep. Shawna, you take the helm." She shot another glance at Keevan and grumbled, "If you figure anything out, you can wake me. Whatever you do, don't go in without me."

As she rose to leave, Nate held up a hand to stop her, frowning thoughtfully at the dark cloud while his other hand absentmindedly fingered the Sigil of the Mysteries hanging around his neck. "...I think maybe we *should* go in there." He turned to Shawna, who had settled into her own control station. "How far in could we get and still get back out again safely?"

Shawna shrugged and was about to respond when Keevan shook his head, almost angrily this time, "Yeh can't do that. It's impossible ta navigate. They say it shouldn't even exist. The whole abyssal Vale defies the laws of physics. The dust's so thick sensors can't see more than a light minute, except in spots next'ta stars where it's cleared out. Our eyes'll only show us maybe a unit or so."

Shawna was frowning and she shook her head slowly. "That's more than thirty light years across. How do we navigate? How do we even tell where the stars ARE in there?"

Keevan turned to her in obvious relief. "Yeh don't. Or not normally. Fer us..." He shrugged. "It's like a great big dust cloud with gravity balls all over it that'll kill us all if we get too close to 'em. Findin' anythin' inside is practically impossible. Yeh can't orient. The Vale was made to stop anybody gettin' in. Only The Keeper knows how'ta do it. Either we get his help or we point in the right direction and hope real hard...then probably die anyway." He shook his head and glanced dubiously over at Nate, "Unless Nate has any bright ideas?"

Nate didn't respond immediately, frowning at the Vale and continuing to stroke the Sigil absently.

Eventually, Laura Gilvers asked, "How far in *could* we go without getting lost? If we knew the coordinates of our destination, could we just point in the right direction and go straight there?" In the two days since they had rescued her from Adamant's sister ship, Resolute, Laura had recovered remarkably. Her cheeks no longer looked sunken, her skin had regained a healthy shade of pink, and her voice was strong. The only obvious sign of her nearly month-long imprisonment was her unwillingness to be alone, even while she slept. She had been bunking in Shannon's cabin thus far and showed no desire to speak of what happened aboard Resolute before they found her.

None of them could blame her, and they all saw the tension around her eyes when she thought no one noticed. That tension relaxed when she looked at Nate, presumably because he had faced and destroyed the Changed that held her captive and murdered her family. Killing a Changed was a rare feat, but no one had ever banished the shade that controlled one before; Nate had.

Keevan shook his head in response to her question, tossing his Universal Positioning Tool back and forth from one hand to the other. "It all moves. Can't tell yeh why or how, but yeh can't just aim for Sanctuary and go straight in. Space isn't...flat in there."

Andrew looked at Nate levelly. "Brightstar, are you sure you want to do this?"

Nate returned his gaze and nodded slowly. "I think we have to."

Andrew nodded back. "You haven't steered us wrong yet. Go ahead, Shawna."

Nate shot Andrew a wry look, but he didn't countermand the order. When they passed into the edge of the great cloud, space behind them lit up in a brilliant reddish hue, fracturing into a rainbow of color around every light source.

Tye grinned. "Well, it's scenic, isn't it?"

After ten minutes had passed, Shawna turned to Nate worriedly. "You have to tell me what you want me to do now. If we go any further, I have no way of navigating at all. Keevan's right. Everything's moving around. I can hardly tell which way we came from."

They all stared ahead in silence at the featureless brown mass of dust for another long minute. Then Nate laughed aloud. When everyone turned to stare at him, he shook his head, still chuckling. After a moment, he reached inside his shirt and pulled out the Sigil of the Mysteries. Then, with the chain still around his neck, he released the sigil. Instead of falling straight down toward the floor, it "fell" straight toward the window in front of them, bouncing slightly as the fine chain went taut.

Nate turned back to Shawna and raised an eyebrow. "The Keeper answered the question for us, it looks like. It's a bit unconventional. I don't have much doubt where it's pointing, though. Think you can follow it?"

Shawna smiled and shook her head. "Dead reckoning would be better than THAT. At least I can guess at a heading maybe."

Nate nodded thoughtfully and opened his mouth to speak, but Shannon was staring at the Sigil, and she asked, "Can you make it send out a beam of light? Right out of the tip?"

Nate glanced over at her and smiled at the sparkle of excitement in her eyes. "I think so." He concentrated and almost at once a brilliant, hand-size patch of glare sprang into being on the main window where the pendant was pointing.

"Ha." Shannon jumped up from the seat she'd been in at the back of the bridge and hurried to her console. A moment later she looked at Nate and asked, "Can you make the beam any smaller?"

"How small would you like?" He raised his eyebrow, still smiling.

"However small you can manage without losing intensity." She didn't look up from her console.

As he concentrated and shrank the bright spot from the size of his palm to something almost as small as the head of a pin, the brightness actually increased.

"That'll do fine," Shannon said, then a moment later added, "Everyone close your eyes."

Everyone except Tye must have done as she asked, because he was the only one who yowled, "Owww!"

Shawna's resulting giggle was contagious, and everyone else started chuckling too.

Keevan opened his own eyes when he laughed, as evidenced by his own similar exclamation. "Voids! Shan, I'm gonna be blinkin' away spots for a week."

Shannon snorted. "Warned you." Then, after a bit more grumbling, she added, "Okay. You can open your eyes now. Nobody stand up while you're staring at the window, though."

When his eyes opened, Nate couldn't see that anything had changed at first. Then he glanced behind him. A brilliant tracery of lines crisscrossed the back wall of the bridge.

"Nate, we need to hang your Sigil right there." Shannon pointed at a spot about an arm's length above the backs of the seats. It was the brightest point on the wall where the spiderweb of light came together to a single clear convergence.

He stared thoughtfully at the spot, "Pretty sure it doesn't work unless I'm wearing it."

It didn't. Nate tried taking the amulet off and as soon as he released the chain it became a dim crystal, obeying the ship's gravity as everything else did. After some experimentation, they discovered that what worked best was simply to have Nate hold the chain at the correct point and allow the pendant to "fall" toward the window, causing the light from the gem to point their way forward.

Shannon turned to Shawna. "I've set it up, sis. You'll have to adjust your heading by where the light is hitting the window, but this will get us close. The photo filters in the window can read the gem's light and it'll give you a heading and declination." She smiled in a self-satisfied way.

Shawna spent a few minutes adjusting their course until the light from Nate's amulet pointed steadily toward the exact center of the window, well above their heads.

Meanwhile, Nate found his arms were tiring rapidly. After holding the pendant in precisely the same position for almost ten minutes, Nate asked, "Could we...take readings or something? I'm not sure how long I can hold this, but I'm sure the trip is going to take awhile."

Shannon shrugged. "It's set to read all the time, but you should only need to hold it up there when sis tells you to."

Shawna glanced back at Nate and nodded. "Let's check it every ten minutes for now." She turned to Andrew. "How fast should I go?"

Andrew shook his head. "Uhhmm." He looked to Keevan. "How far out does the dust clear from these stars?"

Keevan tapped his chin with his UPT. "Maybe a light hour. Maybe more. Depends."

Andrew grimaced. "Not much." He shook his head again. "We need more than three seconds to see a star coming at us, and in that soup we're going to be making one monster of a bow wave."

Shawna frowned thoughtfully. "You're right...but what if we can make that work for us?"

Andrew frowned back, but cocked his head questioningly. "What do you mean?"

Shawna was already busy at work. "We can set it up for feedback. The more dust we burn, the faster we can go. Should slow us down in time if we run into any clear areas."

Shawna got quiet for a moment, then said, "Remember? Dad told us the Retton drive actually feeds on space junk." She smiled, her face sad in a distant way, but still focused on her task.

"How long will it take us to get there?" Tye asked.

"Depends on how far into this muck we have to go," Andrew replied, looking at Keevan questioningly.

Keevan shrugged. "Most of the time, Sanctuary's within a couple'a light years of the Vale's center. Usually. Remember, space isn't 'flat' in here."

Andrew shook his head. "Going to take at least a day or two. Even with Shawna's trick, if we push too hard we're toast. We can only stop so fast."

It turned out that crossing the Vale was supremely dull for anyone not in the navigator's seat. For Shawna, then Andrew, then Shannon after she'd slept, the trip was nerve wracking. The constant laser focus with which they had to watch the instruments, darting their eyes to the forward view from time to time to look for any break or slackening in the murk, left them exhausted after only an hour or two. The fact that such care was necessary was never visually obvious to those who watched from the back of the bridge because the view of their meteoric bow wave, plowing a short-lived tunnel of light through the muddy blackness outside, never changed.

Because they had to take turns navigating and they knew the trip would take several days, Andrew quickly put together a watch rotation. They ran Adamant on a 24-hour day, a fact no one remarked on until most of the group was getting ready to head for the galley for food.

In a puzzled voice, Tye asked, "I thought you were from the Milky Way. What schedule do ships there run?"

Andrew blinked, surprised, then he chuckled. "Earth has a 24-hour day, so that's what everyone's always used. Why? Did New Standard Time take its 24-hour day from somewhere else?"

"Oh. I dunno." Tye looked shocked, as if Andrew's simple question had blown his mind.

Andrew shrugged and made a face. "Ten day weeks are strange. We've always just used the Earth calendar. Granted that makes leap years feel pointless out in space." He paused and shook his head. "When we came here we couldn't change over either. The ship was built to run on Earth time."

"Earth had leap days too!" Tye looked somehow triumphant, as if the revelation vindicated him in some strange way.

Keevan was looking at Tye with a knowing smirk. "Ya gotta think the first settlers just kept doin' things like they were used to, right? It's a wonder we got simple tens for weeks and months instead'a just keeping Earth or Aterria's calendar."

Tye looked thoughtful. "How long IS an Earth year?"

"Three hundred sixty-five days," Shawna said, her eyes fixed firmly on the main window as she was still navigating. "I gather your years are a thousand days? That means I'm only, what? Seven?" She made a half-amused, half-disgusted sound.

"So that means you're twenty-one earth years?" Tye asked. "You don't look more than about four or five." He blinked. "Is that twelve? Fifteen? A hundred years here is like three hundred Earth time?"

Shannon snorted. "We've always aged slow. Nobody knows why."

Tye got quiet. After a pause, he nodded. "Yeah. Me too."

Keevan's wry humor floated back to them as he followed Andrew out the hatch looking for food. "We're all Odds, every one of us... Hadn' yeh guessed? None of us age normally."

Twelve hours after their journey had begun, disaster nearly took them. Shannon was navigating, her concentration already taking an obvious toll, with Nate sitting directly behind her along the back wall. Tye was off to Shannon's left so Nate missed the beginning of their conversation, but when Tye said, "...stupid way to do this," it caught Nate's attention.

Shannon, obviously on edge from focusing constantly on the path ahead, turned to snap back just as Tye reached for her control panel, obviously intent on 'fixing' whatever issue he thought he saw. "What do you think you're..." Shannon's voice was outraged.

Just then, the clouds ahead broke apart and a dim glowing orb swallowed the left side of their forward window. Before they could react, it was already gone, racing past them so close it took Nate's breath away. Shannon turned back in time to see it, and without finishing her sentence, she returned to her navigation, gulping audibly. Tye froze, his fingers still touching the surface of Shannon's control board.

It took Nate a moment to fully process what had happened. Once it sank in, he turned to Tye, fire in his eyes. "Are you trying to kill us?"

"I..." Tye gawped at him, then closed his mouth and shook his head.

"Were you actually trying to change something on her system?" Nate asked. "Besides which... if she doesn't focus, we're dead." Tye winced and hunched his shoulders, still silent.

Nate stopped very still, staring, then said tightly, "Tye, is this really how you want to act? Like an 8-year-old? You constantly play the kid brother. I know you don't look it but you're more than twenty years old. You told me so yourself. Is this really who you are?"

Tye just looked at Nate for a long moment, then he opened his mouth to speak but nothing came out. Nate shook his head.

"You are who you choose to be even more than you are what other people see in you."

Nate stopped again, then he said quietly, "Stay off the bridge, Tye. Unless you can be helpful."

Tye nodded and fled. Shannon remained silent, her eyes glued to the window.

After that, everyone on the bridge kept their eyes glued to the window, and Andrew, Shannon, or Shawna sat with a hand hovering over an emergency stop on the console. As the hours dragged on, Nate and the others felt more and more useless until, sixteen hours after they'd entered the Vale, Laura suggested that they take turns sitting at another control station to provide a second pair of eyes.

Nate and Keevan quickly agreed. After he was told about it, Tye too begged to take a turn.

They all tired quickly. Sitting watching the window with nothing to do while they imagined instant death flashing toward them had a nerve-wracking quality all its own. Only Nate seemed to enjoy being on the bridge. For some reason, the ship's fiery bow wave, showing up as a bright haze outside the window, and the surrounding Vale soothed him. The tension and difficulty that had so closely attended his time at the Ochroleucum, the Telestry's school for young Energematrists, and the trauma of his battle with the Changed turned quickly into a strange peace.

Even when Nate used his ability to see Energematrice6, the power that underlay the universe, the dust outside was a homogenous blur. The ship around Nate was blindingly clear, just as he had come to expect from his Energematrice6 perceptions, and he could focus on any detail to understand everything completely, down to a molecular level. Outside, though, the dust seemed a blur, its individual particles difficult to pick out of the haze. Once or twice, Nate thought he felt something else on the very edge of his perception, but when he tried to focus on it, the feeling melted away. The Vale seemed like home to him somehow, despite its dreariness, and it left him in a contemplative, strangely relaxed mood.

Because he had to check their heading, at first every ten minutes, then, after they determined they were staying on roughly the correct course, every hour or so, Nate napped at the back of the bridge instead of going to the compartment Andrew had assigned him.

After he'd gotten a few hours of sleep, interrupted so he could help adjust their course with the Sigil, Nate finally went to find food himself. The ship's galley was a short walk around Adamant's radius in the direction away from the airlock. He admired the greenery growing on the inside arc of the corridor as he walked. Somehow, the contrast between the Vale outside and the white corridor wall covered in greenery gave him a near perfect mental balance. Adamant had been created by people who spent most of their time in space, and it definitely showed.

The galley opened off the corridor to Nate's left, and it wasn't nearly as big as Nate had expected. There were only seats for eight people total, and they all could have stood around the interior easily if Shawna and Keevan weren't currently on watch together. Andrew, Shannon, Laura and Tye were already seated, with Tye in the furthest seat from Shannon he could get. Tye was subdued, his normal cheerfulness in abeyance, but he still smiled when Nate greeted him. Shannon, too, was friendly enough toward Nate. On the other hand, she was refusing to look at Tye at all.

Andrew motioned to a dish sitting on a counter near where Nate had walked in. "Help yourself. It's some kind of melon, I think. That's the last of what we picked up on Aterria. Other than that, all we have left is fruit and other produce from Shawna's garden. It'd be enough to keep us going, but it gets old fast."

Nate nodded, grabbing a plate from a rack on one wall and serving himself. As he sat down, he realized Shannon had been waiting for him. She looked up with fire in her eyes and pointed at Tye. "He has no judgment or discipline. He nearly got us all killed yesterday. Carl Winton or Dad would space anybody who did what he did."

The whole group was silent, with Laura staring at Shannon in shock. Andrew shot Nate a questioning look as if to ask whether he should step in, but Nate shook his head minutely and Andrew held his tongue. Neither Tye nor Shannon seemed to notice.

After a long silence, Tye spoke up, "I'm...I'm really sorry. I won't do anything like that again."

"You should never have done it in the first place," Shannon said, real vitriol in her voice, then added, "and you really shouldn't have been there anyway." She shot a half-embarrassed look at Nate, but scowled at Tye all the harder.

Tye looked at Nate miserably, but his somber, weary nod looked almost comical on an eight-year-old's face as he said, "I shouldn't have done it...I'm sorry, Shannon." He got up awkwardly then and left the table, heading out the way they'd come. The rest of the group was silent for a long time.

Shannon had actually started to fidget before Nate said, softly, "Shannon, you're going to have to decide which you want more. Do you want to get rid of Tye or to keep me? I don't throw people away because they mess up." He smiled crookedly. "And that goes for you too, you know."

Shannon nodded in acknowledgment and Laura, looking uncomfortable, tried to change the subject. "I like your corridor garden. It has so much more variety than ours did, even though I think ours was bigger."

Andrew smiled. "Shawna has a real green thumb. She's anima attuned and she has a knack with plants. There'd be no way to keep so many kinds healthy without her."

Laura looked over at Shannon, frowning. "What's your attunement? I don't think you've ever told me. Not like we were close, really, but..." She shrugged.

Shannon gave a rare smile. "Pyric. Thankfully I got a useful specialty. I've always liked engines. That's where I learned how to do engineering stuff. I'm not exactly a geotic, but I can get by."

Andrew nodded. "I don't know what we'd have done without her. Dad was Geotic and he taught her a lot before..." His lips twisted and he shrugged. "I'm nephilic. Not sure what I have a talent for. Never had any particular knacks. I guess people listen to me sometimes."

Laura nodded back with a sad, sympathetic smile. "I'm Aqueous." She looked uncomfortable, but after a moment she blurted, "I've got a talent for psi." Andrew whistled and Shannon frowned. Laura hurried on, "I never developed it, but that's how I called to Nate when you all came to Resolute." Nate's mind flashed back to the experience—the eerie feeling of being drawn onward, into the belly of the crashed derelict—and he realized that answered a question that had tickled the back of his mind ever since.

Then they were all staring at him and he blinked. "Uhhh. I dunno."

Shannon snorted. "He's Amasthena. Guess it shouldn't be a surprise if he's got a talent for anything and everything."

The other two nodded and Nate shrugged with a grimace. "If I did, I wouldn't know it. I still can't remember."

They were rising to leave the galley when Shannon stopped Nate as the other two walked out, her eyes downcast. "I'm sorry too," she said. "I was angry with him and, he's so..."

Nate smiled at her gently. "Obnoxious?"

Shannon nodded agreement, smiling crookedly herself and shrugging.

Chapter 2

Over the next three days, Tye spent most of his time sleeping when he wasn't taking his own turn on watch. In Tye's little remaining time awake, Nate noticed he also made a point of helping Shawna tend the corridor garden.

Keevan, on the other hand, mostly withdrew into his own private world. Later on during their second day in the Vale, Keevan joined Nate, Tye, Andrew, and Shawna for a meal of fresh produce harvested from Adamant's corridors. Sitting at the table in the galley, Nate's first taste of produce grown in the ship itself was surprisingly good.

"This is even better than normal grapes. And what is this? Spinach?" he asked.

Andrew nodded wryly. "Yeah. It tastes pretty good until it's all you have to eat for months. It's got enough nutrients in it that you can live on it, though, if you eat enough of the leafy stuff. They had an easier time modifying those."

"Modifying?" Nate asked.

"Yeah. When they left earth they had to modify some of it to add the nutrients we were missing. We still have seeds for some of the ancestral stuff, in case we ever find a place where it would grow, but it doesn't do all that well in space."

Tye shook his head. "I can't imagine how you must have lived."

Shawna grinned. "You think we can imagine how you lived? Being out in the open air is scary. I couldn't even leave the ship on Aterria. And all the people! There are so many people here. When you talk about the Telestry...or the Dominion! How many people are in the Dominion?"

Tye shrugged. "A few hundred billion. Depends on who you believe."

Shawna laughed. "I saw a hundred people together once. But only once. People here have no idea how blessed they are to live so freely."

Tye snorted. "Freely! The Dominion doesn't let people live freely. There are taxes, and registries, and regulations. Just flying around on this ship is more freedom than most people in the galaxy ever have."

Andrew asked quietly, "What about freedom NOT to live on a ship? That's a freedom we've never had."

Tye nodded thoughtfully and Keevan broke in, "Speakin' of the ship, can we see the engines?"

Andrew looked surprised. "The engines...you mean the power plant?"

Keevan grinned, twirling his UPT between his fingers. "Yeah. I've neva seen a ship that actually runs on E6."

"Oh," Andrew said, then shrugged. "Sure. I can give all three of you a tour if you'd like." They all agreed and rose to leave the galley.

Looking back as he led them down the corridor toward the bridge, Andrew said, "When Adamant was built, Bright Future put in twelve private staterooms. You've all seen those. They're spaced around this quarter of the ship." Andrew motioned to his left as he passed the bridge. "And of course you've seen the bridge."

"This hatch," Andrew indicated the one on his right between

the private staterooms that was a deep maroon instead of the usual gray, "is one of two that leads to the power plant and ship mechanisms. I'd like to save that 'til the end."

Andrew continued walking around the ship's perimeter until they reached the airlock. He turned right then, opening the extra-large hatch across from the airlock and passing through. "This is the storage area." He gestured to hatches spaced very close together on both sides of the short, double-wide corridor in which they now stood. "Each compartment's environmentals can be managed separately. Whether we need cold storage, vacuum or zero-humidity, we can get it because these compartments are completely separated from the rest of the ship." Andrew opened one of the hatches and motioned inside, giving each of them a chance to see the mostly bare compartment lined with racks. There was a gap along the left side of the room, and it took Nate a moment to realize that one rack was folded up to the wall. Andrew made a face. "The rest are all jammed full. We emptied that one to pay the port master at Aterria."

Their next stop was two doors further along the main corridor. Andrew opened the hatch and stuck his head through then pulled it back again and stood to the side to let the other three enter. "It's the rec room," Andrew said. "Mostly for exercise, but we have a few games. We've all pretty much done them to death, though." The rec room had a number of devices spaced around the perimeter. Nate was able to recognize a fold-down treadmill of sorts with what looked like elastic bands attached to the sides and a rotary mechanism vaguely reminiscent of a bicycle. There were also weights securely fastened into a rack with a weight bench folded up against the wall next to them.

The next hatch Andrew stopped at was white with a red cross on it. At the sight of the symbol, Tye smirked. "I guess not everything has changed in a thousand years. Is this your dispensary?"

Andrew grinned. "Not the word I'd have used, but basically yeah. We can do a pretty thorough body scan and we have a good suite of medical equipment, but none of us really knows how to use most of it. Thankfully, beyond cuts and scrapes we haven't had much use for it, and Shawna can do more with E6 than any of us could manage with that stuff."

After they were done in the dispensary, Andrew opened the very next hatch. "Most of these compartments are conversion rooms. They can be configured as staterooms or storage or just about anything else we want."

Tye nodded, grimacing in memory. "Right. This is where we stowed all the parts from Resolute." The compartment was half full of a variety of salvage, all secured to the walls and floor with straps next to a smaller hatch, apparently a closet.

They passed another dark maroon hatch and Andrew nodded toward it. "We'll come back here in just a minute. Other than the galley, which you've already seen, the only thing that's left before the power plant is the machine shop."

It was a much longer stretch of corridor before the hatch to the machine shop. Upon entering the compartment, Andrew motioned around at four or five different devices that ranged from puzzling but familiar to completely unrecognizable. Nate thought he recognized a lathe and some kind of milling device, but the other machines were totally unfamiliar to him.

Andrew glanced around the compartment with what might have been regret. "Theoretically, we could make almost anything we need in here, but it's like the dispensary. None of us really knows how to use most of it very well. Shannon learned a little from Dad before he died. I'm just glad Adamant's still in good shape. We'll have to find somebody who knows how to do a real maintenance check at some point. Good as Shannon is, she's no geotic."

Nate nodded and they turned to retrace their steps to the maroon hatch from earlier.

Before he opened the hatch, Andrew turned to them, his face serious. "We can take a look around, but don't get close to anything. This stuff is sensitive, and Shannon will kill me if we break anything...if whatever we break doesn't kill us all first."

When Andrew opened the hatch, Nate could see a long, featureless hallway with another hatch at the opposite end. It was beyond that hatch that everything changed. What registered in Nate's mind first was the lack of light. Every other space in the ship had been bright and well-lit. This compartment, if he could call it that, was dim or even dark, in the maze of recesses and corners leading off in every direction. It was also huge, and Nate realized that the rest of the ship's compartments, all at the same level where he stood, were contained inside this one, which was effectively the entire interior of the ship. All-in-all, Adamant was little more than a metal balloon with little pods welded to the inside perimeter for living quarters.

In front of them at the ship's core, a monstrous sphere leaked multi-colored light from a jagged seam running all the way around its perimeter. When Nate looked at the huge thing through the fields, it was so blinding he quickly released Energematrice6 and blinked his physical eyes in reaction.

Both above their heads and below their feet, huge shapes stretched into the murk. Andrew was pointing at one device after another, some of which protruded over or under the other compartments in the ship.

"...the inertial sump energy converter, the shield capacitors, the field emission controller, and that's the gravity synthesizer." He shrugged. "There's plenty more, but most of it's just names if you don't know what it does. How it works is too much for me most days. If you really want to know, you'll have to ask Shannon."

"What about the engines?" Tye was practically bent over double looking underneath some strange device in front of him.

"Adamant doesn't have engines," Andrew said. "The same field emitters are used for the shields, the drive and the particle collision system." He indicated the sphere in front of them. "That's the power plant, of course. It's the most obvious thing in here. I also can't really open it up and show it to you while we're under Retton drive, and definitely don't get too close." He eyed Tye, who had wandered forward onto the huge chunk of grating that served as a floor for most of the compartment. Tye grinned at him but nodded and came back to stand with the others on the one solid platform that protruded into the great cavity.

"We can even get to the nutrient panels on the corridor walls from here if they need tending. They rarely do, but..." He shrugged. "Bright Future built Adamant so it could be maintained completely in space for as long as possible. There's nothing in here that wasn't made to be broken down and rebuilt, and a lot of it is overdue." He grimaced.

"What's Bright Future?" Keevan asked as Andrew turned back to the corridor they'd entered through.

Andrew shrugged. "It was the name Paul and Carl and Dad and the others took up when they decided to oppose Lastis. It just sort of stuck. There's not much left of it now, I'm afraid. After they left Earth, they would stop in other star systems and set up a base for a year or two, getting further and further away from Sol as time went on. That's when they built Adamant and her sisters. The ships they left Earth with were barely better than the Changed ships. They were slow and clumsy. They learned a lot before they built Adamant, thank the Lightmaker."

Andrew grimaced, showing remembered stress from a time now long past. "The Changed had to build big, clumsy ships though. Dad and the others were strong Energematrists. They'd smash up whatever ships the Changed sent after us and leave them floating in space with all the Changed still in them, then move on to the next base. The Changed built their ships bigger and more powerful. We chose faster and more agile. It worked... for awhile."

They were back in the main corridor by then, and Andrew shrugged, turning away, obviously absorbed in his memories as they headed back toward the bridge. He didn't speak again, but the darkness that haunted his eyes spoke for him.

After their second "day" traveling, Nate's fitful sleep, again at the rear of the bridge, was haunted by terrible dreams. He couldn't recall them when he woke, but he found himself drenched in sweat, his face streaked with tears he couldn't remember crying. There had been a boy...but the dream faded away even as he tried to recall it. Looking up, he caught Andrew grumbling at his console and asked what was bothering him.

Andrew shrugged uncomfortably. "This place is unnatural. It isn't just the gravity. It's..." He rubbed the back of his neck. "It's like it's eating our propulsion. We're only getting seventy percent of our normal acceleration in here. It's just not right."

Nate nodded wryly, still feeling half-smothered by his nightmare. He couldn't help thinking the darkness he felt and the strange physics of their surroundings were connected. "It's definitely strange."

It was Laura who, after they'd been traveling through the Vale for more than sixty hours straight, was the first to see their destination coming on the console and slammed her emergency stop.

Andrew was at the controls, only a heartbeat behind her, but before Adamant could actually come to a stop they had broken through the wall of dust surrounding Sanctuary.

Nate was the only other person on the bridge at the time, a testament to the strange comfort he felt with the surrounding dust. His first reaction upon emerging was surprise at how bright it was. The blue-white light from Sanctuary's sun reflected and refracted from the wall of dust. Even more than a light hour away from the star itself, everything was brilliantly, almost glaringly bright.

"Wow," Laura said.

Andrew was already on ship-wide broadcast. "All crew to the bridge. We made it."

Within a minute, everyone except Keevan had crowded through the hatch, only to stop, stunned, staring at the view before them. It wasn't just that it was bright. It was like being perched on a thunderhead high in the sky on a summer day—if the clouds had all been made of rainbow dust. The star before them was a tiny point of light, almost distant enough to belong to some other system, but it lit up their surroundings so powerfully it hardly seemed like they were still in the void of space.

When Keevan did finally arrive a few minutes later, blinking away sleep, he took one look out the great window and grinned. "Ahhh. Gotta say, no place like home."

Andrew, characteristically, had been focused on more than just the view. "I'm seeing four small inner planets and two giant outer planets. Should only take a minute to get locations on the big man-mades." As the others' dazzlement began to wear off, Andrew nodded. "I'm seeing something big around the second planet and... I'm not sure what that one is—next to the gas giant." He glanced up at Keevan. "Where do we go from here?"

Keevan grimaced. "The only object in the outa' system is Hope, and nobody eva visits. We're headed for the second planet. That's where the Sanctuary is." Keevan's gaze was fixed out the window with something less than eagerness, but he said no more.

"Hope?" Shannon asked, her brow furrowed.

"Yeah. It's the ship that brought us—I mean humans—to the Aurora Galaxy. Paul Casisia parked it here almost a thousand years ago."

Andrew, Shannon and Shawna all stared at him for a moment, eyes wide. "Can... can we go see it?" Shawna seemed almost breathless. Even Tye looked eager.

Keevan laughed grimly, "The council always said Paul put traps everywhere out 'ere. They won't let anybody go ta' look, and before us only the Keeper could get in 'n out of the Vale."

The other passengers all looked a bit crestfallen, and Tye looked at Nate, eyes pleading.

It took another hour to reach the second planet, and as they decelerated into orbit Nate glanced from one to another of his friends with a slight smile on his face. "That was quite a trip." He looked down, frowning, then back up at Andrew, Shannon, and Shawna in turn and gave them each a nod, adding, "Thank you," then turned his gaze back to the planet below. "So Keevan, where should we be landing?"

Keevan laughed. "Oh we don't haf'ta land. They're on the space station...and you might wanna call ahead. They don't exactly have a lotta' guests drop in."

His statement prompted another burst of activity from Andrew. "Nice to know," he grumbled, scowling at Keevan.

As if at Keevan's prompt, a few seconds later they received a hail. It was old-fashioned radio, carrying a video file. With a little effort, Andrew put the video on the inside of the main window. The face that came on screen didn't look quite as young as they did—fourteen or fifteen perhaps, with black hair and a vaguely Southeast Asian cast. When he spoke, it was with the same accent they'd come to expect from Keevan. "Unknown vessel, this's Jesse Galton, son of Teron Galton, Keeper of the Mysteries. Welcome ta' Sanctuary. Please state your business." The face faded out after he'd spoken and Nate turned to Andrew. "Do you have a video pickup?"

"Yeah." Andrew motioned to one of the control stations.

A moment later, Nate strapped himself into the control station. They were weightless again after disengaging their Retton drive for planetary approach, making the restraints necessary, and he was ready to broadcast. "Jesse, this is the vessel Adamant responding. My name is Nate, and I've come to see if Jon and Rachel Casisia are still here. I was informed that the Dominion had taken your father captive. I bring you his Sigil as surety." Nate held up the Sigil, then frowned and shook his head. "I'm truly sorry about the Dominion. Would it be possible for us to meet in person?"

It took only a few seconds to receive a reply. "Brightstar? Welcome! Yes. The Casisias are still here. We've been awaiting your arrival! Please join us at Lighthouse Station! We'll have a berth ready for you."

Chapter 3

Lighthouse Station was set in the most picturesque location Nate could imagine. The nebulous clouds of the Vale reflected their rainbow of light into the system from every angle, leaving a vista without shadows, only multiplying shades of light and lesser light. The planet below was as beautiful as any picture he'd ever seen. It had oceans and continents, deserts and forests, and the colors were almost perfectly contrasted to the brilliant light show of space around them.

Ironically, the station itself was reflective, making it blend into the space surrounding it, refracting the rainbow back to the eye so it merged with the background perfectly. It was hardly noticeable until it actually came between them and the planet.

The station had two great arms that spiraled away from a massive central cylinder, with docking umbilicals at intervals along each arm. They were directed, again by radio, to dock at Umbilical One on Arm A, sunward. As they moved into position to dock, Nate couldn't help but notice there were only two other vessels on the same arm they had been directed to. One was similar in size to Adamant but so crudely assembled it looked almost like a child's toy, molded of cheap plastic. The exterior was blackened and warped, and Nate wondered whether the ship was the victim of many trips through the planet's atmosphere or had been damaged somehow. The other was tiny, its central cockpit barely big enough to hold three or four people. It obviously wasn't intended for entry into atmosphere at all, with spindly, comical-looking connections between its core and other modules.

Andrew's deft touch brought them into their docking station perfectly, but docking still took what felt like a disproportionately long time. Finally, the magnetic grapples securing them to the station were locked in place and tested and an air seal had been formed to the umbilical.

To enter the station, they pulled themselves hand over hand through a heavy articulating tube that looked like nothing so much as a tremendously large ventilation duct. As they neared the airlock, which was open and waiting, gravity began asserting itself upon them. No other space station any of them had seen could boast artificial gravity. It was almost, but not quite, enough to make them pause. They were all ready for a change of scenery, however, and eagerly, or in Keevan's case almost resignedly, followed Nate onto Lighthouse Station.

Nate was the first to cycle through the station's airlock, which was surprisingly only large enough to admit one person at a time. It seemed a strange choke point, and Nate wondered fleetingly why it was so small.

His attention quickly turned, however, to the veritable crowd awaiting him on the other side. The foremost figure among them was an older man with iron gray hair and a stern but friendly look about him. In a huddle around and behind him were six others approximately his own age, four of them men and two women. Standing apart from this group, to Nate's left by the wall, were Jon and Rachel along with Jesse Galton. To his right and behind the cluster in the center, others stood, craning their necks to see or talking quietly to one another as they waited.

When he stepped through the lock and into the room, everyone except Jon, Rachel and Jesse stopped speaking in obvious shock. After a moment, a murmur ran through the crowd. Nate could tell the group was surprised, but exactly why wasn't immediately obvious to him.

Without seeming to notice the others' shock, the gray haired man stepped forward and bowed to Nate. "Lord Brightstar, I am Elder Roderick Jaben. My companions are Bettina Strong, Alden Rebus, Yelena Seiver, Neil Eden, and Regen Sorell. We are the council of Sanctuary and, in the Keeper's absence, we are responsible for Sanctuary. I believe you've already met Jesse Galton and obviously yeh know the Casisias." He smiled at Jon and Rachel. "We welcome you and yours to Lighthouse Station."

Nate nodded to him in return, smiling. "I'm glad to be here, Elder Jaben. I hope my visit will be occasion for celebration rather than grief."

Behind Nate, the airlock opened again and Tye popped through. "I've brought six others with me. This is Tye—Tyler Wrighten. He's most recently from the Telestry's Ochroleucum." As the others came through the airlock, Nate introduced each one. When the airlock cycled for the final time, with only Keevan remaining to join them, there was another murmur in the crowd and Nate turned his head to see Keevan, his own head bent and shoulders slouched, trying to slip out of the airlock to stand behind the others.

He turned back to Jaben and smiled. "And I guess you already know Keevan Raddink."

Jaben's expression was closed, and he gave Keevan a long stare. "Yes...yes, we know Keevan." He didn't comment further, instead turning back to Nate. "We weren't expecting so many of you, but we do have plenty of room. Would yeh care to rest? Are yeh hungry? I know there's much to discuss, and I'm sorry to bring it up so quickly, but if you have any news of the Keeper, we would be in your debt if you'd share. Jesse told us that in your communication ya said his father had been captured by the Dominion?"

Nate nodded. "Telestic Loriden told me before I left the Telestry that the Keeper was in the Dominion's hands." Nate's mouth twisted into a grimace. "He had opinions regarding why that might be, but I don't know anything more than that. I'm sorry."

Jaben snorted. "Loriden....ya haven't put too much stock in his council, I hope?"

Nate smiled crookedly. "I trust the Telestic will see to his own interests and the Telestry's. Beyond that..." He shrugged. "In this case, though, I think he was being honest."

Jaben nodded thoughtfully. Behind him, the expressions and body language of the rest of the council ranged from obvious distress from Elder Yelena Seiver to reservation and doubt in the case of Elder Neil Eden, with several variations between.

Jesse Galton, meanwhile, stepped forward away from the wall and said, "Ya showed me father's sigil when you commed. May I see it?"

Without hesitation, Nate pulled the Sigil from around his neck and held it out for Jesse to take. With real reverence, Jesse took the amulet, which darkened immediately as the chain left Nate's skin. As Jesse cupped the amulet in his hands, slowly, the glow returned.

"It's real." Jesse's face fell visibly. "I mean, I knew..." He shook his head and carefully held the Sigil out for Nate, who hesitated, wondering if he should perhaps allow Jesse to keep it.

"He said it was to be yours," Jesse said, his voice intense, but after Nate took the Sigil, Jesse turned away toward the wall, hiding whatever emotions had momentarily surfaced. As she and Jon stepped toward him, Nate saw Rachel reach over and squeeze Jesse's hand in sympathy, then turn to face Nate.

"It's good to see you," Nate said. Jon smiled and nodded and Rachel stepped forward to give Nate a hug.

"It's good to see you too," she replied. "We've been..." She broke off, eyeing the council. "Jesse told us Hope One is here. That's our, I mean, Dad's old ship. We've been hoping to go see it."

Elder Rebus cut in with a frown, "It's too dangerous. The traps..."

Jesse, in turn, cut in smoothly over Elder Rebus, "The council has yet ta' make a determination as to what course we should pursue. This is one of the matters we hope ta' resolve over the next few days."

Nate nodded thoughtfully, then turned back to Elder Jaben. "Maybe it's time for us to see our rooms? The trip through the Vale was a bit...hair raising. I know Andrew and Shawna could use sleep."

Jaben gestured to the primary corridor leading from the docking arm into the station proper, starting off. As Nate walked beside him, he heard Shannon ask Jesse how the artificial gravity in the station worked.

Jaben must have heard the same conversation because his lips quirked and he glanced over at Nate. "This station was built before Paul ever left us. Some of the tricks he knew from before The Escape...or invented himself." Jaben shook his head. "This station's a marvel. We hardly have the knowledge ta' do maintenance anymore. If it was ever seriously damaged we wouldn't be able ta' fix it."

Nate nodded once more, looking around at the station as they walked. The floor was made of some kind of resinous material with little bits of polished, cream-colored stone embedded in it, resulting in a durable surface that reminded him of hard rubber. The ceiling was higher than Nate would have expected in a space station, made of some kind of smooth white composite, while walls of the same material were colored white at the top, fading to a light blue near the bottom. Everything looked old but well-maintained, from occasional professional patching of the walls and ceiling in a few places to the mechanisms on the hatches leading off the corridor at intervals. Indirect lighting fixtures dotted the upper walls, and it was obvious the station's designers had done their best to make the station feel expansive to its residents, even at the cost of precious interior space.

Nate raised an eyebrow at Jaben. "Keevan said most people live here on the station instead of on the planet. Why is that?"

Jaben smiled wryly. "It's true. The planet isn't a very friendly place these days. We're told it used ta' be cooler. It was almost as nice as Aterria, even. When Paul put the Vale in place, the sunlight reaching the surface increased drastically." He smiled ruefully. "Unintended consequences. The reflected light raised the average temperature thirty degrees. It's still of use to us, of course. We get most of our food from the planet. The heat doesn't keep us from growing crops and livestock there." He shrugged. "It's enough ta' keep us all fed, and a few hardy souls live there full time. It's not for the faint of heart though."

Jaben looked around at the people walking with them. "We have a few thousand people aboard Lighthouse. We've only filled up the lodging twice in our history, and it's been almost a hundred years since the last time that happened. There are always a few who want ta' leave in every generation, and the Keeper made sure none of us ever felt like we were in a prison. He always took anyone who wanted ta' leave into the Outside. A few even came back." He glanced back at Keevan, trailing well behind the rest of the group alone.

Nate nodded. "I don't suppose you do any trading here? Not as if you get many unexpected visitors."

Jaben laughed. "Only once in our history, before you. The famed visit of Siever Radding, the Wild Man. The Keeper brings in a trader or two sometimes, you know. Now before Paul put the Vale in place, we had a pirate ship threaten the station once. Of course, Paul was aboard at the time, so it didn't go very well for them."

Jaben continued to talk of times past while they walked, but Nate was only half listening. There was something that felt right to him about this place. It was clean—not just physically, but in a way he couldn't quite express. The people in the crowd that followed them were friendly and happy, laughing and chattering to each other as they walked. A few wore tools on their belts, but there were no weapons in sight anywhere. The few pieces of jewelry he saw were simple and tasteful. One woman had a necklace with a crystal cut similarly to the Sigil of the Mysteries, though smaller. There was no pretension of power or bustling obliviousness. Once or twice as he walked, Nate heard the sounds of children playing down a side corridor. Nate already loved this place and its people, despite what he could sense was a council so set in their ways and used to the rightness of how they lived that they would perhaps sooner die than change.

In a sense, they were right. They were set in their ways because their ways had worked for a thousand years. They were happy because the way they lived was simple and they loved each other. He could see it in how the people walked—obviously together, obviously part of a whole. Their community wasn't perfect, but it worked.

At first, Nate felt a warm happiness inside, like a glow surrounding him as he walked. Then he recognized what he was feeling and his guts twisted. He could feel at home here.

When they reached their rooms, Nate's impression that the people weren't pretentious or power hungry like those at the Telestry was confirmed in another small way. Jaben showed him into his room first, then bowed again, looking embarrassed. "It's the best we have. The station was built for colonists, not for visitors I'm afraid."

Nate looked around the simple room, plain but sturdily furnished, and shook his head, smiling. "This will do perfectly. Thank you."

Nate later discovered that they had arrived in the middle of the station's "night" cycle, and thus he overslept their normal wake up time by several hours. Again, he found himself caught in a nightmare from which he could not wake. What finally roused him was a banging at the door to his quarters, cutting through the darkness in which he was trapped.

As he tumbled out of the low bed, Nate felt a strange sense of duality, as if his mind were in two places at once. He was so clumsy in getting to his feet that it took all his concentration just to stumble over to the door. He leaned on the wall, gathering himself before he finally opened it. When he did, Rachel burst through like a towering storm cloud. She swept past him into his room, her expression thunderous, only to stop dead still when she realized the lights were still out and he was blinking away the remains of his troubled sleep.

"Ohh. Uhh..." Rachel cleared her throat and Nate could see her face going a bit pink even in the dim light. Outside in the corridor, he heard Jon burst out laughing. A moment later, Jon followed her into the room as Nate turned on the lights.

"Ohhh, Rach." Jon said through his last gasps of merriment.

Nate was grinning also as he turned to Rachel and raised his eyebrows in question. "So... Good to see you. What's up?"

Rachel swallowed audibly then nodded and turned to him, her obvious embarrassment once more giving way to anger, though more controlled now. "They won't let us go!"

"Go?" Nate asked, his eyebrows raising further. "They're trying to keep you here?"

"No, no! They won't let us go to the ship!" Rachel was seething. "That snake Rebus has led the charge against us ever since we got here. I think they decided to quit waffling because you finally showed up, but they went into closed session this morning and they decided not to let us go! Jesse said he was the only one who voted for us."

"Jesse's on the council?" Nate asked.

"Of course. He said they were 'concerned about what trends it might encourage.' Hope One is the only home we have left!"

Nate nodded slowly. "Andrew picked it up on sensors when we were coming in."

"It's orbiting the big gas giant. It's just not right! Hope One was Dad's, and now he's gone and it should belong to us!" Rachel seemed on the verge of tears now.

Nate frowned. "So are they guarding it, then?"

Rachel snorted. "They can't even get close to it. 'The Vessel' is protected. Dad was the one who set up defenses for it. He told them there was a shield around it, and there are probably traps too. They couldn't get to it if the Dominion were invading and all their lives depended on it."

Nate nodded thoughtfully. "You're right. They can't stop you. You DO have a right to go. I'll ask if Andrew will take us."

Rachel blinked at him. "But... Oh."

Nate looked at her again, questioningly. "Did you agree to abide by their decision?"

Jon smirked. "Hardly. She was ready to throw them all out an airlock. She probably could have done it too." He grinned at her.

Rachel was deflating visibly now, and she looked embarrassed. "I'm sorry, Nate. I shouldn't have..." She trailed off with an uncomfortable shrug.

It was Nate's turn to snort and he smiled, shaking his head. "It's okay, Rachel. Now that I'm awake, can you tell me what happened after I left you?"

Rachel shrugged. "There's not much to tell. Teron brought us here. He taught us more about the Schemic and how to imprint while we were on the way. When we got here, he got called away again after only two days. The Dominion must have taken Malak when he left the Vale."

Jon made a face. "The council all followed him around like puppies. Then when he left they started acting like they run the show. Really they're just snarling at people behind his back."

Nate stared at him soberly. "Something tells me that will have to change sooner than later." Then something occurred to him and he turned to rummage through the few belongings he'd brought aboard Lighthouse Station. "I didn't get a chance to show you this, before. It's the letter The Keeper gave me when we first met...It's from your dad."

Jon and Rachel both crowded in closer to read as Nate sat down on the bed, considering.

From Paul Casisia to the coming Brightstar. (Written on the eve of the Disappearance.) Preserved by Teron Galton - 610 NST

I do not know who you are, but I know that you will come.

My compatriot, Siever Radding, tells me he has seen a vision of a great light, hurtling into our universe, bent upon defeating the enemies that beset us from every side. Siever may be odd, but his visions have never failed to come to pass. Thus, I write to you, Brightstar, to give you whatever blessing I may and perhaps to arm you against the evils you will face.

I have all but lost hope. The Nosufer, the Ilvayn, and especially the Opterans plague me. Even those who are still truly human are fractious. All the mortal powers are like flies, waiting to bite me the instant I turn my attention to something more important.

It has been a thousand years since we fled, and we brought so little with us. Our history has been lost. I have only the dreams to remember Earth, and they are nothing but terror. I thought we had left Lastis Ralond and his ilk behind when we escaped Earth-that-was. I was wrong... or perhaps I misunderstood the threat from the very beginning. I fear I have failed this universe, over which the Lightmaker set me as guardian. They have won. All I can do now is to delay Them.

But I didn't set out to complain to you of my own problems. I feel the burden of the looming darkness. I had to warn you of the evils I have failed to overcome. I do not foresee this universe becoming safer when I am gone. I hope I may forestall its destruction, but I cannot imagine prevailing against the many-headed voidspawn that besets us. For every head I cut off the beast, it grows two more. I must leave vanquishing it to you.

I have entrusted this letter to Teron, my son in all but blood. You see, They have taken even my children from me. If you are able, do me this one service: find them. Find Jon and Rachel. Free them from their prison. I know they will fight at your side.

Look for the Mysteries. I have hidden them well, but allow

Hope to lead and you will find them. They may aid you in your fight. The Mysteries are far too powerful for me to allow them to fall into Their hands.

I thank you, Brightstar, for your part is to complete the task that I have so thanklessly begun and at which I have so spectacularly failed.

Truly Yours,
Paul Casisia, Guardian of the Remnant

As they finished reading, Nate was frowning thoughtfully. "Do you suppose he was talking about Hope One? Could he have put something aboard?"

Jon and Rachel looked at each other for a moment. Rachel's eyes were full, but that didn't stop her from nodding decisively.

"If he left us anything, it's definitely aboard Hope." Jon's certainty was no less than Rachel's, and Nate nodded in return.

"All the more reason to pay a visit." He raised an eyebrow at the other two. "Do you know where we could get some food?"

Chapter 4

They met Andrew, Shannon, Shawna, and Laura in the nearest of the station's cafeterias. There was a small crowd of locals who stared after them with curiosity, but kept their distance.

After they sat, Rachel launched into an explanation of her problem over the station's lunch hour. Andrew frowned thoughtfully as she spoke, then nodded when she finished. "So the council doesn't want you to go. What did he say?" He inclined his head at Nate.

Nate gave him a rueful smile. "I said we might be able to talk you into taking us if I ask nicely."

Andrew laughed. "Adamant's yours. You don't have to ask. I'm pretty sure even Shannon's on board now." He looked over to his sister with a questioning expression.

Shannon sat for a long time as the silence grew more and more tense. Finally, she said, "I do want you to stay with us, Nate, even if that means Tye stays too."

Nate smiled more broadly. "I'm glad to hear it. Something tells me trying to find a ship as fast as Adamant would take me clear to the Milky Way."

The silence returned then, though it was less hard-edged than before, until Shawna cut in, "Didn't you say 'the vessel' belonged to Paul Casisia? I'd like to see it. He was Dad's best friend."

Rachel looked over at Shawna and her jaw dropped. "Your dad was Jim Logan? But...but that's impossible!"

Shawna immediately looked abashed, but Nate chuckled. "You haven't properly met Jon and Rachel yet, have you? You came on board after I did last night."

Shawna's eyes widened. "Wait, Jon and Rachel Casisia?" All three of the siblings and Laura were staring wide-eyed at Jon and Rachel now, with something like awe.

Laura said, "We've heard stories about you and your dad our whole lives. Everyone still wonders what happened to you. Most people think you're dead."

After that, it took a full half hour to tell Jon and Rachel how the four had come to the Aurora galaxy and then explain to the others how Jon and Rachel had been imprisoned for over a thousand standard years in crystal and Paul had gone no one knew where.

When they finished their stories, Jon and Rachel were looking back and forth between Nate and the others while the four from the Milky Way stared at Jon and Rachel in turn.

"You killed a Changed?" Jon asked, eyeing Nate with surprise and wonder.

"And he banished the Shade inside it, too!" Shawna exclaimed.

"Guess that explains why none of you have a Rechemacula, too," Jon said. That required a whole new round of explanations and left the Logans and Laura all staring at the pattern that was visible above Jon, Rachel, and Nate's collars thoughtfully.

For his part, Nate was glad the other diners were keeping a respectful distance. The rumors and explanations that would have to follow such revelations would be...interesting if anyone overheard them.

After a moment, Andrew looked at Nate, "So when do you want to take them? We could go right now if you want."

Nate shook his head. "How about tomorrow?" He looked at Jon and Rachel. "I'd like to spend some time here today, and I'm going to inform our hosts of our plans before we go."

Rachel looked blank as she absorbed his intentions then stared at Nate wide-eyed, laughing aloud. Andrew gave Nate a dubious frown. Nate smiled crookedly. "A little humility would go a long way for this council. Give them a chance."

With lunch finished, Rachel led them to the station's conclave, the great hall in which the people of Lighthouse Station had public forums and discussions. The massive amphitheater also served as their center of education. When they arrived, the afternoon lesson was just beginning. The conclave was at the very heart of the station's central core, and it was bigger around than Adamant, even if the ceiling was only two stories high at the very center.

As Shawna first walked into the huge room, she stopped suddenly, breathing hard. When Shannon touched Shawna's shoulder with a concerned look, she shivered and looked down at her feet. "It's so big..." After taking a deep breath, Shawna looked up again, her jaw firm, and started walking forward once more.

"It's the first day of the month," Rachel said. "They told us they teach the story of The Betrayal and The Escape on the first day of every month so everyone remembers it."

Tye waved at them from a seat near the bottom center of the amphitheater-shaped room and they went to join him as others trickled into the chamber. All four of Nate's friends from the Milky Way stared around unabashed at the crowd.

Laura was the only one of the four to speak, but she clearly voiced what they were all thinking. "SO many people! Is this what a city is like?"

Tye laughed and shook his head. "Not even close. Just wait til you see a real planetary capital."

Andrew frowned as he gazed around thoughtfully. "We were in Casisia City, but we never really left the ship. Looking out at it from the bridge is nothing like being a part of it." He smiled at Laura. "You should have seen it! A real city! With people walking around in the open AIR!"

Meanwhile, Elder Bettina Strong stood at the podium, paging through an ancient-looking paper book that was nearly the size of the podium itself.

"Today..." Her voice boomed across the conclave, taking advantage of a room shaped with acoustic properties man had been using since before history was recorded. Nate could see she was giving herself a slight boost with Energematrice6 as well. The room grew silent instantly as she paused for a moment, then continued, "Today, we remember the story of The Betrayal, the great Sin that damaged humanity forever and the monsters who perpetrated it upon us." Her voice had a cadence and tone that was stilted, and Nate realized she was reciting as much as reading.

"In ancient days," she continued, "humans inhabited only one world—Earth. There was harmony and prosperity among the people. In those days, we had not been given the use of the Fields or driven to break ourselves upon the uncaring rock of entropy in its use. All was at peace."

Next to Nate, Rachel snorted quietly. She leaned over and whispered, "Harmony and prosperity? A thousand years sure changes a lot." Her words didn't carry far, a testament to the room's design as much as her low tone. Nate gave her a quelling look and she shrugged, grumbling a bit under her breath.

Elder Strong was still speaking. "In the laboratories of Earth, they developed many strange technologies. Foremost among these laboratories was Dyna Syntronic, and it was their scientists who first discovered Energematrice6.

"Paul Casisia was one of the warriors assigned to protect this ancient laboratory, and it is from his lips and his writings that we remember.

"It was then the Betrayer made himself known—Lastis Ralond, the bringer of entropy. He took the seed, the kernel of power that allows the fields to be touched. He stole it from Dyna Syntronic Laboratories. Upon it he worked the wiles of ancient Medicine and it became a disease that spread across the face of gentle Earth. The princes and powers of the world attempted to defeat Lastis, but to no avail. His preparations were too perfect. As the world fell to his dreadful disease, Lastis took control of everything.

"But, as is His way, the Lightmaker raised up a tiny force to stand against Lastis' might. Paul Casisia and Carl Winton led Bright Future against Lastis and the forces of darkness. Though they struggled against the tyrant, their fight was hopeless. Lastis' control of the world was too strong for mortal men to break. It was then, in humanity's darkest hour, that Paul led the survivors to use the marvelous technology of Dyna Syntronic, building space vessels that would allow them to leave their dying world.

"But Lastis was not to be beaten so easily. He too had built such a vessel, and he sent Lana Trent to destroy Paul and his tiny group of refugees. She caught them beyond Earth's moon and engaged in battle most terrible. Lana used her tremendous grasp on Energematrice6 to hold their ships fast and destroy them one by one. Then, when all seemed lost, Paul used his own tremendous power to whisk his forces away from the home they had always known into the darkness of the Between.

"They traveled through the great darkness and the Lightmaker was with them, for it was here they came, to Aurora, our new home."

Three seats down from Nate, Shannon shook her head slowly. "This is weird," she said. "We all thought they died..." She frowned. "...And Rachel's right. This story got twisted." He barely heard her, but a sharp glance from Elder Strong showed that she'd caught more than Nate had thought possible. She stared at Shannon for a long moment with a strange look on her face, then said, "We have with us today Jon and Rachel Casisia and the Brightstar himself, so named by the Keeper. Perhaps one of them has some insight to share with us on The Escape or The

Betrayal?" She sounded both serious and curious, and for a frozen heartbeat, Nate was petrified. Then he nodded slowly, rising to his feet.

Nate felt to his very core that he needed to speak to these people, that this was his purpose in the Vale, but he didn't know what to say. Lightmaker...what now? As he ascended to the podium, Nate grasped Energematrice6 and quickly copied what he saw Elder Strong doing, holding just enough power to amplify his voice for those at the edges of the amphitheater.

Elder Strong stepped back from the podium to make room for Nate, standing at a respectful distance, and he nodded to her as he turned to survey the room, searching for something to say. Finally, in the moment when he needed it most, clarity descended upon him and he saw his purpose, his whole purpose, as he had once before when he first found himself in the Aurora galaxy, on the vessel Ocharist. This time there was no doubt that what he saw came from somewhere outside himself. Whether it was the Great Schemic or the Lightmaker or some other force that had implanted the knowledge in his mind before he ever appeared in the Aurora Galaxy, he wasn't sure. He knew this story–the true story, uncorrupted by the passage of time or the flawed perspectives of its storytellers.

When Nate began to speak, he was quiet at first. "People of Lighthouse Station, I'm glad to be here. If I had a place of my own in this galaxy, I would be happy to claim Sanctuary as home. The people of Sanctuary are a breath of fresh air to me, after having spent my last month at the Telestry.

"As Elder Strong said, Earth was the ancient home of humanity. However, human nature has not changed in the thousand years since The Escape or even in the period before it, The Betrayal.

"Human nature was just as dark then as it is now. Earth was a terrible place of war and famine and death. As if man is not evil enough on his own, even in the time before The Escape the people of Earth were haunted by the Shades, evil beings that, in those days, lived in..." Nate paused, searching for a way to describe the reality of how the universe was folded and set upon itself, then shrugged. "They lived in what you would think of as another dimension of space, the Twilight, from which they can see our universe but we cannot see theirs. The Shades blinded the people of Earth to reality. The Shades used every trick and deception they could contrive to convince humanity to kill each other for sport.

"Dyna Syntronic was a laboratory, as Elder Strong said, and they discovered Energematrice6, how the world is built of and upon it, but it was then that the Shades saw their opportunity and Yimakh, the most powerful and evil of all the immortal beings that live in the Twilight, hatched a terrible plan. It was Lana Trent who stole the technology that brought the fields to the hands of men and took it to Lastis Ralond.

"In those days, the world was torn by war and strife, stirred up at the bidding of Shades they couldn't see and didn't believe in. Lastis determined to put an end to war, and he made a bargain with the Shades. They gave Lastis the knowledge to create injections that imbued himself and a chosen few of his lackeys with the power to manipulate Energematrice6.

"Carl Winton was Lastis's chief lieutenant. He saw the great evil Lastis was creating, how Lastis would take power for himself and use it for whatever purpose he chose. With the Shades at his back, Lastis' grip on the world would be stronger and more evil than ever before. It was then the Shades' deeper plan became reality. Yimakh provoked a fight between Carl and Lastis, and with Yimakh's connivance from within the Twilight itself, their titanic struggle blasted a hole—a puncture through the fabric of space into Twilight. In its own struggle to puncture reality itself, Yimakh twisted the fabric of being, and it was this abomination that entwined entropy with Energematrice6.

"You see, Energematrice6 was not intended to be used by humans for their own power. Nor was it intended to bring a premature end to those who did have the means to use it. From our side, the puncture was invisible, both to us and the Shades themselves. It only allowed passage in one direction. It was not the effect that Yimakh had intended, and once a Shade passed through, it became trapped on this side of the rift.

Even this was enough to give the Shades direct access to humanity, and they took full advantage, manipulating our genetics and creating monsters the likes of which we had never imagined. After his fight with Lastis, Carl saw that Earth's plight was dire. He knew Yimakh would not rest until it controlled every living human, for it is jealous and despises us with a hatred that knows no limit.

"In desperation, Carl took the injection Lastis had made and created what today you call 'the Plague.' The Plague was a mercy in disguise, conceived by the Lightmaker and unleashed on humanity by Paul Casisia and Carl Winton. It was the Plague that gave us E6. It restored the balance between the powerless people of the world and Lastis and his chosen friends."

Nate stopped for a long moment, then shook his head. "It was Paul who decided the people must flee. When Carl escaped from Lastis in the aftermath of their battle, Paul enlisted his help to build the ships that would take them away from Earth and the terrible destruction of the Shades."

"Building the vessels in secret as they did was a tremendous, costly effort, and Lastis hunted Bright Future relentlessly. As Elder Strong said, Lana Trent caught them in space, but The Escape was no intentional exercise of Paul's might." Nate smiled wryly. "In the battle that raged between Paul and Lana, with so many of the refugees already in hibernation for what they thought must be a voyage of decades, space was rent by fire and destruction. Raw E6 was unleashed in ways that had never been tried before. What you call The Escape, given by the mercy of the Lightmaker, seemed no more than an accident to Paul and his passengers. Instead of the destruction that was intended, a path was opened from the Milky Way to the Abyss here in Aurora.

"It was thus that the first colonists came to Aterria a thousand standard years ago, only a hundred fifty Earth years for the Milky Way."

Silence reigned across the amphitheater as the people digested Nate's words. After giving them more than a full minute to think about what he'd said, Nate spoke again, "The puncture is still open. The Shades can still escape Twilight, though they still may not return to their proper realm, and from within the Twilight their elders can reach into Aurora itself. In the Milky Way, humans are hunted like animals across the stars and made into monsters if they're caught.

"And the truth... Even here, the truth has been lost. The people of Aurora have forgotten. Entropy strangles them in their youth, and they squabble over power just as their ancestors did on ancient Earth. It is for this reason I have come here." Nate's eyes were downcast when he finished, but after a moment he raised them again, catching every eye he could in an audience that now seemed vast. "The Lightmaker always provides a way out, and there is always a path to redemption. There is also a cost, and a choice to be made." Nate stepped back from the podium with a nod to Elder Strong, then took a position to one side of her.

Elder Strong turned her head to give him a long, measuring look, but didn't move. The crowd was murmuring around him, with more and more hostility bubbling up to the surface the longer he listened.

One man called, "No respect fer Tradition!"

Despite the general conversation among the crowd, which did not rise above a murmur, the few who rose to their feet to approach the center of the room seemed respectful enough. The first to reach the dais stepped up to the podium and turned to look back at Nate. "Thank you, Brightstar," said the young man, barely older than a teen himself. "My name's Ilvin. I was... I was wonderin'. Would ya be willin' ta' answer some questions?"

Nate nodded and stepped forward to clasp his hand. Then the young man smiled at him and said, loud enough for everyone to hear, "Ya spoke of Shades. We have a few stories about beings like that, and ya said they can reach into Aurora, but could ya tell us, can the Shades reach us here in the Vale? Paul's great gift has protected us fer centuries. Are we ta' fear Them even here?"

Nate nodded again, then amplified his voice once more to be sure all would hear. "Ilvin, I'm happy to answer your question. When Paul put the Vale in place, he set protections around and upon it. It is possible that the Shades could reach you here from the Twilight, but only if someone willingly allowed them access. The galaxy outside the Vale on the other hand..." Nate trailed off, looking troubled.

"As to whether they could come here from the Milky Way, the answer is yes, but only if someone shows them the path. The passage between the Milky Way and the Abyss is sealed, and only a few know how to find it. The Shades do not—or did not until recently." Nate turned a thoughtful gaze to Andrew and his sisters.

The next question was the worst that Nate had to answer, and the only one that really captured the mood of the crowd. A short, angry woman all-but screeched at him, "Ya think ya can just show up and contradict a thousand years of history! Who do ya think you are?"

Nate's gaze was firm as he scanned the audience. "As to whether my words are true, I give you only the knowledge the Lightmaker gave to me." This didn't seem to help his case with the crowd, though the rest of his questioners were unfailingly polite, creating a strange contrast with the underlying atmosphere.

The next question came from Alina, a middle-aged lady with frown lines between her eyes. She actually curtsied when she stepped forward to speak. "Ahh... Brightstar, could yeh tell me... We've long been taught that Energematrice6 represents balance, that good and evil, light and darkness, past and future all find their balance in the fields..." She shrugged helplessly.

Nate nodded. "What exactly are you asking me, Alina?"

Alina frowned for a moment, then she said, almost desperately, "Energematrice6 is not just for physical power. It's our spiritual source! How can it never have been intended for us ta' use it?"

"Ahh," Nate shook his head. "E6, like the rest of the universe, was made by the Lightmaker, a tool for His own use, and for those to whom He gave the means. Any who find their spiritual source in the Fields and not the Lightmaker are lost...and," Nate's lips quirked but his eyes were full of compassion. "Looking to E6 as your source of balance is like looking to a hurricane for strength. Strength it may have, but not for you to borrow."

The third question was from an old man, so stooped and wrinkled his age was impossible to guess. He stared at Nate, almost bleakly, and said, "Yeh've given us much today. How do we live with this? Do we spend our days in fear, knowing such a great evil is just outside our door?"

Nate nodded respectfully to him and was silent in thought, then said, "When The Escape landed on Aterria, the people asked for a way to live with their new power. Paul gave them the Tenets, but they could not live by them. Humanity faces defeat and destruction in the Milky Way. Here in Aurora, you cannot see further than your own gain, whether in the power-hungry Telestry or here, where you huddle behind a wall of dust in fear of what the outside world may do to you."

Nate paused, looking over the gathered people. "The time is coming for the people of Vale and Telestry alike to be renewed and equipped to defeat the enemies that have awaited them for so long. That is my purpose in this galaxy. First, to see truth restored to you. Second, to equip you for the battles that lie before you. Third, to face the enemies you cannot."

For almost a full hour, Nate answered question after question, looking to satisfy each of his questioners as best he was able. Their hostility never really abated, instead trailing off into sullen silence. When finally no more came forward, Nate stepped down from the dais to return to his friends. They too were rising to leave when Nate made it back to them, but he saw Elder Rebus approaching from the other side. When he reached them, Rebus gave them all a smile, while Rachel glared at him and Jon watched with a frown.

"So glad ya came," Rebus said. "Tell me, do yeh think us backward here in Sanctuary?" There was something malicious behind his eyes, and his bait was so obvious as to be rancid.

Nate stared at Rebus for long enough to make him uncomfortable, then said, "I think lies, even polite ones, are an abomination. You tell me, are you really glad we came?"

Rebus looked shocked for a moment, then dropped his act entirely, turning his previous question into an accusation. "Ya come here, to the most sacred and protected place in the entire galaxy, speaking down ta' us—the keepers of the histories—as to inferiors. Your arrogance is tactless and juvenile."

Nate stared at Rebus, expressionless. "Again, you fail to value truth over your own ego. To answer your other question, Sanctuary is a healthy place....mostly. I'm glad I came."

Rebus rolled his eyes sarcastically. "And what will yeh do next? Begin yer campaign to bring down the Dominion, I suppose?"

Nate snorted. "You suppose a great deal, Elder Rebus." Nate gave Rebus a long look as his friends filed out of their seats past him, craning their necks to see his interaction. Finally he asked, "I understand you've decided not to use Sanctuary's resources to help Jon and Rachel reach Hope One?"

Rebus nodded, his eyes sharpening once more. "That's correct. The council determined the risk ta' public stability, not ta' mention ta' the Casisias themselves, was unnecessary at this time. As the keepers of the relics left ta' us by Paul, such is our right."

Nate frowned slightly. "Andrew and his sisters have graciously agreed to allow us the use of Adamant for the visit. We'll be going tomorrow. If you would inform the rest of the council, I would appreciate it. As Paul's heirs, such is *their* right."

With Nate's final words, Rebus looked ready to explode. He remained silent, however. Whether it was from shock or simply because he was strangling on his own rage wasn't clear. Then, another voice spoke from Nate's right, "So. Yeh've decided ta' flout the council's authority?" It was Elder Jaben, standing just a few paces away, his own expression a thunderhead of disbelief and righteous anger.

Nate considered his words for a moment, then shook his head. "Jon and Rachel are the last living colonists to leave Hope One, as well as Paul's heirs. If anyone has a right to it, they do.

Even if the council wanted to claim jurisdiction, could you reach it?”

Jaben’s frown deepened. “The Vessel’s been inside Sanctuary ever since Paul left. At the very least it would be courteous ta’…”

Nate shook his head again, more firmly. “Elder Jaben, I understand that your people venerate Hope One and you don’t want it disturbed for that reason if no other. As far as I’m concerned, that’s not enough to overcome the Casisias’ need or their right to see it, and I don’t need anyone’s permission to take them there.”

Nate saw the instant when Rebus’ expression went suddenly from thunderous to crafty. As if something new had just occurred to him, Rebus said to Jaben, “Ta’ the contrary, I think this is a capital idea.”

Jaben stared at Rebus, bewildered. “What?”

“I do!” Rebus nodded. “They must, of course, take a member of the council with them ta’ be certain nothing is disturbed on The Vessel.”

Jaben continued to stare, as if he had never seen Rebus before, then understanding seemed to dawn. “And you wish ta’ be that council member?”

Rebus’s eyes widened and he laughed as if the idea were ridiculous. Like the rest of his persona, it was an act, and Nate felt as if he needed a shower. “Of course not! You and I are too old for such a thing. Young master Galton is a much better choice. Don’t ya agree?”

Once more, Jaben looked confused, but he shook his head in irritation. “I don’t see that we have the capability ta’ forbid such an expedition at any rate. If Jesse wants ta’ go, he may, of course.”

Frowning, Nate nodded. “We’d be happy to have him.” Nate wasn’t sure what Rebus’s game was, but Jesse Galton had so far seemed solidly on their side, and having him along for such a trip might actually be to their advantage.

After a moment, Jaben sighed. “Will you at least promise ta’ leave it intact when ya finish?”

Nate looked to Jon and Rachel, his eyebrows raised. Rachel glared at Jaben but nodded reluctantly. Jon just shrugged. Nate said, "I don't think any of us wants to destroy it."

Jaben looked grim. "That will have to do, I suppose." He paused, then sighed again. "The reason I sought you out was actually unrelated. How much do you know of Keevan Raddink?"

It was Nate's turn to frown. "He was the first person to find me when I awoke aboard Ocharist. When he asked to join us, he told me he had been sent to spy on me by Loriden, but originally the Keeper sent him to spy on Loriden."

Jaben shook his head. "Ta' my knowledge, the boy was never sent anywhere as a spy." He grimaced. "I say boy, but Keevan is at least fifteen standard years old. He ages...differently. As many would put it, he is an Odd. He was exiled for being a troublemaker. We hoped a dose of the outside world would cure him. His bloodline comes straight from 'The Wildman' and his family's always been... troubled."

Behind Nate, Tye laughed. The others all looked blank. Nate glanced over his shoulder at Tye, who grinned. "The Wildman was the one who first prophesied about you, Brightstar. He came through The Escape on the same ship Paul Casisia did. Hope One, I guess, and they say people who came through The Escape were never quite right. He was extra special though. The Telestry kicked him out three times. They finally killed him when he came back again the fourth time. His name was Seiver, right? Seiver Raddink?"

Jaben smiled at Tye's insouciance. "Radding, actually. The name changed on the third generation when Seiver's son left a bastard and wouldn't claim him. Keevan's mother and sisters still live here, but the council asked him ta' leave after he tried ta' sabotage Lighthouse Station two standard years ago. He did relay some information ta' us about Telestic Loriden's plans, once." Jaben's mouth twisted. "We ask that you take him with you when you leave."

Nate nodded. "Keevan's already said he's coming with me." He frowned. "Has anyone seen Keevan since we got here?"

Jaben shook his head sadly. "He's been with his mother and his sisters since he arrived. Hasn't come out of their quarters once, though his mother and sisters were all here a few minutes ago."

They spent the rest of the station's "day" cycle exploring and talking with the people. Shawna even found the station's head gardener and swapped some seeds with him, trading two of the varieties they grew on Adamant for a vine fruit she had never seen before but that he promised would survive in null gravity for long periods. Jesse also invited all of them to join in an Energematrice6 practice session that was held in the conclave after the station's final meal of the day. Nate, Shannon, Rachel, and Tye all attended, and though Nate couldn't say he learned much, he was again impressed by the friendly, genuine attitudes the people of Sanctuary showed. Despite the general atmosphere, however, Nate was left with an uneasy feeling that night as he drifted off to sleep.

Chapter 5

Nate's next awakening was even worse than his previous one. He had the exact same dream as before, smothering him with terror and darkness. This time, as he struggled to break sleep's iron grip, he remembered—deeply and completely—what happened before he came to the Aurora galaxy. Father.... Adrienne... himself. He remembered the incessant crackling of nail guns invading his consciousness. He remembered beating his head against the wall until the dull ache drove out the intrusion. He remembered leaning on Adrienne, stumbling down the hall to collapse on his bed, mentally and physically broken.

Alone in his quarters on Lighthouse Station, Nate wept as a reality that was now unimaginably far away asserted itself upon him so strongly that he wondered what was real. What was this world? His friends? E6? Which of the two was his memory and which a dream?

Gasping, Nate sat on his bed with his back against the station's wall. The knowledge of who he was—who he really was

—was inescapable, bringing an all-too-familiar, clumsy near-paralysis. The strange sense of two minds trying to meld together, one broken and one whole, made it nearly impossible to move. He panicked, and suddenly his body was a cage again. There were no words for the horror, the stark contrast between this bright reality he'd had for such an infinitesimally short time, being whole and capable and...what he was in that other place—what he really was. And now that world was invading this one. His horror deepened as he saw what would happen, what his friends would say and the destruction that was waiting for them at every step. He was too important here to be the weak link. He would turn this whole universe into a disaster. He would fail. His mind whirled around and around, caught in a pattern that was a finger's-breadth from overwhelming him.

Desperately, Nate reached out and opened his mind to the fields, looking for something, anything to break his mental loop. What he found—what thrust itself into his mind—was the Great Schemic, its pattern looping through him and into the universe, reaching out to draw everything into focus from a perspective far greater than his own.

Nate understood patterns. They were like his native tongue, a language he knew instinctively. This pattern was familiar to him, like the sweat and leather smell of father's coat when he hugged him, but so much more it was beyond expression. It gave him a perspective different from anything he could have imagined and showed him his life—his lives in both realities—in a new light. For a single crystalline moment, broken pieces came into alignment and his panic subsided into wonder. He was part of a perfect design—a perfection he couldn't even fathom.

Then the clarity was gone, but the sense of wonder lingered. Like holding on to father in a strange place, it allowed him to hang on to his sanity.

There were two realities. The two of him were really the same person. One was caught in a paralysis he couldn't cope with, while the other led a tiny group of truly extraordinary people into the teeth of a universe determined to destroy itself.

Nate laughed aloud then, realizing that the pool of memory in the back of his mind, now quiescent, still guarded its secrets. The patterns his unconscious knew so well, that he had seen with such clarity for a blazing instant, were still just beyond the reach of his conscious mind. Lastis, the Telestry, the Dominion, the Changed and their masters in twilight—the whole puzzle was both firmly before him and tantalizingly beyond his grasp.

Nate sighed. At least he hadn't panicked and made a giant hole in the station...or even fallen over. Nate slid off his bed and onto his feet. Everything he did here was so effortless...so different from what he'd known his whole life. Trying to shake off the last of the double-minded feeling, Nate headed out the door, making his way to the same cafeteria as before.

His friends were already there, excited for their upcoming adventure. Soon Jesse Galton joined them, and they proceeded to Adamant as a different kind of unease stole back into Nate's awareness. Something about their situation was bothering him. Tye volunteered to go fetch Keevan while Andrew gave Jon, Rachel, and Jesse a short tour of Adamant, which began with a rather necessary explanation of where the ship and its passengers had come from.

When Tye and Keevan returned, Jesse was saying, "And this type'a vessel's still standard back in the Milky Way? Here, we stopped building E6 machines nine hundred standard years ago. It was a pretty dark time after everyone got settled on Aterria. They weren't too keen on E6. It's what originally drove Paul and the first settlers out here ta' Sanctuary, actually." He made a face. "No one was safe using E6 for a hundred years after The Escape until the first generation had all died off except the really strong Sixers."

"Sixers? You mean Energematrists?" Laura asked.

Jesse nodded and Tye frowned at him. "And by really strong Energematrists... You mean the Odds?" Tye asked, a smirk lurking behind the innocence in his voice.

Jesse looked uncomfortable, but before he had to answer, Andrew shrugged. "We don't build many ships back home anymore. Most of that stopped when we couldn't get more people off Earth about forty years ago..." He hesitated, then finished, "The ships we do have mostly belong to family groups."

As they all settled in, Andrew took the forward chair with Shawna on his right and Shannon on his left as usual, while the others scattered across the acceleration couches spaced along the back of the bridge. They didn't fill up the seating, though it was over half full now, and Andrew took a careful look around to be certain everyone was secured before he sent the signal to Lighthouse Station to release the docking clamps. Nate stared into the rainbow of color being refracted back to him through space as they gently pushed away from the station, unable to keep from wondering what might happen here at Lighthouse while they were gone.

The trip to the furthest giant planet took almost an hour, most of which was spent maneuvering and matching trajectory, first with the planet, then, after their sensors localized it, with Hope One itself. The vessel was actually at a Lagrange point between the huge gas planet and its largest moon, positioned away from any other predictable object that might dislodge it. Andrew brought Adamant to a stop rather abruptly when their destination was still too far away to see out the main window except when Shawna changed the view to show them the scanners. The gas giant itself, Sanctuary V, filled one side of the bridge's great window, its clouds a psychedelic blue that outshone even the rainbow of reflected light from the Vale.

As Nate stared, surprised, Andrew looked around, holding a hand to his head and said, "Nate, I'm suddenly getting a headache. Really suddenly. This isn't normal. Do you think there's something over there...?" He gestured in the direction they were pointed. When Nate looked around the bridge, he saw that the only three besides himself who weren't showing some sign of pain were Jon, Rachel and Jesse.

Nate frowned for a moment in thought, then nodded decisively. "Don't get any closer." He looked around again. "Tye,

Keevan, Laura, Shannon, Shawna, are you all feeling the same as Andrew?" There was a chorus of assent and a few nods, and Tye let out a low moan. Nate addressed Jesse and the Casisias, "We need to figure out what's going on here." With that, Nate opened his senses to the fields.

At first, Nate saw nothing he could identify as unusual. The planet and the moon were too far away for him to perceive normally with Energematrice6. He would have had to work to change his perspective in order to see them, though he thought he could if he tried. Looking around again, he realized he couldn't even see Hope One yet. Shrugging to himself, Nate began a systematic examination of the bridge around him. He couldn't sense any Energematrice6 intruding on them that wasn't a normal part of their surroundings. Nate shifted his perspective to a smaller scale and found the same. Nothing was out of the ordinary. Granted, 'ordinary' was a cacophony of confusing streams of power and massive, glowing fields surrounding every object in view.

After a minute or two, Jon said, thoughtfully, "Look at me then look at Tye. I can't quite tell what's wrong, but something's off."

The two were sitting next to each other and Nate did as Jon suggested. The sense of something not quite right was immediate, but what it was or what might have caused it eluded Nate. For almost another full minute, Nate watched the flows of Energematrice6 moving through the ship and the people. It was a pattern. Something...

"The Schemic!" Jesse exclaimed just as Nate himself realized what he was watching. What he saw was the web of Energematrice6 that drew itself through and around every person on the bridge. The power that streamed through himself, Jon, Rachel, and Jesse was smooth and even. That which flowed around the others seemed agitated, almost vibrating with the difficulty of its passage.

Nate had never actually seen how the Great Schemic connected him to the universe. He'd never known to look for it, but there was no doubt that's what he was looking at now. It arched off of him and away in all directions, so confusing and yet perfect that he couldn't comprehend what he was perceiving, but he was left almost gasping in awe. The pattern, as he could see it, was repeated infinitely, scaling both up and down until it was infinitesimally small, its twists and whorls always repeating. After a long moment, he realized that the streams of power were going off in too many directions. It was more than a three-dimensional object, so much more so that he got lost looking at the tiniest part of it, and only he, Jon, Rachel, and Jesse were linked by it. Jon and Rachel obviously saw it too. Everybody else was hunched over in pain or actively holding their heads in their hands.

Jon's face was a study in awe, and Rachel said, "I didn't realize... It's like... it's holding the whole universe in sync!"

Rachel smiled wistfully. "Dad must have keyed the space around Hope One somehow. It's only us four who have the Schemic, and it's only letting us go near it."

Jon shook his head. "Dad was always so clever with this stuff." He eyed Tye, then let out an exclamation "Voids! It's like he's going out of phase!"

It was true. Tye's body blurred briefly, as if he were preparing to vanish into nothing.

Nate turned to Andrew, who was now holding his head in both hands with his eyes squeezed shut. "Get us to at least twice this distance from Hope One, Andrew," he said. "We need to talk."

It actually took almost another half hour for the others' headaches to fade, and Nate had Andrew move them even further away, almost as far from Hope One as it was from the gas giant, just to be certain they were clear of the effect. The explanation of what the Great Schemic was took another half hour, and by the time they finished Nate was glad to have Jesse along. If anything, he was even better than his father at explaining the Schemics, and when he'd finished, everyone sat around the bridge staring at each other.

"So you're telling me," Tye said, "that this 'Schemic' was reaching all the way out from 'The Vessel,' which we couldn't even see yet, and making us phase out of the world?"

Nate snorted. "The Schemic is part of the whole universe. It was the force bending the space around Hope One getting at you. Obviously, its aim is to make sure everybody belongs to the Schemic before they can enter, but that wasn't the Schemic itself. It was one of Paul's traps." He grinned darkly. "I'd hate to think what would happen to somebody who had imprinted a different schemic."

"Yeah, that." Tye said. "So what now?"

"Well," Nate said, "either every one of you adopts the Schemic or we turn around and go back. We can't ask anybody to endure THAT, and we weren't even close yet. I get the idea the closer we get the more effect it's going to have."

Everyone was silent for what felt like a long time, then Laura asked quietly, "You were imprinted with the Schemic?"

Nate nodded and held up the Sigil of the Mysteries. "It's what lets me use this, and... It's more than that." After another moment's thought, Nate asked all of them to open their senses to the fields. Andrew was visibly reluctant, but they all did, and Nate told them how to look at him in order to "see" the Great Schemic. When he returned his attention to the group, he could see Andrew sweating. Jon, Rachel, and Jesse watched with knowing smiles while the others were all raptly focused on the incredible pattern of the Schemic—all except Keevan. He had turned away and was gazing across the bridge, obviously a million miles away. After a few long seconds, Andrew looked at Nate, almost pleadingly, and Nate nodded. Andrew, too, turned away in relief and Nate made a note to himself to ask about it later.

Meanwhile, he turned back to look at Keevan, who was still staring across the bridge, playing absently with his UPT, and asked, "What's on your mind?"

Keevan shook his head as if it was too much to put into words. "They gave us all the opportunity ta' imprint, ya know? They spent hundreds of hours teachin' us about it."

He glanced down at the device in his hands, still twisting it back and forth. "I got this when I was just a kid on Lighthouse Station. A trader gave it to me. I think he saw how badly I wanted to be free—to see the galaxy. I neva liked it there, even when I wos a kid... You realize I've neva actually used this? It's a Universal Positioning Tool. Could save a thousand coordinates, and I've neva done it even once."

Keevan looked over at Nate and made a face. "Ya' know, I'm not really sure why I hated Sanctuary so much. I was a nephilic with a knack for stealth and a Raddink besides. They neva' trusted me. Not really. so I guess I neva' really trusted them." He shook his head.

"You have a chance for a fresh start." Nate said. "What do you want to do?"

Keevan shook his head again, glumly. "Not sure." He turned back toward the great window to stare at the billowing clouds of dust and reflected light surrounding them.

Of the three girls, Shawna was the first to break her trance-like absorption into Energematrice6 and the Schemic. She immediately looked at Nate and said, "I'm in. You'll have to ask Andy and Shan, but..."

Andrew broke in with a nod of his own, "Yeah. I'm in too." Over the next few moments, Shannon and Laura both snapped out of their own absorption and agreed as well.

Five minutes later, Nate finally got tired of waiting for Tye to finish his examination and he walked over and poked him. Tye blinked and grunted, then grinned at Nate. "Yeah, Okay. That's amazing. I want it."

Nate snorted, then turned to Keevan. "Well? You want us to take you back to Lighthouse?"

Keevan's mouth twisted. "Well, they sure don't want the loiks of me back at lighthouse, eh? I'm in."

Nate turned to Jon and Rachel. "Did the Keeper teach you to imprint?"

Rachel nodded. "Jesse knows how, too."

With Jon, Rachel, and Jesse to do the imprinting, waves of blue and green Energematrice6 raced across Adamant's bridge one after another. It was only a few minutes before Nate could see the same indescribable web linking all of them. It was another few minutes before they had all re-seated themselves and were ready to try a second approach to Hope One. After they had settled in, Andrew glanced back at Nate. "How do you want to come at this? You said there are traps? I don't suppose the Schemic was all we have to worry about?"

Nate shook his head and looked over to Jon and Rachel. "I don't know. You two have any thoughts?"

Jon and Rachel both shook their heads in turn. After frowning in thought for a moment, Rachel said, "Dad didn't think in straight lines. If there was an obvious way to do something, he found another. The only thing to expect is that it won't be easy."

Even as Rachel finished speaking, Andrew was shaking his head in puzzlement. "There's something wrong here. Our sensors can't get any resolution on Hope One." The view in the main window changed abruptly and a blurry silver tube appeared before them. The details of the image were completely lost in noise, and Andrew shook his head again. "I have no idea why it's doing this. I can't get any read on what's interfering."

Nate nodded slowly. "Get us close enough to see it. If anyone sees anything strange, call out." Andrew nodded in return and the fuzzy image slowly began to grow as their speed increased. Andrew was also the first to spot the anomaly. His exclamation was only a bare instant ahead of several of the others, however.

Behind Hope One, directly in front of them, a spiraling web of light appeared, shaped like a disc. It was tiny at first, but grew before their eyes, twisting and writhing, the density of its lines growing as it did. The disc quickly expanded past the edges of the window. Then, Shannon let out an exclamation. The view in the main window changed again to show the entirety of the disc, now recognizable as a half-sphere, its near edge spiraling inward again as if to wrap Hope One inside a ball.

"It's closing!" Andrew said. It was true. The spiral had created a giant circular hole on their side of Hope One that was narrowing before their eyes. Its rate slowed as the hole continued to shrink, but at their current speed they definitely weren't going to make it through.

"We need to stop," Jon said.

Instead, even as Jon was speaking, they accelerated. The view before them leapt closer as the spiraling edges of the hole closed more and more slowly, and they were still accelerating. Andrew bared his teeth, his gaze fixed on the portal in front of them. They WOULD make it now. It was plain.

"No, NO. STOP!" Jon called, panic in his voice. "That IS the trap."

"He's right. Something's up." Tye added.

Andrew looked around and Nate nodded. "Stop."

Andrew let out a muffled exclamation, but he slammed a button on his board and they stopped fast enough that the g-forces left them all woozy. The hole in the web hung before them, as if waiting, still several times the size of their own vessel.

They all sat and stared for a long moment, then Andrew exclaimed again, "Abyss. I think you're right."

Without anyone quite noticing, their view of Hope One through the mesh of the cage had come clear while the portal ahead was still blurred. Oddly, when he looked at the portal through Energematrice6, Nate saw nothing, as if the portal really was a hole in the field ahead.

"How could you tell?" Nate asked Tye.

Tye shrugged. "I told you I specialize in Electricity? Something's not right with that portal. Something's in the way."

Jon broke in again, frowning. "I think I know what it is."

Nate raised an eyebrow questioningly. "Oh?"

Jon shook his head. "It's a toy, but... Here, look." Jon held up his hand and closed his eyes, then said, "Slap my hand." Nate tried to do so, swatting at his palm, only for his own hand to come to a complete stop a full hand's breadth in front of Jon's, as if it had hit a wall. It even felt like hitting a wall.

"Dad taught us how to do it when we were kids," Jon said. "Now, move your hand really slow. Touch my palm." Nate did so, very slowly moving his palm in to touch Jon's open hand. Everyone was staring at Nate and Jon with fascination, and Andrew had a queasy look on his face.

After a long moment, Nate withdrew his hand then tried again to slap Jon's palm with the same result as before. Shannon cut in, "That looks like the same principle Adamant uses for its particle collision field."

"Oh?" Nate asked.

"Yeah," She frowned at him thoughtfully. "You know how we set it up to slow us down when we stopped hitting high concentrations of dust on the way in? How the dust was just vaporizing when we hit it?" Nate nodded, and she made a face "That wasn't just magic or something. The ship has a collision interdiction shield. If we hit something the size of your head or smaller, we just vaporize it instantly. Without that, we'd look like a strainer in no time. Hitting a bit of dust going that fast would make a hole clear through the ship and us too."

Nate turned back to the screen in front of them and he whistled. "So if we'd run into that "portal" at any speed, we'd have been a bug on a windshield." Everyone was looking at Nate with perplexity when he turned back to the others, and he shrugged. "Point is, it's a very good thing Jon stopped us."

Shannon was frowning, though, and she shook her head. "You can't stop an object that's within even a few percent of the same size you are with one of those. Lots of little objects, sure, but not big ones. It uses the mass of the ship to absorb the impact. If the field didn't just burn out, it would have vaporized both ships."

"What if..." Rachel pointed behind them, at where the moon would be, "What if Dad used E6 to hook the field into the moon? Would that do? Then he made the big energy field show up as bait."

Shannon snorted. "Oh yeah. That'd do it." She nodded to Nate. "I don't know what bugs or windshields are, but I definitely don't fancy having my particles scattered across the solar system. Just one question. How did he keep it from showing up in the fields?"

Jon and Rachel both shrugged and shook their heads. Rachel chuckled. "Dad's tricky like that."

Nate grimaced. "So if we move forward very slowly, we should be okay?" Nate asked.

Shannon shrugged. "Sure."

Nate looked over at Andrew. "Go ahead and try it."

Andrew nodded and soon they began moving forward again at such a slow pace they couldn't gauge their movement by the vessel ahead of them. When they reached the "portal," the blur filled their window.

A moment later, they were through, with the only effect being a tingling sensation that passed through Nate's body and, judging by their expressions, everyone else as well. Shortly after, the gently glowing Sigil around Nate's neck brightened, and he could see a similar glow from Jon and Rachel's amulets. Then, the sensation abated and the amulets all glowed even brighter.

"Well, then there's that." Nate stared down at the Sigil of the Mysteries, his expression halfway between grim and satisfied. "How much you want to bet we'd be in serious trouble right about now without these?"

For the space of a breath, everyone on the bridge stared at the three pendants, their eyes wide.

The rest of the long, slow trip to Hope One was, ironically, completely uneventful. Andrew opted to keep his acceleration low, just in case the collision field operated inside its original radius. Shannon explained that their ship's own collision field would react if something accelerated too quickly within its own radius, and Nate didn't object. He suspected that particular danger was past, but better to be safe. The pendants continued to glow painfully bright the entire time, their light a testament to their presence in some sort of Energematrice6 trap that Paul had set up almost a thousand years ago. Outside the ship, the luminescence of the strange wire frame sphere that marked the collision field hung in space around them, while the magnified image on their main window had finally come clear.

Three endless hours later, they finally pulled up near enough to Hope One to get a useful unmagnified view of their goal. It was a long cylinder with a simple cone at one end, totally unremarkable except for the rainbow of colors that reflected from its shiny exterior. Rachel gazed at the sight wistfully as the view continued to grow.

As they got closer Nate realized the vessel must have been much larger than he originally thought. Jon pointed to a tiny spot at the base of the vessel. "That should be the airlock." Nate nodded thoughtfully. If true, that meant their own Adamant was smaller than the diameter of the cylinder that made up Hope One's body.

"So that's what they all came to Aurora in? All our ancestors?" Tye asked. That put the vessel in perspective for them, and it bestowed a sense of reverence as well. As they approached the airlock and slowed to a stop, Andrew said, "Jon and Rachel need to go. Maybe Shannon too?"

Nate nodded, "I wish we all could go."

Shawna made a face. "I dunno. You sure there's nothing...bad over there?."

Nate grimaced. "We don't know, do we? Even so, we probably won't get another chance like this."

Andrew shrugged. "I'll stay and take care of Adamant. Shawna should go."

Nate nodded again. "Yep. In fact, everybody except Andrew should come."

They all donned environment suits, and as they prepared to move into the airlock, Shannon patted Nate on the back. Her wicked amusement transmitted clearly across the comm.

"Try not to break your suit this time, Nate."

Chapter 6

They crowded out the airlock to make the short hop over to Hope One. A spacewalk outside was somehow a much different experience than being inside the Behemoth. The infinitude of space had a weight that drove itself instantly into the consciousness, even inside the Vale with the tremendous dust clouds surrounding them on every side, refracting rainbows from the incredible power of Sanctuary's blue-white sun. They all felt it, as attested by the silence over their suit radios once Adamant's airlock had opened. Each of them pushed off gently from Adamant toward the airlock on Hope One, which they could already see had handholds surrounding it. They reached it one by one and they all managed to grab on without trouble.

By mutual unspoken agreement, they allowed Rachel to examine the airlock's controls. After a brief once over, she announced, "It's coded."

There was a moment of silence, then Jon said, "Try Trisha."

"Oh," Rachel said. She keyed something in the light on the airlock glowed and it slid open, silent in the vacuum. "That was mom's name," she said after a short silence. "Dad must have expected it would be us. I mean, I know Teron said he had, but…" She trailed off and pulled herself forward into the airlock.

Considering the size of the ship, the airlock was surprisingly small, barely big enough for five of them at once. As it cycled, Shannon remarked, "It's amazing that this stuff still works. It's been a thousand years, right? And that's like three thousand earth years." She looked a bit overwhelmed by the sheer amount of time.

Rachel shook her head, half smiling in memory. "Dad always had a knack for leaving things so they'd work when they were needed. It was one of his talents. Besides, null gravity makes a lot of difference, and it's all been asleep."

Laura commented, "I think there's even air in here. Not sure whether it's breathable."

A quick look into the fields confirmed that she was right, and as the airlock opened into the ship itself, Nate unsealed his helmet. The air inside Hope One smelled like machinery and old grease, but Nate didn't have any trouble breathing it, and light flooded into the airlock from the corridor beyond.

After a moment, Jon noticed what Nate had done and he frowned. "You know that could have killed you, right?"

Nate grinned crookedly and popped his helmet loose completely. After a little consideration the others followed his example and Nate said thoughtfully, "The others should be through soon enough. I'm not sure about you guys, but since the air's good I'm going to leave my suit here."

Nods went around the group and all five proceeded to strip their suits off. Once the airlock had cycled open again and the rest of the group was busy stripping off their own suits, Rachel turned down the passage to her right and began pulling herself along via handholds recessed into the wall. Jon, Nate and Shannon followed silently, with Jon behind Rachel and Nate bringing up the rear behind Shannon.

The lights in Hope One came on well ahead of them and went off again once they had passed, but even in the space directly around them the ship's corridors were dimly lit. Some of the lights had failed with time, and a thin layer of fine dust had collected on every surface. Nate had no idea where it might have come from, but they stirred it up as they passed, making him sneeze now and then, following as he was.

The trip from the airlock took what felt like an age, and they made it in silence, buried in their own thoughts. Finally, Rachel came to another closed hatch, which she took only a few seconds to open. The corridor beyond turned at a right angle and Nate realized that what they'd been pulling themselves along was actually a ladderway. Hope One had been built vertically with the nose pointing upward. What they were entering now was actually a short corridor that crossed the width of the vessel, with a hatch to either side of them and another pointed toward the nose of the craft when they reached the center of the corridor. Rachel stopped again and spent a longer time with this hatch.

Just when Nate was about to ask what she'd found, Rachel smacked the hatch with one hand and, with a resounding crack, it sprang open.

Rachel looked back at Nate with a wry grin. "Aqueous's privilege. The lock was frozen and it's our ship." She made a face as she ran a hand over the warped hatch frame.

Nate blinked in surprise. "Aqueous?"

"Didn't you know?" She shrugged. "Aqueous specializes in mental or physical force. I got mostly the physical." Rachel pushed through into the next room, which would actually have been above them, Nate realized, if the ship had been oriented properly in a gravity well. It was unmistakably the bridge, and as he followed the others through, Nate looked curiously around. Unlike aboard Adamant, the control stations here were arranged in a circle, and the room's 'ceiling' was further away than either of the walls, suggesting to him that they must be right in the nose of the craft near where the cone came to a point.

All of that was pushed out of his mind by the curious mass in the center of the room. Dominating the massive bridge was a giant cloud, or so it seemed at first glance. The lights mounted around the perimeter of the room and at the control stations didn't illuminate it perfectly, but even so he could see that the roughly spherical mass nearly filled the space, with tendrils and arms extending toward the control stations that ringed the bridge.

Nate and the others had all caught hold of something, whether the room's broken hatch, in his case, or the nearest control station, in Jon and Rachel's. Shannon was hovering near the wall, her head cocked, staring at the thing.

"It's the Vale," she said, wonder filling her voice.

"I wondered what Dad did to create it," Jon half grumbled. "Looks like we get to see that at least."

Cautiously, Rachel reached forward from where she clung to the control station and passed her hand through one tendril of the cloud, her eyes glued on her hand. No swirl of dust followed her movement. Was the cloud a projection? A hologram?

"Can't feel it," she said.

Nate opened his senses to the fields and examined the cloud. The most obvious feature was a pulsing—a vibration—that brightened and darkened the cloud almost too rapidly to perceive. He watched it, fascinated, as the seconds passed and the cloud shifted slowly, waves flowing across its surface. It was an intuition as much as anything that connected the pulsing and the movement in his brain, but suddenly he could see it clearly. The cloud moved the tiniest bit with each pulse of light. It was the light that was causing it to shift and change.

A sudden suspicion crossed Nate's mind and he pushed off gently from the hatch where he clung toward the cloud. It took a moment for him to reach it, but as he passed into it he heard Shannon and Rachel exclaim in surprise.

Rachel called out, "Voids, Nate. Be CAREFUL." Then his vision was blocked completely. He could still hear without significant muffling, and he could breathe just fine, but his sight was completely obscured by the brownish cloud. Even worse, his Energematrice6 sense was flooded with the strobing energy that brought the cloud to life.

"Well, if there's anything dangerous in here, I'll definitely be the first to find it," Nate said wryly, a tick late. "even if I can't actually see anything."

Drifting through the cloud, Nate moved his arms back and forth, feeling for anything solid in the murk. Just when he thought he must be almost through the other side, Nate found what he was looking for with his chest, crashing into it full-on without any kind of warning. The air rushed out of his lungs. Even in zero gravity, inertia had its way. He flailed instinctively, grabbing for the thing with his arms as he bounced off and managed to wrap them around it, pulling himself in. At such close range, the pulses of light that were obviously coming from the thing he'd wrapped himself around were blinding to his Energematrice6 sense. From this range, he could actually feel the energy flowing out of the object into the cloud as if it were moving through his own body. As his mind traced the threads of power, he could distantly sense connections between the cloud around him and the unimaginable vastness of the Vale itself.

Any detail was lost to him at first glance. The pattern was too complex, and the pulses were too intense. It was like being blinded by a strobe light while trying to read fine print. He gasped, sucking air back into his lungs, then refocused on the object—it felt like a big ball—that he was hugging against his chest. He could see the Energematrice6 flowing through the ball, from the center to the outside then back to center again, as rapidly as the strobing, brilliant pulse of energy went through the cloud that represented the Vale. Obviously, it was the source of that dazzling incandescence, but looking inward Nate could see that the Energematrice6 ran through uncountable tiny channels in the crystal globe. They stretched inside to outside, outside to inside. The channels were both many and one, a collection of myriad tiny veins that were just that, a collection, and that collection was a switch, or possibly a gate. He took in the totality of the object in the tiny space between flashes before being blinded once more. Some of the channels were closed; more than half, even, but the rest... Hoping he was right, Nate pushed on the collection of channels with his mind and both the flow and the strobing suddenly stopped.

Nate blinked, staring at Jon, Rachel, and Shannon. The cloud was gone. Nate moved his head, the motion causing him to drift.

His arms were still wrapped around the crystal globe, which was now free of whatever had bound it to the center of the ship.

Everyone was speechless as Nate began to slowly tumble. Then Rachel said disbelievingly, "I hope you meant to do that. Something tells me Sanctuary's not gonna be real pleased."

Nate shook his head. "I just made it go passive. I don't think I actually shut the Vale off...not exactly." He paused, then added, "Maybe if we brought it back, and gave it to the council? Or..." He trailed off thoughtfully.

Rachel shrugged, but nodded in acceptance. Meanwhile Shannon had pushed off from the wall, flying toward him. She reached out an arm to him and he grabbed it as she floated past, allowing her to pull him into motion toward the opposite wall, one arm still wrapped around the globe.

When Nate finally managed to catch hold of a control console after pushing off the opposite wall, he took a moment to catch his breath. Then, he unwrapped his arm from around the globe and actually looked at it, allowing it to float in front of him in the dimness of the bridge. Even without his Energematrice6 sense, it was breathtaking. If someone could have made a marble the size of a beach ball, then put a living, moving replica of the Vale inside, that was what he beheld. Through his Energematrice6 sense, it was even more spectacular, if for different reasons. Energy in a thousand shades flowed through a myriad of intricate patterns inside it. Nate imagined if he could see the electrons moving through a computer, this was what it might look like.

They all stared at the object for a long time, spellbound, until Jon finally asked, "So now what?"

Nate looked over at Jon, his mouth twisted into a wry grin. "I think we'll take it with us. It may come in handy."

They were still staring at the globe, enraptured, when Laura poked her helmetless head through the hatch. "Ahhh. There you are. The others are right behind me." She eyed the globe in front of Nate, her eyebrows raised. "Looks like you already found something, huh? It's pretty."

Shannon snorted. "Yeah, he found it alright."

Then Tye, Keevan, Jesse, and Shawna were all crowding through the hatch into the bridge and exclaiming over the globe. Tye immediately pushed himself off the doorway toward Nate in an effort to see it more closely, which ended with Nate trying to grip the console with his legs while holding the globe in one arm and attempting to catch Tye with the other. Then came Shannon's acerbic account of how Nate had come into possession of it, with more emphasis than Nate would have liked on how he'd had no idea what he was doing. She finished with a grin in his direction that made it clear she was mostly teasing him.

There were a few good-natured jibes and Keevan moved to examine the globe himself, eventually asking, "What's our objective? We dunno how much air's left in this heap. Can't be more than a few hours, roight? ...Unless the scrubbers are still running." He looked doubtful.

Rachel huffed. "Heap nothing. She's been sitting here for a thousand years and she's still holding air! What other ship can you say that about?"

Keevan shrugged uncomfortably. "Sorry. No offense. I been hearin' talk about 'the vessel' my whole life. I was practically expecting somethin' magical. My own fault, really."

Nate shook his head wryly. "Let's have a look around and see what's here. Anything Jon and Rachel want to look at they can. It's their ship and their show."

The others agreed and spread out to try the other hatches along the corridor leading to the bridge. The first find came almost immediately. Rachel stuck her head out of a compartment at the end of the hall, calling for Nate. Of course, everyone had to gather again to see what she'd found. Inside what, according to Jon, used to be the captain's private office, metal loops lined one wall. Each loop had a pendant attached to it, much like those that graced Jon and Rachel's necks. There were three empty loops at one end of the row, but ten of them were still occupied. The pendants' gems were identical in shape to Jon and Rachel's, but each had a different color that caught the light from the room's ceiling fixtures.

Jesse stared at the row of pendants, his eyes widening. "Paul's Amulets! He made twelve of 'em before he finally created the Sigil. Dad always said they're the most powerful E6 artifacts in the galaxy." He paused for a second then shrugged. "At least, they're the most powerful ones that Paul left behind. Dad was always a little afraid've what Paul might'a made and neva talked about."

Nate pulled himself to a stop at the desk by one wall and looked at the Amulets thoughtfully as the others crowded into the room behind him and Rachel. Noting the three empty loops and the glow coming from the pendants around his, Rachel's, and Jon's necks, Nate called back to the rest of the group, "One for each of you, I think. I'll carry the rest for now."

Tye was, of course, the first to reach them, and after passing his hand over each of the gems, he picked out a light blue crystal that instantly began to glow when he put it around his neck. Tye's eyes grew large and he looked at Nate. "This is so much power! I'm like five Energematrists now! Fifty!"

Tye was right. When Nate looked at the Amulet using Energematrice6, it was a very curious object indeed. Like Nate's own Sigil of the Mysteries, it looked almost like an inverted funnel, or maybe a concave lens, bending the fields as they streamed through it, focusing and multiplying them dramatically.

Nate snorted. "Lightmaker help us all. Remember what I told you about power, will you?"

Tye nodded, grinning, and pushed off for the door, obviously intent on seeing what else he might find.

The others made picking theirs into a ritual of sorts. Shannon was next, passing her hand over each one, frowning, feeling how each interacted with Energematrice6, and settling on a pink crystal so dark it verged on red. Each in turn did the same. Shawna took the deep green amulet. Keevan took a gray one that barely glowed, even though it seemed just as potent as the others. Laura took a long time when her turn came, eventually choosing a dark blue gem. When his turn finally came, Jesse hesitated, clearly uncertain. Nate frowned thoughtfully and looked Jesse directly in the eyes. "Jesse Galton, will you follow me? Even if it means leaving Sanctuary and all you've ever known?"

Jesse gulped visibly. "I... Yes. Yes, I will."

Nate inclined his head, accepting the promise. "Take one."

Jesse's amulet was dark red, leaving four—soft purple, yellow, brown and turquoise—unclaimed. Nate finally approached, taking those that remained and slipping them carefully into his pocket.

The next find was less interesting for most of them. Jon called out to Rachel from the room that had been their father's as the head of the colony expedition. When she got there, they both bent over a piece of paper pinned to Paul's desk. Nate glanced into the room, but seeing what they were about, he left them to it.

Meanwhile, Shannon had, characteristically, been checking to see if the vessel was functional and to what degree. Nate found her back on the bridge, shaking her head as she paged through screens on an ancient monitor.

Nate grinned. "Bit dated, huh?"

Shannon glanced up at him and returned his grin. "Oh, sure, but I expected that. I'm just amazed at how close the basic design of this system is to Adamant. It's almost like they were built by the same person." Her lips twisted. "Might have been, I guess. No way to know, really, but yeah. I know how it works."

As if on cue, Tye poked his head through the hatch. "Shannon thinks she knows everything." He grinned cheekily at her. "And she's almost right."

Shannon snorted, but she laughed despite herself as Tye pulled his head back out into the passage.

Nate smiled at her and she nodded wryly as if Tye had made a point. "I really don't mean to be a know-it-all." Her lack of defensiveness and Tye's obviously friendly attitude lit a warm glow inside of Nate. Maybe they really *had* been listening to him.

He nodded back and raised his eyebrows. "So, where do we stand?"

Shannon shook her head. "I wouldn't want to try to move Hope. She's been sitting too long. We obviously have auxiliary power, but it's using an E6 field tap that's so primitive it makes my hair stand on end just being in the same ship with it. If we turned it on it might work...or it might not work—catastrophically." She shrugged. "Not really sure what you want to do."

Nate frowned thoughtfully. "What about the defensive systems? Are they patched into the computer?"

Shannon shook her head again. "Nope, and that's another reason I wouldn't want to move it. Who knows what would happen if the collision system really is tied to the moon? Wouldn't even care to guess."

Nate nodded. "I think we'll leave it here...WITHOUT messing with the defenses."

Shannon agreed, and Nate went to search the next deck down with the others.

Chapter 7

There were two other notable finds over the next hour. Most of the rooms they checked had obviously been used for colonists first, with the mounting points and plumbing for cold sleep chambers still sticking through floor and walls, capped off or coiled and secured with ancient, congealed rigger tape. There were also dust patterns on just about every surface that showed they had later been used for storage, probably of artifacts that Paul eventually removed, based on half-visible shapes in the dust.

As he emerged from the crawlway to yet another deck below, a sharp exclamation drew Nate down a main passage. A moment later the cry repeated, even sharper and more insistent. "No! Don't!" It was Shawna's voice. Again, Nate followed her cry to a completely unmarked side chamber that at first seemed exactly like all the others. The walls and ceiling were the same as any other compartment, but then Nate saw something that instinctively made him reach out to grasp a handhold in the corridor wall. In the center of the room a column of something shiny jutted out of the floor. It wasn't metal—some kind of glass or crystal perhaps?

Atop it sat a gem that was roughly the size of Nate's head. It was so dark that it drank in all the light that surrounded it, looking more like a hole in reality than a crystal. Nate could see its facets only on one side, where the light reflected faintly from the sheer surface.

The more immediate concern was Keevan, who stood transfixed before it, his hand outstretched. Nate had arrived just in time or he might not have believed what he saw. Wisps of darkness reached out from that pitch-black void to meet Keevan's fingertips, as if drawing him in to touch it. He might have been sleepwalking, his motions slow and clumsy, as he shuffled toward the strange object. Then he did touch it. When his skin contacted the gem, his body went completely rigid.

His head swiveled slowly, menacingly toward Shawna, who stood just out of Nate's view from the corridor, inside the edge of the doorway. The voice that issued from Keevan's lips was far too deep for his small frame. "***So*... *Long*... *In The Darkkkkkk!***"

Shawna was silent, as if whatever she saw in Keevan's eyes had rendered her speechless.

Nate's mind was racing, but he too was frozen in place, not sure how to respond.

Keevan spoke again. "***I* *Am* *Jozriel.***" Then, after a moment, "***How Did You Come To My Prison, Human?***" Shawna let out a strangled gasp, but still didn't speak. With barely a pause, Jozriel spoke again, its tone unmistakably impatient. "***Humans... Were it possible I had forgotten how stupid and weak you are? Though the Maker's fiends locked us away so *Long* ago, still I should have remembered*.**"

Nate stepped forward into the doorway, so he could see Shawna clearly. She was gasping and clutching at her throat, and some movement of her hand must have brought the amulet hanging there to the creature's attention, because its next words seemed almost excited. "***What...* *What is this??* *Who** made you, little pretty?* *What luck!* *Hmmmm... Locked away, I see... But such power...* *Such.... Power!*"* The final, almost reverent note of Jozriel's monologue was cut short as Nate drifted forward through the doorway and Keevan's head whipped around to stare at him.

It was, indeed, his eyes that shocked Nate the most. They were completely black, sucking in the light like the gem to which Keevan's hand was still affixed. His face was stuck in a rigid, grinning mask, almost like a caricature of a clown. Nate shivered involuntarily as those eyes widened even further, the horrifying light-devouring blackness eating yet more of Keevan's face. The harsh, sibilant voice, still far too deep and completely wrong for Keevan's vocal chords, assaulted him directly. **"*Who are you?...* *What...ARE You?***"**

The huge, black eyes narrowed, which felt somehow even worse than before, as if all the malevolent attention in the universe was focused through their slitted aperture. **"*Yoou??? The One?? I should have guessed!!***"** It paused, thinking, then howled. **"*But... How can this be? Do They know?? Did They foresee?!?!***"**

He stared for another long, frozen moment and let out a shriek so unearthly that Nate and Shawna both gave a violent start. **"*The Wyrm tricked me!!! From the very beginning, it knew. Even before I was cursed to sightless imprisonment in this mortal hell!! For this, my children—my race—will die? This cannot stand! It must not stand!!***"**

With that, Keevan moved so quickly Nate barely registered what he was doing. He certainly didn't have time to react before Keevan had lifted the enormous faceted gem and hurled it straight at Nate's head.

Instinctively, in the nick of time, Nate reached up to slap the huge gem out of the air, but was barely fast enough. There was a brilliant flash when his hand contacted it, leaving spots dancing in his vision, and somehow the flash reached beyond the spectrum of visible light. Nate's awareness of Energematrice6 was pierced with the same bright hole as his vision. The black gem, meanwhile, clanged off the metal bulkhead to his right and floated off into the middle of the room.

Keevan dove for the object with a cry, but Shawna saw what he was doing and pushed off to intercept. She slammed into him, and the two hit the bulkhead in a tangle of arms and legs as Nate's vision began to clear.

Keevan squawked, "C'mon Shawna! We gotta take it with us! It's callin' to me, I'm tellin' ya!" He tried to disentangle himself, his eyes still fixed on the gem floating across the room behind Shawna.

"Keevan!" Nate barked, "What in the void is the matter with you?"

"Nate! Help!" Shawna's tone was fearful and she clung desperately to Keevan's arm.

Nate pushed off toward the gem where it floated across the room. As he traveled, he turned slowly toward Keevan, rotating his body. When he spun past, something in the surface of the gem caught his eye and seemed to stare back at him, leering. There was no time to wonder over it, though.

"Keevan! Snap out of it!" Nate's tone was commanding, but Keevan continued to babble.

"We've gotta take it with us. Can't yeh see? It's..." Keevan cut off as Nate came between him and the gem.

"I think not." Nate said. "In fact, Keevan, go see what else you can find. Now."

Keevan frowned and started to open his mouth again, but then he really saw the look on Nate's face, and finally awareness penetrated his near-mania. He blinked in surprise, then frowned uncertainly and shook his head, as if to clear it. "I guess... Yeah, okay." He turned reluctantly away and pushed off toward the hatch where they'd come in, rubbing his palm.

Shawna turned to stare at the gem as Nate touched down on the "wall" and rebounded back toward the door, his own wary gaze now fixed on the gem as it floated in the back corner of the room. She asked in a quiet voice, "What? What...is it?"

Nate's expression was bleak. "I'm not precisely sure, but I don't think it's something I want any of us touching ever again."

Keevan didn't wait for them outside the hatch, instead swinging into another room down the corridor.

Once he and Shawna were both outside, Nate closed the hatch himself and locked it, keying a code into the electronic lock. Shawna looked at Nate, frowning. "Was that... One of Them? Caught in that gem?"

Nate stared back at her, frowning in thought, then shrugged. "Or something worse. I wish I knew...or maybe I don't." He shook his head. "No safer place for it than here, and I'm not taking it with us."

One final find, from Laura, distracted them. She came from another room, yet another level down, holding what at first looked like a fist-size cylinder. When she handed it to Nate, however, it became obvious that it was a set of disks, bound together by an unseen force. When Nate examined the object with Energematrice6, he couldn't tell whether it was intended to use the fields directly or simply drew on them to retain its integrity. There was Energematrice6 flowing through it, but the configuration was strange, and it didn't respond to Nate's prodding. Nate shrugged and agreed that it too should be taken along.

The room in which Laura had found the disks was another puzzle. It was a storage room, but none of the other objects inside were directly linked to Energematrice6 in any unusual fashion. They were just ordinary gems or simple machines, like a microscope and a bank of decrepit computers.

A cursory examination of the rest of the ship yielded nothing of note. They were all getting tired, but Jon and Rachel were still in their father's old cabin.

When Nate went to check on them, he found them just sitting, staring at a metal ring that hung in the air between them. It was a plain band with no inscription or markings, but tears spilled from Rachel's eyes and hovered in tiny droplets around her face. Jon looked heartsick.

Rachel saw Nate and she let out a choked sob. "It's his wedding ring. He left it for us. He's gone." She broke down again, crying quietly.

Jon grimaced, then said without looking at Nate, "He loved mom so much. He never let her go. Even though she died when we were too young to remember, he talked about her all the time like she was still there."

Nate closed the hatch behind him and floated there, looking at the ring thoughtfully. After a long moment, Jon continued, "The fact that he left that for us means he really thought he was going to die. There's no other reason he would have done it." He turned toward Nate, his face drained of color.

Rachel dashed the tears from her eyes, using one hand to steady herself, and shook her head. "He can't be. He just can't. We'll find him."

Nate pushed off gently from where he clung to the hatch and caught himself next to Rachel, then enfolded her in a hug made awkward by the lack of gravity. "Is that what he'd want you to do?"

Rachel sighed. "No. Of course not. He told us NOT to, but we can't give up on him."

Nate bit his lip, but he shook his head. "Rach, you're not giving up on him. If I know you at all, you never will, but you only have so much time in this world. What was your dad doing with his time?"

Rachel raised one hand in denial, but then she looked Nate right in the eyes and he could feel her heart breaking as she answered, "He was fighting against the evil Lastis released into the world. His whole life, that's all he did—fight to save people from it and fight it himself, but there was never anybody to look after HIM."

Nate nodded, frowning. "So what did he want you to do?"

Rachel shook her head, obviously resisting what she said even as she said it, "He always said, 'There are only two paths in life. We can fight against evil or fight for it, whether by action or inaction.'" She stopped for a moment, then looked at Nate through tear-fogged eyes. "He said those were the only two choices we have."

Nate nodded again, grimly. "He was right...and so are you. Someone should take care of him." Nate paused, giving Rachel another squeeze then reaching over to lay a hand on Jon's arm. "Be sure what you choose to do doesn't waste the time you have."

Rachel finally hugged Nate back, fiercely. When she stopped, Nate released her, allowing himself to drift toward the ceiling as she turned to regard her father's ring again, her face finally relaxing. Nate pushed off of the ceiling to flip himself around and move toward the door.

Behind him, Rachel said quietly, "He wanted us to help you, when you arrived, and we will."

He turned his head as he reached the door and nodded to her with a grave, quiet smile. "We have so much to do, you can't even imagine."

The trip back to Adamant was mostly uneventful, though they could find no simple way to move the artifact that controlled the Vale, which was christened unimaginatively by Tye the 'Globe of the Vale.' After some discussion, Tye volunteered to hold it while they towed him across the gap with a length of line. That accomplished, they went through the process of cycling through Adamant's airlock yet again. Once back aboard, Nate went to secure the Globe of the Vale in his own cabin.

At first, he couldn't find an appropriate place to put it. It was just large enough that none of the storage compartments, even the closet, would fit it. Eventually, he decided that securing it to the sleeping couch with the restraint netting was his best option.

That done, he made his way to the bridge where Andrew was examining the others' amulets with fascination. Smiling, Nate offered him a choice of the remaining four. Andrew looked nervous at first. Even quickly passing his hand over each to feel the Energematrice6 flowing through them left him sweating, but he seemed genuinely grateful when he chose the yellow amulet. He put it on, and it lit up with a soft golden light.

"Andrew," Nate asked, "what's bothering you?"

Andrew's lips twisted. "I used to be good at this."

Nate simply waited while Andrew sat staring at his new amulet.

After a long moment, Andrew said, "I almost killed myself. We always just called it overexertion. It's what you call entropic shock. It was when we were running away. Back...home? Makes me wish I had one of those." He eyed Nate's Rechemacula dolefully.

Nate nodded, and Andrew shook his head. "It was...bad. There was no time to rest when I did it, and ever since..." He shook his head again. "Ever since, I can hardly stand to open my senses to it. I know it's all in my head, but I just can't."

Shawna spoke up from where she was strapped in. "Andy, you saved us so many times. Whatever you can't do, it's not because you're weak."

Andrew barked a laugh. "Oh I don't have any regrets. I did what I had to do, but now?"

He shrugged helplessly, then looked up into Nate's eyes. "I can barely stand to even look at it now."

Nate nodded. "We'll find a way to help you. There isn't time right now, but we will find a way."

Jon looked at Andrew sadly. "I can't heal entropic shock, you know. I've tried."

Tye snorted. "You and everybody else." He smiled sympathetically at Andrew. "Just be glad you didn't hurt yourself physically. The physical part is even harder to heal than the mental part. The professors could help people whose minds were...stuck, like yours."

As they all secured themselves for travel, Rachel stared through the great window at Hope One from two seats to Nate's left. "I almost wish I could stay."

Next to her, Jon asked gently, "And do what, Rach?"

She shook her head mutely as Laura laid a hand on her arm from the other side. Laura's eyes were more than a bit haunted as she turned to Rachel. "I know how you feel." She squeezed Rachel's hand.

Jon, too, squeezed her hand and Rachel turned her head to give him a crooked grin. "At least we're not trapped in a crystal anymore."

"Speaking of which," Nate was frowning. "We had a little incident aboard Hope." He relayed to them all what had happened with Keevan and Shawna and the black gem. When he'd finished, Keevan was staring at him as if he'd never seen him before.

"I don't remember any 'a that." Keevan shook his head, absentmindedly rubbing his hand. "I swear. I would never." He looked troubled, and shook his head again, almost reflexively.

Nate nodded grimly, "It was messing with your mind. If you'd seen what we saw... Well..." He shrugged.

Shawna looked scared, presumably at even the memory of what had happened.

"I'd never..." Keevan seemed almost desperate now, and Jesse reached over to lay a hand on his shoulder. "It's all right, Raddink. Ya have friends around yeh."

Keevan looked at Jesse, nonplussed, and laughed aloud. "Imagine! A Galton saying that. ...Ta me! Am I dreamin'?" Jesse smiled, but Keevan's own gaze had turned inward, presumably to his own memories.

After regarding Keevan thoughtfully, Jesse looked over to Nate. "I'm glad ya asked me along, Brightstar."

Nate looked at Jesse quizically. "I asked? ...That was Rebus' idea." His lips twisted ironically. "Not that I mind having you along. You were more than welcome."

Jesse had gone pale, though, and he shook his head. "We have to get back. Rebus is up to something, and we have to stop him."

Nate sighed, returning Jesse's alarmed stare with a resigned one. "We'll head back, but based on what you just said, Rebus was trying hard to get you out of the way. Don't be surprised if our welcome is worn out."

Jesse shook his head again, stubbornly, "My father would never allow something like this. Rebus is goin' too far."

When they had all settled in, Andrew took the helm to head them all back toward Lighthouse Station. The trip back through Hope One's collision field was slow and might have been painfully dull if they weren't all exhausted from their search. As it was, every one of them was in a near-stupor as Andrew inched them back out of Hope One's field then turned his attention to navigating around the primary toward Lighthouse Station.

As they traveled, Nate studied the clouds of the Vale around them. Was there less movement? Less density? He wasn't certain, but it seemed to him that there must be. Or he was imagining it. How could he compare when he hadn't known to look in the first place?

Chapter 8

After they left the collision field, it took an hour to get back to Lighthouse Station. When they arrived, they docked at their previous berth and again waited for the docking mechanisms to complete their seal. As they moved to debark, Nate traded a glance with Jesse, then said, "You should all stay here... except Jesse. We'll go see whether we're welcome anymore."

Andrew looked at him askance. "Is that wise?"

Nate read agreement with Andrew in the eyes of several of the others, but he just shook his head. "What do you think they're going to do?" Andrew didn't look convinced, but the rest of the little group didn't follow when Nate turned and pushed himself toward the airlock. As he hit the button to open it, he turned back to them, his mouth quirked wryly. "One way or another, I doubt this will take long."

When Nate emerged from the airlock into the station, there was, again, a greeting party. This time, however, it was two of the council members with no crowd or fanfare. Elders Rebus and Eden stood stiffly, their backs straight, and Nate couldn't help feeling that they were looking down their noses at him from the very instant he left the airlock. Nate also couldn't help noticing the two security guards that loomed behind them, their faces blank.

"Nate," Rebus said, stepping forward. "The council would ask that you and any of yer companions who wish ta' come back aboard Lighthouse Station accompany us ta' a full council session."

Nate's eyebrows rose and he frowned, but then he nodded thoughtfully. "I can do that."

Immediately upon following Nate out of the airlock, Jesse saw Rebus and Eden and scowled. "Are you two making trouble again?" He looked over at Nate. "I wondered if I should have stayed here just to see that they couldn't do anything...stupid."

Rebus smirked. "The council's convened and waiting. Best come along, Jesse."

Nate spent the ten minute walk in melancholy contemplation. He had enjoyed his comparatively short stay on Lighthouse Station, and he got the distinct feeling that time would soon be coming to an end, whether he liked it or not. By contrast, Jesse was visibly fuming beside him.

As they approached the conclave, its main door now guarded by two strong-looking men, Nate laid a hand on Jesse's arm. "Let me do the talking." Jesse nodded reluctantly as they were ushered through.

"...urge you toward reason." Elder Strong was speaking as they stepped into the conclave, but she broke off at the sight of them. The podium had been removed, replaced by chairs for each member of the council...except Jesse.

Rebus and Eden led them down the main aisle toward the council, which sat in a semicircle facing them, with two empty spaces. Looking awkward, Rebus and Eden hurried down the aisle to take their places in those empty chairs, leaving Nate and Jesse to walk the last few yards by themselves. Nate glanced over at Jesse and smiled crookedly, continuing to move at a dignified pace. The auditorium around them had fewer people in it than the last time they had gathered, but the mood was ugly. From Jesse's dark glances around, Nate suspected the crowd had been gathered a bit...selectively.

When he reached the dais, Nate stepped up onto the circular platform in the center of the room directly across from the council and promptly sat down cross-legged facing them. Most looked a bit shocked as he did, evidently having expected him to remain standing like a criminal come for justice. Elder Jaben frowned thoughtfully and Elder Strong's eyes widened and crinkled at the corners. She managed to suppress her smile, but it was a near thing.

Jesse stood for a moment, looking around at the council with a mixture of confusion and hurt, hardening into a deep anger. As Jesse took a position beside Nate, also cross-legged, Jaben spoke, "Nate, we find that there is some...question regarding your status and we wish ta' make a formal inquiry—"

Rebus broke in. "How rapidly do ya age, boy?"

Jaben gave Rebus an annoyed look and continued as smoothly as he could. "There are allegations that you're..." He paused uncomfortably, "an 'Odd.'"

Jaben's discomfort intensified, but he soldiered on. "There's also been suggestion that you're not, as claimed, the Brightstar." He trailed off, frowning at Nate.

Nate nodded slowly, then shrugged. He looked Jaben in the eye. "I am who I am. You can call me whatever name you choose. It was the Keeper, your own leader, who gave me this." He held up the Sigil of the Mysteries, which glowed softly even in the bright light of the auditorium. "Tell me, from where do you take the name 'Brightstar?'"

Surprisingly, it was Eden who spoke in response. "From the prophecies of the Wildman, Siever Radding." His eyes were fixed on Nate as he continued. "Many know of the prophecies of Radding, given at the Telestry. We take the name Brightstar from his most famous prophecy, 'Darkness before you and chaos behind you, in hubris and weakness the bright star will blind you.'"

Eden looked at Nate hard as he continued, "What few know is that we, too, were given a sign, when Radding pierced the Vale upon his third Rejection. The words have been preserved, passed down through the council and through my own family. They are not known widely—have never been spoken before a full session of the council, even, but they have been kept as a surety against the day of Brightstar's appearance."

Eden paused, likely reciting in his own head. When he spoke again, he was obviously quoting long-rehearsed and oft-repeated memory. "Like a filing to the lodestone, the light of goodness draws him. His only home within the Vale, an elder spring of truth and lore. To the people he gives praise and to council respect and honor their due."

As Eden finished, Rebus rose to his feet. He had obviously been waiting for the cue, because he pointed accusingly at Nate. "Disrespect. Disrespect is all yeh've shown the council! 'Elder spring of truth'? Fah. The drivel ya spread among the people is as foul as you are, Odd! Brightstar ya most certainly are not!"

Beside Nate, Jesse jumped to his feet. "You would defy my father openly!?! When he returns—"

Nate interrupted Jesse without seeming to raise his voice, but still driving past his outburst, "Peace, Jesse."

Nate shook his head slowly, then looked each member of the council in the eye in turn before he spoke. "What exactly were you expecting? Am I too young? Too strange?" He paused in thought, then shook his head again. "'No prophet is accepted in his own country.' The Wild Man was rejected by the Telestry, not once but three times for giving them more truth than he gave to anyone else in the galaxy. Likewise, I gave you the truth more plainly than I may anywhere else, and you reject it." There were mutters from the audience behind Nate, and the council's faces grew, if possible, even more stony than they had been before.

Jaben shook his head in rejection. "Ya defied the council directly, Nate 'Brightstar,' and your... history lesson... left more unrest among the people of Sanctuary than we've had in my entire lifetime."

Nate rose to his feet. Though he was still shorter than any of them, seated as they were in their tall council chairs, Nate might have towered over them. "Long after this universe is lost to memory, an unwelcome truth will still be the most potent insult it is possible for one person to offer another. Ancient lore from

Earth itself tells you that wisdom loves correction, but a fool wants nothing more than to hear his own words in another's mouth."

Rebus looked on the brink of speaking again, his face growing red, but Nate continued. "The truth is that the people of Sanctuary lead the most privileged life in the galaxy. Because you are protected by the Vale, unopposed and unassailable, this council has become arrogant, even if your people are not.

"I paid you every respect you deserved. You cannot say the same about your treatment of me. Just as your prophecy says, I gave this council a come-down, exactly as you were due. It was the greatest gift I could offer you."

Apparently, Rebus could take no more. He broke in, yelling, "Take him!" With this utterance, Rebus's eyes changed, his pupils stretching into vertical slits. He stepped forward and stared into Nate's eyes, his voice dropping to a near whisper, "I know what you ARE...'Brightstar'."

Behind Nate, several people from the crowd rose up and stormed up the stairs while Nate stood frozen, his gaze locked with Rebus's, his attention shattering. Rebus knew. Nate could see it in those exsect eyes. He knew about both of Nate's worlds. He knew what Nate really was.

Then Rebus's cronies were around Nate, seizing him by the arms and around the middle, hefting him easily above their heads. For a moment, Nate was afraid they were going to actually tear him apart. He instinctively tried to seize Energematrice6 to defend himself. His mind was stuck in the same paralysis that was so familiar to his body in that other reality. He could see Energematrice6 as clearly as ever, but grasping it was so far beyond him in his shattered state, he didn't even know where to begin. He could no more use the fields than he could have done a handspring or even tied his own shoes in that other, impossibly distant world. Terror and confusion enveloped him as his helplessness struck home and he thrashed uselessly.

"Ta' the locks!" one of them yelled. There was a general roar of approval and the whole mass started moving, carrying him along. From where he was held above the crowd, as if from a world away, Nate could see Jesse's mouth drop open in shock. He also caught a glimpse of Rebus' gloating sneer. As the crowd turned, now joined by others from the surrounding amphitheater, Nate heard Jaben trying to impose his voice over their roar without success.

Nate's own shock at Rebus' revelation and a gut-wrenching feeling of failure prolonged his paralysis. The same four men held him over their heads, carrying him bodily through the station while the rest of the mob forced gawkers out of their way.

More than once as the eternity of the next minute or two wore on and a sense of unreality overcame his paralysis, Nate tried again to use Energematrice6, hoping to simply incapacitate the mob that carried him down the corridor. They were none too gentle, and the only thing he was certain of was that they were up to no good. If they were on their way to the airlock, as their words had suggested, that most likely meant another trip through the vacuum without gear. Over the time it took for the mob to reach the nearest airlock, on the opposite side of the station's hub from where Adamant was berthed, Nate struggled savagely against the wall that kept him from grasping the fields. Even as his shock wore off, something else stopped him. At first he thought it was the same paralysis that had gripped him when Rebus had caught his eyes, and the same sense of horror and failure reached up to strangle him. Slowly, he realized It wasn't. He could see Energematrice6. He had opened his senses to it, but something was stopping him from using it against these people. The realization of what that wall was came to him in a flash as they rounded the last corner and he saw the airlock ahead of them. It was the Great Schemic itself. With that realization, Nate's focus came clear and his grasp of Energematrice6 was instantaneous. His original instinct, to stop the mob that held him, was still impossible for him for reasons he couldn't quite understand, but he prepared himself for what he knew must be coming. When they reached the airlock, one of their number had run ahead to cycle it open, and they shoved him unceremoniously inside.

Well, Nate thought, *a little space walk isn't going to hurt me, whatever they might want.*

As the door was closing, he shaped the fields and, with his hand on the outside door, created a bubble around himself as quickly as he could, starting at his head and rapidly inflating to hold the rest of his body. This time, he didn't have to create his own air, only envelope the air already around him to hold it as the airlock depressurized.

He had barely finished when, a few seconds later, the door between him and the vacuum simply opened. Someone must have hit an emergency evacuation button, because the airlock hadn't cycled. The air was still inside the chamber, until suddenly it wasn't. The explosive decompression ripped Nate out of the airlock and tossed him into space, his bubble intact.

The worst part was the tumble his ejection put on him. He was both spinning and slowly somersaulting head over heels, and he had to close his eyes as they disagreed violently with his inner ear about what to do with his last meal. It took a few precious seconds for him to recover his equilibrium and start using small body movements to counteract his tumble.

Nate couldn't help the disorientation he had to fight, and it was a tremendous effort to maintain his little bubble of air. Still, being unprotected in the vacuum couldn't completely distract him from the raw majesty of the rainbow dust cloud, which seemed to hang just out of reach all around him. Nate's involuntary gasp of wonder was shockingly loud within his tiny bubble.

Then, his eyes caught a flash of fire from across the station where Adamant was berthed. The entire station lurched and Adamant shot away, wreckage from the station's docking clamps and umbilical tumbling in its wake. Nate chuckled darkly. Obviously Andrew had heard what happened.

As he watched, Adamant turned gracefully and came straight back toward the station, then, after what must have been a hurried discussion among its pilots, straight toward him. As it approached, it occurred to Nate to wonder whether they could actually see him. He didn't want to wind up splattered across the front of the vessel.

After thinking for a moment, Nate raised his hand and let loose a pulse of Energematrice6, focused in a bright blue-white flash. Over the next few seconds, he repeated the flash several times until it became obvious that Adamant was slowing to a stop in front of him. Another moment's thought led to a carefully crafted blast of air as a makeshift directional jet, adjusting Nate's trajectory toward Adamant's airlock, then several more strategic blasts as he approached.

Once he was at the airlock and able to grab a handhold, it took what felt like no time at all to pull himself inside and re-pressurize the lock. As he sagged inside the airlock, Nate's gorge rose again. He felt sicker than he'd have thought possible considering that he hadn't actually been exposed to vacuum.

As the air pressure rose around him, Nate finally released the bubble he'd been holding around himself with a gasp of relief. Containing a breathable bubble of air in a vacuum required tremendous energy, even without creating the air himself. When the inner airlock opened, he found Jon, Rachel, Shannon, Shawna, Laura, Keevan, and Tye all crowded around the hatch, their expressions ranging from enraged to anxious.

As they caught sight of him, their expressions all relaxed. Nate grinned weakly, then pulled himself through the inner airlock and felt his body spasm. His neck and shoulder were afire again too. When had that happened?

If there had been gravity, Nate would have fallen. He gasped and doubled over, and his body made another attempt to empty the contents of his stomach.

Nate somehow managed not to crash into anyone, but he felt hands on his back and shoulders and he heard Jon exclaim, "He's hurt! That's entropic shock!" Then a wash of power flowed through him and the sickness and disorientation retreated.

After a long, nauseous moment, he looked up into faces that were even more concerned than before and shrugged. "How'd you know they were throwing me out?"

Keevan sneered and waved his UPT in the direction of the station. "Those old buggers were bound ta' do somethin' stupid like that. Jesse's on the com. We should let 'im know we've got yeh here safe." He turned to stare at the airlock, facing back toward the station, his shoulders hunched, a confused mix of emotions playing across his face.

Nate nodded faintly and reached out to push off the wall as they all headed for the bridge. By the time he got there, he was feeling almost normal besides a bit of lingering nausea. Facing him on the window as he entered the bridge was a semi-transparent projection of Jesse.

Upon seeing Nate, Jesse's eyes widened. "Nate! You're okay?"

Nate smiled mirthlessly. "Seems like it."

"Well, I'm glad you're okay. It looked like they spaced you." Jesse shook his head in obvious disgust.

"They did," Nate said, his smile going crooked, still without humor.

Jesse's forehead wrinkled and he grinned. "Well, that's something." Then he frowned. "I should be out there with yeh." He glanced around himself at whatever was outside the video pickup, his face stony. "There's certainly nothing left for me here."

Nate's smile turned into a grin and he raised his eyebrows. "C'mon out, then."

Jesse snorted, then, seeing that Nate was serious, he blinked uncertainly. "How did ya...?"

Nate nodded. "Make a bubble around yourself while you're still in the airlock. Might be hard to hold your focus, but the amulet will give you plenty of power." Jesse hesitated, and Nate grimaced. "We can't afford to hang out here long, and there's no way they'll dock us up again. Make your choice, Jesse Galton."

Jesse returned his nod. "I'm on my way." He turned and the screen went black. Nate motioned to Andrew at the controls. "We need to get down there. Everybody strap in or at least grab onto something. Andrew, get us as close as you can without actually bumping them."

They did have to strap in before Andrew maneuvered, but once they were secure Nate went down to the airlock to receive Jesse. Sitting there in front of the closed lock, he opened his senses to the fields and focused. It hurt a little, probably from the entropic shock, but he managed, and when he tried he could actually look THROUGH the airlock door. It was almost a full minute before he saw the airlock across from them open and he hissed. Jesse's bubble wasn't strong enough, and molecules of air were rushing through it like a strainer, each one clear to Nate's enhanced senses.

As Nate watched, it flexed and started to distort. Nate set his hand against the corridor wall and reaching out, he pushed against Jesse's bubble where it was deforming, using his own concentration to help Jesse steady himself.

There was a moment where nothing changed, but then Jesse's bubble stabilized and tightened and Nate felt him push off toward Adamant's airlock. A few seconds later the airlock began to cycle.

Jesse was gasping as Nate had been when the airlock opened, but Nate thought it was more from terror than entropic shock. Over the next few seconds, Jesse's breathing went back to normal and everyone—Tye, Shannon, and Keevan had come down to see what was going on—headed back for the bridge.

After they were settled into their seats, they all just looked at each other, taking time to assess their situation.

It was Jesse who finally broke the silence, "Thank you all...and particularly thank you, Nate." He looked uncomfortable. "I should'a been able ta' handle that bubble. It *was* within my power. I guess I could use some practice."

Nate nodded with a genuine smile. "You're welcome."

Andrew stretched in his chair and leaned over to look at Nate. "The question is, what now?"

Rachel was staring at Lighthouse Station, tightly-controlled rage behind her eyes. "I just want to poke holes in that tin can. If only there weren't innocent people over there."

Jon grunted and laid a hand on her arm. "But there are, Rach." Rachel nodded sharply and the two shared a look.

Nate glanced through the window at the space station and sighed. "It's a good question. We probably shouldn't hang around here, though. I'd rather not wait for Rebus to come up with another stupid idea." For the first time, a sharp prickle of anger hit Nate, but he shook his head, pushing it away.

Jesse smiled darkly. "Rebus's in trouble. He didn't have the council's approval for what he did, even without me there ta' keep an eye on him."

Nate snorted. "Not surprising. Maybe the others will have the backbone to hold him accountable. I still don't have any particular interest in hanging around. Anybody else?" Nate raised an eyebrow and looked around the bridge to see universal head shakes from everyone.

Tye grinned. "So what's next? ARE you going after the Dominion?"

Nate snorted again, but he didn't answer directly. Instead, he turned to Andrew. "How are we for supplies? There are ten of us now."

Andrew shook his head. "Air and water are fine, but we'll need food. We should have enough salvage left to trade for whatever we need, if we can find a place that will accept it."

He looked around to see if the others had anything to contribute. After a moment, Jesse said, "We have ta' get out of the Vale first."

Nate looked thoughtful—then his mouth quirked ironically. "I think I can fix that problem." He got out of his chair and left the bridge. A short while later, he returned carrying the crystal globe from his room. Several sets of eyes widened and Jesse sucked in a sharp breath.

"Ya can't! ...I mean, please... Take some time ta' think about this."

Nate sent Jesse a hard stare as the prickle of anger returned even stronger. "Oh I have, Jesse." Then, he forced himself to let the anger go, and sighed. "Do you really think the protection

Sanctuary has been under is beneficial without the Keeper to shepherd people in and out of the Vale?" Jesse blinked, opened his mouth to reply, then closed it again. Nate shook his head. "There will never be a 'good' time for this, but your people have been isolated for too long. Even if...your father...were still here, this state of affairs can't go on forever. We can't really protect people from the universe. We can only prepare them to face it, and I saw how many Energematrists you have aboard Lighthouse. Do you really think they can't defend themselves against pirates?"

Jesse sighed and shook his head. "They're really not gonna like it." His mouth twisted wryly. "Ya might be right, though. Maybe it's time for Sanctuary ta' rejoin the rest of the universe...and the Telestry too."

Tye laughed darkly at that, but Nate ignored him, grasping Energematrice6 and feeling for the channels inside the globe. Then, he nudged them into reverse.

For a few heartbeats, nothing happened, but soon the globe began to glow and pulse brilliantly in the visible spectrum. Nate opened his senses to the fields and gasped. The crystal looked like a hole in space, sucking in a tremendous amount of Energematrice6 from all around them, and the flow was actually increasing. It was more Energematrice6 than any of them could handle, even with the amulets, flowing into the globe every second.

They all stared at the artifact, marveling at it, before Jesse spoke, "Now we really need ta' leave. Lighthouse Station is armed, and if they figure out what you're doing, they may fire on us."

Nate nodded and looked to Andrew. "Let's get clear of Sanctuary. Head for the dust cloud. I have no idea how long this is going to take, but you can bet it won't be fast."

Chapter 9

Waiting for the Vale to clear was frustrating. They had no real indication of what the progress actually might be, so all they could do was wait. The null gravity wore on some of them. Jesse and Tye seemed particularly affected, while the others were mostly bored.

A few hours after they eased away from Lighthouse Station on a slow trip to the system's dust cloud boundary, they received a transmission from Elder Jaben, which Nate took on the ship's bridge.

The transmission was delayed because, again, the station used light-spccd transmitters. When Jaben's face came clear, the recording said, "Brightstar, I wish to extend the council's—and my own—abject apologies for what happened to you...for what we did." He looked pained, but shook his head. "Not to excuse my own part in this, but I allowed Alden, former Elder Rebus, to manipulate me into that sham far too easily.

"I can at least report that Rebus and four of his associates are to be tried for attempted murder. Both Elder Rebus and Elder Eden have been removed from their council seats, effective immediately." The already-tight lines on Jaben's face tightened even further. "When we arrested former Elder Rebus, we discovered...far more than we would ever have guessed." Jaben paused as if not sure how to continue, then shook his head and shrugged helplessly.

"We discovered that Alden Rebus was on the payroll of Drake Loriden and had been for some time." Exclamations rose up all around Nate, but he was silent, digesting the statement's implications. He understood his friends' shock. Rebus's position on the Lighthouse council made such an entanglement with Loriden a true conflict of interest... maybe even treason. But how could Rebus even communicate with Loriden? Nate frowned in puzzlement.

Unaware of the group's response due to the long light-speed communication lag, Jaben continued and Nate got his answer. "Rebus had an Energematrice6 communication device that must have been built shortly after the Escape, before Energematrice6 machines were destroyed." Jaben shook his head. "We certainly have no such technology...or weren't aware of it until now."

Jaben looked down at his hands. "Again, I apologize, though such a gesture seems futile. I've no idea how the situation reached this dire state." He looked back up at the camera. "If ya wish ta' return to Lighthouse, I will offer you my resignation personally and you and Jesse Galton may oversee the selection of a new council at your discretion."

Enough time had passed that Nate was feeling the full force of anger from being spaced. A part of him very much wanted to take Jaben up on his offer, and to punish Rebus, perhaps by subjecting him to the same treatment Nate himself had been given. The thought made him smile grimly, but he forcibly pushed the anger aside, facing the situation coldly and clearly.

From across the bridge, Jesse shook his head sadly. "He's a good sort, really. Too patient and not nearly suspicious enough, maybe, but a good sort." Keevan snorted in obvious disagreement, but said nothing.

Nate queued up the control station he'd taken in order to respond, and said, "Elder Jaben, while I appreciate your apology, I don't foresee returning to Lighthouse Station in the near future."

He paused, then said evenly. "I've also made a decision. During our time on Hope One, we found the artifact that holds the Vale of Mysteries in place around Sanctuary. I've deactivated it. The Vale is currently dissipating. We don't know how long it will take, but expect the position of Sanctuary to be exposed within a few weeks at most. I leave to your discretion whether you resign, but I think your people might benefit from your leadership, and you personally might find some measure of redemption if you choose to remain at the head of the council."

Despite what he'd said to Jaben, Nate couldn't help taking some dark satisfaction in his message. There was a certain undeniable symmetry to the situation. They had tossed Nate out an airlock, intending to expose him to the vacuum. He, in turn, removed their protection and exposed them to the rest of the galaxy. Nate felt doubt prickling along the edges of his certainty, finally, as his anger subsided and he thought about what the newly-exposed Lighthouse Station would likely face, whether from pirates or more territorially-inclined powers.

When Jaben's reply arrived, almost twenty minutes later, his face was bone-white and his voice was panicky, "My lord Brightstar, we have detained Rebus and the others and he WILL stand trial. Is there anything else we can do in apology for our mistake—anything that might convince yeh ta' change your mind? We are not prepared for such exposure. The Keeper is GONE! We will be destroyed! We..." Jaben shook his head, looking horrified and bewildered, and after a moment of helpless silence the transmission ended.

Nate's reply this time was gentle, "Elder Jaben, I had decided even before we returned to Lighthouse that the time had come for Sanctuary to rejoin the galaxy. Throwing me out an airlock made it easier, but I would have done it anyway. You need the broader galaxy and it needs you. I think you underrate your own resourcefulness and capability. I know for a fact that you have many Energematrists among you. I do recommend you prepare for visitors, welcome or otherwise."

Nate paused, then smiled a genuine, if wry, smile. "Believe it or not, I wish you the best. I did not make my decision out of spite. Lightmaker watch over you, Elder Jaben."

It took twenty more minutes for Jaben's reply to come, leaving Nate plenty of time to question his own decision. Was it really too late? Could he return the Vale to its former state? Jaben was right that an entire planet and the station it supported were at stake.

Still, Nate hadn't made his decision lightly. It really was high time Lighthouse Station rejoined the galaxy. And there was the matter of the Vale itself...

When Jaben's reply finally came, his face was drawn but he looked resigned. "Very well. I thank you for the kind words. They are more than we deserved under the circumstances. Lightmaker watch over you also, and for Jesse, I want yeh ta' know—we'll all miss ya. Jaben clear."

In the aftermath of Jaben's call, everyone on the bridge was silent for a long time.

Nate found himself reflecting on what had happened aboard Lighthouse Station and now, in hindsight, feeling another flash of anger toward Rebus and wondering in turn what instructions Drake Loriden had given the corrupt elder.

Keevan interrupted his thoughts, blurting, "I gotta learn'ta keep my abyssal mouth shut." He was looking down, and Nate stared at him in perplexity. Keevan squirmed under his gaze, then continued, "They got t'me, Nate. While we were on Lighthouse, Rebus found me... I... I let some stuff slip that I shouldn'a."

Nate's eyebrows rose and he stared at Keevan, waiting for him to finish. After a moment, Keevan continued, shamefaced. "I told 'im yeh'd killed a Changed. I told 'im yeh'd banished the Shade. When ya' escaped from Loriden, I mean. Then...I told 'im the Logans were from the Milky Way. I didn't mean it. It slipped out. Rebus an' one of 'is goons got me alone. They were tryin' ta make me help 'em." Keevan paused again, uncomfortably, then added. "They neva told me what they were plannin'. I'd never 've kept somethin' like that from ya if I knew."

Nate's piercing stare morphed into an exasperated sigh. He shook his head and grumbled, "I know you told me you were a spy even before we left Aterria, but really? You just blurted it out to the first person who asked?"

Keevan shrank into himself. "But... it was Rebus." His protest sounded almost desperate. "He's council...I mean, I grew up 'ere."

Nate held up a hand to stop him. "So it wasn't the 'first person who asked.' It was a councilman from your home who you'd known most of your life, and probably been bullied by before." Keevan started to open his mouth to answer, but Nate shook his head and held up his hand once more. "We have to figure out how to keep you from spilling the beans when somebody you know shows up." Nate grimaced and shook his head again. "In this case, I don't think you've done any particular harm though." His grin morphed into a smirk. "I can only imagine the confusion that particular report is causing back at the Telestry, and I suspect they would have found out anyway. Somebody's going to discover Resolute at some point."

Keevan stared blankly at Nate for a moment. Then a wave of relief crossed his face and he nodded. "Yeah. I gotta learn ta' keep my mouth shut."

Nate sighed and nodded. "And Keevan...I didn't escape from Loriden. I left." Then, angling to lighten the mood, Nate looked around with a whimsical grin. "Anybody else have any admissions while we're about it? Somebody stow a Changed in one of the cargo holds?"

To his surprise, as he looked around at the faces of his friends, Shawna wouldn't meet his eye.

He stared at her, not entirely sure what to say, until she blurted, "I kept the piece of the black gem."

Nate's eyebrows climbed his forehead once more and he just continued to stare at her as his stomach did a flip-flop. Keevan's admission had been disappointing, but not particularly damaging. Shawna's left him a bit stunned and even more uneasy. Keevan, on the other hand, was sharply interested. His eyes fixed on Shawna and he seemed about to say something, then changed his words at the last moment.

"What piece?"

Shawna bit her lip and tears came to her eyes. She held out her hand to Nate, obviously clutching what he assumed must be the shard of the black gem.

Nate hesitated, then reluctantly held out his hand, asking, "Why, Shawna? Why did you bring it?"

"I... I... I don't know." She was caught between utterly embarrassed and, somehow, confused. "Something came over me. ...I still don't really understand it."

Nate stared grimly as she set a short, sharp piece of what felt like broken glass carefully into his palm. Immediately, on contact with the shard, Nate shuddered as...something...seemed to stare at his back. Feeling as if he'd been bitten, he dropped the black shard on the console in front of him, which caused the sensation to disappear as quickly as it had come, then returned his gaze to Shawna, now feeling troubled.

Hesitantly, she asked, "Was it...well, watching you, too?"

Nate nodded thoughtfully, eyeing the irregular piece of crystal without speaking. He really wasn't sure what to do with it. His first instinct was to toss it out into space, but at the thought he got an immediate check. Some instinct told him that would be a bad idea. He stared at the shard for a long moment, then caught Keevan looking at it as well and grimaced.

Shawna cleared her throat and asked, "So who was watching us. Could it be this Drake Loriden? I mean, I don't know..."

"O'*course* it is!" Keevan's exclamation was short and sharp. "Loriden's got 'is fingers in every pie! Why wouldn'it be?"

"How would Loriden have access to an artifact that's been in Hope One since Dad...left?" Rachel obviously stumbled over the last of her thought, but she shook her head to emphasize the point. "I could see an artifact coming from Lastis Ralond...or Hillman maybe." Her eyes were dark as she uttered the final name.

"Or someone...or some*thing* we've neva seen before." Jesse put in. "Drake Loriden's only one of the major powers in the galaxy, even as leader of the Telestry."

Keevan scowled. "Don't sell 'im short. Loriden's got a longer reach than ya' think."

Nate shrugged. "No way of telling without actually trying to follow the link back to whoever controls it...and that seems like the worst idea of all. For now, I'm just going to put it away. I'll figure out what to do with it later." He unstrapped himself from the console, then grabbed the shard once more, grimacing as the sense of being watched returned. He pushed himself toward the main hatch leading into the corridor. As he turned to head toward his own compartment, Nate heard someone behind him and turned his head to see Keevan. His hand tightened on the shard, remembering Keevan's reaction to holding the black gem on Hope One.

Keevan stopped at the hatch, though, seeming hesitant. A few seconds passed before he called after Nate's retreating form, "Thank you...For not leavin' me behind."

Their first day of waiting for the Vale to dissipate was spent recuperating—Nate from his entropic shock and the others from their long day exploring Hope One. Near the end of the ship's day, Andrew stopped next to Nate where he sat in the galley and slammed a metal cube down on the table in front of him. It looked heavy, even though it was small enough he could have held it in one hand. He looked up at Andrew, who was actually scowling at him, feeling a bit like an animal that had wandered onto a busy road in the middle of the night, transfixed by oncoming headlights.

"Use that for your extropy instead of our shade-blasted walls, would you?" Andrew grumped.

Nate's eyebrows rose. "What? Extropy??"

Andrew glowered at him. "You left a nasty hand print in the wall just inside the airlock from your stunt with Jesse, and there's no way I can fix it. Any time I try to do anything, the surface just flakes away. I'd have to strip it back a full inch just to stop it from crumbling every time I try to clean it. That's without even mentioning the one you left in Laura's room."

"Oh." Nate winced and nodded, then picked up the cube in both hands. It fit on one palm but it was so heavy it took both hands for him to lift it. "I take it this is for me to destroy instead of the walls?"

Andrew nodded back. "Tungsten. Should soak up plenty of extropy."

"Extropy. Got it." Nate grinned. "I'll try to avoid messing up the walls from now on if I can help it."

During the second day of waiting, Jon took Nate aside to talk. When they reached Nate's room, it took awhile for Jon to find the words he wanted, but eventually he said, "That was entropic shock...when we got you inside. You could have died if you were out there much longer, Nate."

Nate frowned and shook his head. "I don't understand it myself. If I did, this would be a lot easier. You know my memory isn't whole." He felt troubled, as if his mind were far away, on something else.

Jon nodded slowly, then asked, "So what ARE you planning to do? You don't seem keen on going after the Dominion."

Nate grimaced. "Seems like everybody else wants me to go after them, doesn't it?"

Jon grinned. "Something tells me that what 'everybody wants' doesn't really play into your plans."

Nate shrugged. "It's what everybody needs that has me concerned...and most of them don't even know what that is." He stared at the Globe of the Vale, securely tucked into the netting in his couch, and shook his head slowly. "I can see everything so clearly...the big picture, I mean. I can see it like it's right here in front of me.

"Loriden...the Dominion, they're only the tiniest part of this. What I can't always see is the part I'm to play in it all, not until the time comes. The Lightmaker's plans are beyond me, but when I need to move, it's like when you went with the Keeper. I KNEW the time had come for you to go and that I couldn't. There was no doubt in my mind. Before that moment, I had no idea."

Nate reached into his pocket and pulled out the three amulets that remained unclaimed from their visit to Hope One. "I still have these. That means there must be more of us, and beyond that, I have to tell people."

Jon looked at Nate curiously. "More of us...what do you mean? And tell people what?"

"More Odds, I suppose?" Nate sighed and shook his head, then grinned crookedly at Jon. "I have to tell them what's coming, but they wouldn't believe me if I tried. People are too comfortable. Some of what's coming is bad." He paused and his eyes grew dark. Then his grin returned. "Some of it's good, too, but so much will just be...different."

Jon frowned, seeming a bit worried. "Nate, if anyone in the galaxy is ready for you, it would have to be the people here—in Sanctuary. What sort of welcome do you think we'll get anywhere else?"

Nate shrugged and headed toward the hatch. "I think it's time we restocked Adamant. After that?" His eyes were distant as his grin faded into grim sobriety. "Lightmaker only knows."

Part 2:
Purpose

Interval

Her nervousness was obvious as she opened the door and quietly stepped inside. That was just fine by him. It wouldn't do to let one's associates get comfortable. Comfort bred weakness.

The windows at the top of the great spire glinted all around them. The air was cold, up so high. Allowing the grand office to remain cold as well had been a conscious decision long ago, when his hold on power had been less secure—when even this world was still dangerous. It had been a statement, then. Now it was merely habit, but it suited him. There was always the danger of getting too comfortable himself.

She actually bowed before she spoke. His lips tightened ever so slightly. The news must be dire.

"My lord, we've looked everywhere. I'm... I'm afraid they've escaped." Dread thickened her tone and she glanced reflexively up at his face.

His laughter was genuine, for once. It rolled up out of his belly to fill the space around them with his merriment and her eyes widened. Not what she had expected.

"...My lord?"

"Yes, yes. Of course they've escaped. But one of ours went with them this time!"

She paused then, uncertain, and he enjoyed the touch of fear that still lingered in the air.

After a time, he continued, letting a trace of annoyance slip through his calm, "Can't you see what this means? It means we can follow them!"

"Yes, my lord. The effort is proceeding apace. The Brotherhood is spearheading recruitment and the draining of the Sol..."

"No, no, you fool." He frowned as she cut off abruptly, then began again after a long silence, "We can follow them NOW. We needn't wait for a gate. Don't you see? The great masters have shown us the way! When they pierced the barrier between our worlds, they gave us the pattern. Now all we have to do is follow it!"

He saw understanding take hold and he nodded almost gleefully. It had been so long, and the answer had been in front of him the whole time!

"But...My lord, what about last time?! We still don't know what happened!" For a split second, he considered putting her in her place, but her horror was genuine, so he simply stared at her, his gaze hard.

After a long moment, he saw her swallow uncertainly. Then her posture firmed and she simply looked him in the eye. He nodded once more. "Paul Casisia is dead, and his obnoxious protege...well. He can no longer interfere. Our path is clear."

"In that case, my lord, how should we..." She trailed off, still uncertain.

He stroked his chin, thoughtfully. "That. That is the difficulty. Now we know at least two of the rebels got through..."

Chapter 10

When the Vale started to visibly clear almost fifty hours later, they all gathered on the bridge for the spectacle. They could actually see wisps of the cloud around them sucking inward before disappearing into nothing, and they watched for nearly a half hour as the last of the Vale finally disappeared.

As the final streamers were fading away, Andrew eyed Nate. "So, where are we actually going?"

Nate looked around, then shrugged. "What we need is a resupply. Does anybody know where the nearest port is?"

Jesse's mouth twisted in distaste, but Keevan nodded almost excitedly. "Yeah, that'd be Bounty. If ya' pull up yer magic star chart, I can show yeh where it is."

Jesse eyed Keevan with some irritation. "It's pirate-infested."

Keevan looked almost shocked. "It is not! I been there. They're a bit...unconventional, but they're not pirates!"

Jesse didn't look convinced, but before he could speak again Laura piped up from one side of the bridge. "What are pirates?"

Jesse turned his head to stare at her, dumbfounded. "Whadda ya mean, what are pirates?"

Laura blushed and started to mumble something, but Shannon turned to her with a smile and said, "Don't worry. We didn't know either when we first got here."

Jesse shook his head. "I keep forgetting."

"Pirates," Tye said grimly, "are people who hurt other people so they can take their ships and cargo. Sometimes they even space them." He didn't go on, but from his tone of voice it was obvious that something in his past gave him more than just a theoretical knowledge of the subject.

Laura looked horrified. "But... People spacing other people just to take their stuff? That sort of thing hasn't happened since before The Betrayal!"

Tye scowled. "It happens here."

Laura shook her head in disbelief as Nate looked to Jesse. "What makes you say it's pirate infested?"

Jesse frowned. "That's what everyone at Sanctuary always said."

Keevan scoffed, waving his UPT in front of him in a gesture halfway between fidgeting and emphasizing his point. "Ya' mean that's what the council told yeh. Those old hulks wouldn't know a pirate if he came up and bit them on the collective hinder."

Nate held up his hand to stop the conversation and asked, "Keevan, if they're not pirates then what are they?"

Keevan shrugged. "They just...don't like authorities much. They wouldn't steal from yeh unless maybe yer flyin' a Dominion tax ship."

Nate nodded. "Good enough. And while we're there, let's get a real star map." His mouth quirked. "Not that your sensor composites aren't great, but it would be really good to know where we're going."

"And some real food too," Tye added. "You were right, Andrew." He made a face. "The spinach gets old after awhile."

After Keevan and Jesse examined Adamant's original sensor composite map and found what they both agreed had to be

Bounty, Shannon told them the trip took a full day even at maximum Retton drive.

It was an uneventful trip compared to their voyage inward through the Vale, with none of the white-knuckle attention that going through the muck had entailed.

"All hands, disengaging Retton drive in ten minutes," Shawna's voice warned them when their trip was nearing completion. Nate was on the bridge with Andrew, Keevan, Laura, and Rachel, with the rest of the group variously sleeping, going through inventories to make lists of supplies they needed, or spending personal time elsewhere on the ship. The second planet from the system's primary was the only inhabitable world, and Andrew set them on a course for it without commenting or asking for instructions.

As the Retton drive disengaged and he finished adjusting their course, Andrew looked at Keevan quizzically. "So do we dock at the space station? Or land on the planet?" Andrew asked.

Keevan shrugged, waving toward the window in front of them with his UPT. "People don't wanna' live without gravity, and since Sanctuary has the only space station I know of with artificial gravity, people tend ta' make their homes and do their business down on the surface. The only people who use the space station are industrial haulers and the loike."

Andrew nodded and made some minute adjustment to their course, then asked Shawna to look it over for him as he glanced over at Nate. "What did you have in mind when we land? Do you want to find a place to sell our salvage? What do people use as currency here?"

Keevan shrugged again. "Everybody takes Dominion marks. There are others, but the Dominion has the best reach, even on Bounty." He glanced at Nate. "If it's all the same, I know a few people 'ere. I think I can handle the salvage."

Nate nodded. "All yours. Andrew, you may want to stick around and help. I don't know what the custom is with unloading, but I suspect having locals aboard Adamant unsupervised may be a bad idea. See if you can find us a decent star map and more provisions too, will you? I'm gonna look around the city."

Keevan gave a wave of agreement and shortly after they received a hail, which Andrew answered, adjusting their course once again to follow flight control's directions to an unoccupied berth at Bounty City Space Port.

Even before they'd begun re-entry, Keevan took advantage of a weightless moment to cross the bridge to a control station. By the time they landed, he was happily tapped into Adamant's comm system, looking up his contacts.

After they touched down, Nate unstrapped and stood up to stretch, then made his way off the bridge. Jon, Rachel, and Tye were all in the corridor outside and they eyed Nate quizzically as he passed.

"We're heading out to see the city," Shannon said from behind him. Nate turned to give her and Laura, who had both followed him off the bridge, a half smile as Rachel and Tye both perked up at the news.

"I wanna come too," Tye said.

A moment later, Rachel chimed in with a somewhat more dignified, "I'll come."

The space port outside was much like the one on Aterria, composed primarily of a giant paved landing field, centered on a flight control hub. Unlike C-City, however, Bounty City fully surrounded its space port with warehouses and import/export companies.

Making sure to stay well clear of other vessels, Nate headed out of the spaceport to the north, toward the city center.

Their little group stayed close, partly because they could sense Laura and Shannon's discomfort at the tremendous amount of open space around them and the increasing crowds as they left the spaceport.

Nate caught Laura looking around in wide-eyed amazement, and smiled at her. "Are the open spaces getting to you?"

Laura smiled in return and shook her head. "I know Shawna has agoraphobia. Not me. I'm just amazed at how many people there are. I thought Lighthouse Station had a lot of people on it. I never thought this was even possible."

Shannon nodded a bit less happily. "Yeah. It's amazing they don't... I dunno, kill each other or something."

Tye grinned, obviously enjoying the girls' new experience. "They do, you know. Sometimes. There's at least some murder in all cities." Shannon looked shocked, staring at Tye in horror. Then her expression faded into wariness and she stared around suspiciously, causing one nearby pedestrian to actually shy away from them.

Tye laughed. "Not often, and usually it's people who know each other. Murdering strangers just doesn't happen much unless they're caught in some kind of crossfire, especially kids." He made a face.

Nate eyed Laura then asked, "Your psi talent—what does it show you in a place like this?"

Laura made a face. "Well, I'm getting a little emotional overspill. There are a LOT of people, but I told you, I never trained it." She shrugged, still looking around in wonder. Shannon's suspicious watchfulness had subsided a little after Tye's explanation, and it looked like the girls were slowly getting accustomed to the crowds.

As they walked, Nate noted the people around him. They didn't have the friendly, curious look the people of Sanctuary had, but all of them were cheerful and courteous enough. The obvious bifurcation of the society on Aterria between Telestics and everyone else was nowhere to be seen, but perhaps, he thought wryly, that was because he wasn't in the company of a high ranking Telestic.

Sure enough, it wasn't another full minute before he spotted a figure in Telestic's robes, cutting a wide berth through the crowds that packed the street. Nate saw his friends were all looking in the same direction, but none of them commented beyond a quiet snort from Tye as they passed.

After they'd been walking for a few minutes, Laura asked aloud, "How do these people govern themselves? There are just SO many of them."

Tye laughed. "Most of the worlds around here follow the Telestry's model, even the ones that aren't actually Telestry worlds."

"What does that mean?" Laura's tone showed clear interest.

Tye shrugged. "Well, they mostly don't have governments. The Telestics enforce the laws and help settle disputes. People pay them for their time when they render a service, and mostly nobody crosses them. Local stuff, like policies, are mostly discussed at the conclave."

"They all have conclaves, like Sanctuary?" Laura asked.

Tye nodded. "Yeah. That's where all the important stuff gets handled. They tell stories there, too, like on Sanctuary."

Tye stopped for a moment, then laughed and made a face. "Before I joined the Telestry I saw a re-broadcast from the conclave on Skelter at Aterria's conclave. It was pretty awful. Usually conclaves only broadcast to their local solar system, but sometimes if people really like something or really hate it, they'll rebroadcast from other systems." As they'd been talking, they were approaching an amphitheater that they all immediately recognized as an outdoor rendition of Lighthouse Station's conclave. Instead of being built above ground, this one was open to the air and set down below ground level with obvious provision for lighter material to be extended over the top to create a roof.

Shannon glanced sidelong at Nate and snorted. "At least here they don't have an airlock to throw you out of."

Nate laughed then shook his head and smiled grimly. "Touché. This is what I came here to do, though. I have to tell them what's coming, and this is where we start."

Rachel looked across at Shannon, her eyes dark. "If somebody does try something, well, we came with you this time."

When they had descended the steps from the rim of the conclave to the center, Nate took his place in the waiting area below the speaker, a Telestic with robes that marked her as senior among her order.

She was practically haranguing the crowd as she spoke, her voice shrill, "...of Bounty, you accept the services of the Telestics, but what of your duty to the Telestry? We who have given our all in service of the people, pledged our very lives to the Telestry, are in our hour of need. What have you done for us? A pittance for the tithe and you count yourselves well-served? Balance requires more than this!

"The day may come when we are not here to be your guardians or magistrates! What will you do then, you who have so little gratitude? Upon the next full conclave, we demand your support! Bounty must join the Telestry!"

With that, she stepped down from the podium and settled herself in a nearby seat set apart from the rest, obviously a place of honor, perhaps reserved for the one in charge of seeing that speakers did not become too unruly or overstay their welcome.

Nate's lips twisted ironically as he stepped up to the podium. He began with a long, thoughtful look around the amphitheater, which was neither packed nor empty. Evidently there were enough locals who could spare the time to frequent the conclave to keep it busy even on a business day. The crowd obviously wasn't expecting much from a boy of barely twelve, as they saw him. They were laughing and talking, completely ignoring him. The previous speaker, now settled in her seat, eyed Nate doubtfully, but no one else was there to speak and she didn't seem prepared to try to stop him.

Nate began in a tone that cut through the noise, providing himself with an unobtrusive boost through Energematrice6 as he had at Sanctuary, "I have a tale for you of the time before The Escape." He paused for effect and the crowd began to quiet.

He looked across the conclave, meeting the eyes of as many in the audience as he could, "Before even The Betrayal, the way men lived was very different than it is now."

After another short pause to let the crowd quiet the rest of the way, Nate could see he had their attention, and he began in earnest, "Before Energematrice6 came to the hands of man, people measured their power over one another by other means. For some, it was how expensive their ground car was. For others, their house. For the very powerful, it was how much gold they held."

A ripple of laughter spread across the crowd and Nate smiled a crooked smile. "You laugh because gold is so common today, but this was before space was firmly within humanity's grasp. There was no mining of asteroids or moons, and the only gold men could acquire was pulled out of the depths of the Earth, with great labor and toil. And so, men measured their power by the size of their stack of shiny metal, and those with great amounts of gold treated the others as slaves.

"Society was different when there was no nuclear fusion, and men were used as beasts of burden, women as household automata, simply because they had less gold than their neighbors or their masters. Society was different, but people were the same. All they needed was an excuse to hold others as lesser than they."

Nate shook his head. "Then the virus came. One day, the greatest standard of power was gold. The next, it was Energematrice6, and then a man's worth could be measured by how much power he could personally control. The world changed overnight, and those who had treated their neighbors as worthless were suddenly the lowest slaves themselves." As he spoke, Nate raised his hand and a great ball of light grew above it, growing brighter and brighter until the audience was forced to look away. Then, the light faded and Nate stared around at the bedazzled crowd. His eyes raked them, looking for the few who showed no signs of bedazzlement, the Energematrists, and staring them down, one at a time.

A moment later, Nate shook his head again. "As it was before, so it will be in the time to come." He paused and looked around slowly once more before continuing, "Those who hold great power because of their ability with Energematrice6 will lose that power in time. Take care, you who lord it over your neighbors because of your strength in the fields. The time will come when you will be brought to serve, willingly or not, and woe to you who treat others as lesser because of a power you were born with. There is always a reckoning.

"In the end, Energematrice6 is a tool, nothing more. What matters is whether it's used to aid people or enslave them."

Nate paused, reflecting on how many things would have to change for people to be able to accept what he had really come to do. There was too much that opposed him, and there was the enemy, unseen but always present. That enemy was the other reality these people couldn't even imagine.

When he continued, Nate barely knew what he was saying, only that those enemies were in the forefront of his consciousness. They needed to be told. He spoke about the proper use of the fields and recounted again how Energematrice6 had been given to men by the Lightmaker to prevent all of society being enslaved by Lastis and the shades. Most of all, he spoke about the shades and their Changed, and the threat they posed.

As time passed, the conclave began to fill with more and more people, as those in the audience contacted friends or, perhaps, those who were watching the rebroadcast came to see for themselves. By the time Nate finished, almost two hours later, every seat was full.

As Nate stepped down from the podium, the crowd was completely silent. Slowly, a few people began to applaud, then a few more. Soon, the crowd was on its feet as Nate strode away from the podium. The noise was deafening, and it continued even as Nate neared the exit.

As he passed, a man leaned out of his seat and grasped Nate's arm, calling out above the roar, "Are you telling us the Dominion will pay for what they did?"

Nate stopped and looked down at the man in his seat, cocking his head. "The Dominion? What did the Dominion do?"

The man looked surprised. "Why, they killed all the Telestic trainees! Hadn't you heard? The Ochroleucum is empty and the Telestry's been humiliated!"

Nate stared at the man, dumbfounded. Behind him, his friends had all stopped and Rachel, at least, had heard what the man said. Nate didn't move for so long that Tye came up behind him and poked him. Nate didn't respond and by now the man who had grabbed Nate's arm was looking more than a little uncomfortable under Nate's blank gaze.

Rachel looked over at Tye and jerked her head at the man who had spoken. "He says the Dominion killed everyone at the Ochroleucum."

Tye's eyes went wide and he looked at the man. "Do you know why? Did they say why they did it?"

The man was looking at Nate with realization now instead of discomfort, and he nodded. "Yeah. They said the Telestry was harboring the Brightstar."

Nate sucked in a sharp breath but didn't say anything. There was a small crowd behind them now, so after a moment Rachel put an arm on his shoulders and gently guided him forward. The whole group started moving and didn't stop until they were outside the conclave, walking down the street.

When Rachel finally released him, Nate stopped again. He glanced over at Rachel, a sick look in his eyes. "It's because of me."

Rachel shook her head grimly. "Not your fault. It was the Dominion. Come on, Nate."

Nate nodded. "Still because of me." He shook his head in turn. Rachel opened her mouth to speak, but nothing came out. The others were clustered behind them, equally silent.

Then, with none of them knowing what to say, a small voice just in front of them piped up, "You look sick. Are you gonna puke?"

Chapter 11

Nate blinked and glanced up to see a small girl, no more than a standard year old—three or four Earth years—staring boldly up at him from about ten feet away. She frowned at him, then ran forward and threw her arms around his legs, hugging him. The young man of about twenty who was standing behind her, half turned away and talking to someone else, tried to turn back and catch her, but he was too slow.

Then he looked at Nate with a rueful smile and said, "I'm so sorry. She likes to run off."

Nate shook his head, still unable to find words, but the girl looked up at him again with a frown. "Are you okay?"

Nate laughed aloud and bent down to return her hug. "I will be. What's your name?"

"Tasia." The girl bent her head backward until she hung over his arms with her hair dangling almost to the pavement, then wriggled out of Nate's hug to dash back to the man behind her.

Nate looked up with a wry smile at him as he stood up again. "She seems to know exactly what to say. How old is she?"

The man laughed, a happy, jovial sound. "That she does. She's nine months, standard." He shook his head in exasperation and twisted around to lay a hand on the girl's head.

He held out his other hand for Nate to shake and said, "I'm Jack. You met my daughter Tasia, and this is my wife Hannah." He gestured to a young lady behind him.

Nate nodded to Hannah, then turned back to Jack, his smile a bit more natural. "That was the best medicine I could imagine, and I really needed it."

Jack looked at him quizzically. "Oh? How's that?"

Tye piped up from behind Nate, "He just found out the Dominion killed all the students at the Telestry because of him." Everyone turned to look at Tye, with the rest of Nate's party giving him the evil eye while Jack and Hannah's eyes widened in surprise.

"Well," Tye said, "It's true."

Down the street, a disturbance unsettled the crowd. At first, it wasn't obvious what was happening, but something had made the people mill about. Then the crowd began to scatter.

Out of the mass of humanity, a tall, dark figure shot toward them down the street like a meteor across the heavens.

Jack was eyeing the crowd, now actively diving for cover. His gaze settled on the onrushing figure, still a long way off, with barely-disguised worry. "We need to get off the street. That could get...way worse. Will you come home with us?"

Nate looked over at the others, frowning. "Go with them. Make sure they're safe. I'm staying for now."

Tye gave Nate a sideways look and opened his mouth to speak, but Rachel preempted him, "I'll stay with him. The rest of you go."

Jack seemed surprised, but Shannon quickly nodded and led the way down the street with Hannah close behind, holding Tasia by the hand. Jack and Laura were on their heels, though Jack looked back over his shoulder, obviously confused, as they hurried away.

Nate turned back to the rapidly-approaching figure, mentally preparing himself for whatever might come. The figure was glowing with a light Nate had never seen before. A halo of tattered energy followed it, as if it were a black hole, vacuuming in all the Energematrice6 around it.

Working quickly, instinctively, Nate raised a shield around himself and his friends, then twisted the weaves of Energematrice6 into themselves as tightly as he could. It was like trying to tie a dainty knot with handfuls of garden hose. As the figure closed, Nate marveled again at how fast it?...he? was moving.

Then there wasn't time to marvel anymore and Nate strained, bringing the weaves of power tight together.

He saw the figure's teeth bared as it closed—its head was strangely misshapen, looking almost like that of a dog, and its eyes glowed electric blue. Its skin was pale, ghostly even, and just as it reached them Nate thought he saw its lips curling in contempt. The glimpse only lasted a bare few seconds before it leaped into the air, straight for Nate's shield. Then, those inhuman blue eyes went wide in shock and it bounced backward.

The shield might as well have been a trampoline, and whatever the creature was, it flew back dozens of feet to skid across the pavement.

Nate snorted in amusement. The dog creature was strange, and its features left Nate with an odd, visceral discomfort. He didn't feel fear, though...only curiosity. "I don't think he was expecting that."

Next to him, Rachel grunted. "I think... he's a Nosufer. I didn't know any of them had made it to Aurora." She grimaced. "I guess...Dad said they had in his letter, didn't he?"

Nate's gaze tracked to the crowd beyond the creature—the Nosufer—and his eyes narrowed. Two small groups ran well ahead of the rest, next to each other but obviously not together. They were still a long way off.

Now, the Nosufer sat up slowly, looking dazed. A panicked look crossed its face and it glanced back toward the crowd, then around at Nate, its eyes wary.

Rachel grunted again, sourly. "They were calling them Vampyrs back on Earth, before we left... Supposedly they drained the life from people using Energematrice6. I don't think any of us ever really believed it, but..." She scowled at the Nosufer, which was rising to its feet now. "What do you want to do?"

Nate stared into the creature's electric eyes for what felt like a long time, his memories giving him a rare glimpse at the vast tapestry of reality he'd seen once upon a time on the Telestry vessel Ocharist. Nate murmured almost to himself, "Born of three peoples, claiming none. A spark of light, spawned in deepest night. Such a long, long road..."

The creature started, then spoke aloud as if it had heard him, though it still stood far out of earshot. It called, "What do you know of me, human? Why are you not terrified?" The Nosufer shook its head, bewildered.

Nate laughed grimly, then again, almost merrily, "I know more than you would find comfortable, I suspect."

The Nosufer walked toward them, more slowly, though it glanced behind and once more quickened its pace at the sight of the crowd, still streaming toward them, now alone where the two streets crossed.

When it reached them, the strange dog-headed being reached a hand forward to trail its fingertips across Nate's shield, his touch almost a caress, and its eyes went distant for a long moment. When its eyes opened again, they were wide in surprise. "Bright One, who are you? ...WHAT are you?? In the dream... You could be a thousand shining stars! It is—it MUST be YOU that I have been seeking! I saw you from Home. You are the reason I came to this place!"

Nate looked at the Nosufer and shook his head almost sadly, compassion in his eyes. "I have nothing to offer you, child of the Reaper. The Lightmaker sent me for the wayward children of fallen Earth."

The Nosufer looked aghast, his head dropping, then shook himself like the canine he bore such an eerie resemblance to, "Would you deny the dogs even the crumbs from the master's table, Bright One?" His electric blue eyes fixed on Nate as if his very life depended on the answer.

Nate stared back for a long time as the crowd finally began to draw near, then nodded slowly. "Very well." He looked at the onrushing crowd. "Don't do anything. I'll talk to them."

The Nosufer turned to stare at the crowd, uncertain. The two groups leading the charge were clearly visible now. One was made up of six Telestics, both men and women in their distinctive embroidered robes. The other was a group composed completely of men in black and gold jumpsuits. Their leader had a shiny disc fastened to the forehead of what looked like a skull cap. The two groups were both running flat out while still keeping a distinct distance from each other.

Nate stepped past the Nosufer, moving to meet them. Rachel stayed by his side, though she craned her neck, trying to keep the Nosufer in sight even after they'd passed.

The two groups came to a stop at almost the same time, their members already gasping questions at Nate past their exertion.

"Has it hurt you?" The man with the silver disc on his forehead could at least speak clearly.

"Step...Aside!" The Telestic was breathing so hard that his demand came out half-strangled and it was all Nate could do not to chuckle.

Instead, Nate asked, "What do you want with him?"

The man with the silver disc gaped, "That is a Nosufer! Are you mad?"

The Telestic grunted in something far from amusement. "Stupid child!" Nate saw the man reach out for Energematrice6 and snapped his own shield back into place instantly, protecting himself, Rachel, and the Nosufer.

The one with the gold disc snarled and took a step back, but he wasn't reaching for Energematrice6 himself as far as Nate could tell.

When Nate's shield sprang into existence, the Telestic really looked at him for the first time and Nate gazed into slit-pupiled eyes, their owner gone completely still in shock.

What happened next was as confusing as it was quick. Simultaneously, there was a bellow from behind Nate where the Nosufer stood and the Telestic with the exsect eyes said, "YOU!" The man smiled, then, completely without humor, and pointed his finger directly into Nate's face. "I KNOW what you ARE!"

Again, Nate was stunned. There was no doubt in his mind. This being, whatever it was, knew him. It knew...too much. It knew everything.

There was a blur in the corner of Nate's vision and the Nosufer rushed past him to slam into the Telestic. Then, the Telestic was simply gone. Where he had been only a pile of fine dust remained in the relative shape of a human body.

Nate and everyone else watching were thoroughly caught by surprise, and they stared at the Nosufer standing over the Telestic's remains, a snarl fixed on his face as his head whipped around in all directions. His eyes had changed from electric blue to red. Pure rage seemed to ooze from him, forming a haze in the surrounding air.

Everyone else acted at the same time. The Telestics' shocked silence ended with a collective roar of outrage and they each unleashed a different form of Energematrice6 on the Nosufer. The other group had dropped into defensive positions and were pulling out weapons of some kind.

No longer protected by Nate's shield, the Nosufer took the Telestics' attacks on its own, which flickered for a moment, then strengthened under the assault instead. The Nosufer turned on the Telestics, snarling, but he didn't spring upon them as he had their leader, holding back despite the red madness shining from his eyes.

Nate shook himself, gritted his teeth, and drove past the shock.

The Nosufer's shield was strong, but just to be certain, Nate pushed his own incalculably stronger shield past the creature, once more leaving himself, Rachel and the Nosufer protected from both the Telestics and the other group, which was now beginning its own assault. They had dropped into prone positions behind their leader, who crouched in front in a defensive posture, a strange Energematrice6 shield emanating from the bright disc on his forehead.

Then, they opened fire with weapons Nate hadn't even realized they were carrying. Simultaneously, the Telestics released another wave of various colors of Energematrice6. All of it impacted Nate's shield over the space of less than a second.

By this point, Nate was so accustomed to using the Sigil of the Mysteries that he had automatically created his shield through it, and the level of power it provided was tremendous. His shield shrugged off the incoming attacks without him really noticing. Even so, the impact of energy and projectiles on the shield was a bit shocking, and the sound of shrieking energy and a spatter of impacts assaulted his ears.

Rachel snorted. "Now what?"

Nate sighed and shook his head, then turned to address the Nosufer. "Go. I will see you again, boy from the darkness."

The Nosufer seemed startled, but nodded and leapt forward past Nate and Rachel to continue on his original path through the city.

Turning back to the two groups in front of him, Nate folded his arms and scowled. Some members of both groups were still attacking his shield, while others gaped at the Nosufer's retreating back. It took almost a full minute for the remainder of both groups to stop attacking his shield.

Eventually, there was silence and Nate asked, "Now what?"

Everyone started speaking at once. All five of the remaining Telestics began to yell at the tops of their voices, and the leader of the other group, with the silvery disc on his head, started to speak as well. Apparently realizing there was no way he would be heard over the Telestics, he stopped, spat on the ground, and raised two fingers to his lips to let out a piercing whistle.

At once, the Telestics quieted and the man sneered. "Sixer rabble." He turned his attention to Nate and asked, "What have you to do with the Nosufer, child?"

Nate frowned. "I've never seen him before today." He could practically feel Rachel's sardonic grin beside him, but she didn't speak.

The man nodded sharply and motioned for the rest of his group to follow. Then, he stalked forward past Nate and Rachel and began sprinting once more in pursuit of the Nosufer.

One of the Telestics gabbled, "But... but his shield!"

Another cursed and motioned. "Come on! We can't let the brotherhood get it! We'll deal with the boy later!"

Then, the Telestics too sped off after the Nosufer, three shooting constant glances back over their shoulders as they ran.

Nate and Rachel both stared after them for a moment, then looked at each other, their expressions somewhere between amused and disbelieving.

Before they could reorient and move, a head poked out of a side street and Tye was motioning vigorously for them to join him.

Rachel sighed, exasperated. "Can't he even *pretend* to do what he's told?" Nate smiled at her ruefully and shook his head. They hurried to join him, though, and found the entire party waiting barely a block away, past the intersection.

Tye's first question, as the three rushed to catch up with the rest of the group, was excited. "Did you get to see the Nosufer?" Nate nodded thoughtfully but didn't speak, and after a pause, as they were drawing toward the others, Tye asked, "That was the Order chasing it, right? I didn't know the Order was on Bounty."

They had rejoined the group, and everyone turned to follow as Jack and Hannah led the way toward a side street.

Hannah had apparently heard the question, and she turned her head to answer, one hand holding her daughter's. "The Knights of the Order don't like Telestics trying to get Bounty to join the Telestry. Bounty is one of only a few neutral ports that are left in this part of the galaxy—that means they keep a sizeable presence here, for deterrence if nothing else." She shook her head and picked up Tasia to increase her pace.

A few minutes later, Tye looked at Nate, who was walking beside him, and said thoughtfully, "I wonder what happened to Bundy...and the Proctor." He paused, then added contemplatively, "I hated it at the Ochroleucum, but thinking of all of them dead is awful." He paused again, then grimaced. "I never thought I'd say this, but I sort of hope he got away."

Nate stared at Tye in surprise then smiled. "I do too, Tye. I do too."

It took another ten minutes of walking to reach Jack and Hannah's house, which was small, even by the standards of the city's center. There was barely room for all of them inside the main room, and Nate found himself marveling at the couple's friendliness. They didn't even know him or the others. Why would they offer strangers, a group of children who were obviously Odds, hospitality? As if in answer to his question, the plaque above their door caught his eye. "What you do for others must also bear its fruit in you." It was a simple thing, the words inset into wood with a carved edge.

As they spoke over the next few hours, Nate came to realize that in their genuine kindness and generosity the saying fit them perfectly.

When Nate and the others returned to Adamant later that day, they found Keevan and Andrew loading the last of their provisions. Keevan was smirking a bit, twirling his UPT between his fingers triumphantly, when they walked up to the boarding ramp.

Nate raised an eyebrow. "You seem pleased."

Keevan grinned. "Yeh might say that."

Behind Nate, Shannon snorted. "Well then tell us why. Don't just stand there and smirk."

Keevan's grin turned sheepish. "Yeah. Alright. We got it all! Bounty's scrapyards didn' know what half the junk off'a Resolute was, but they knew they were lookin' at tech they'd neva seen before. We made more than I eva thought we could."

His grin widened again. "An' you should SEE Shawna's new star map!"

Ten minutes later, they were all looking at the star map projected on Adamant's bridge window. It had various territories demarcated by networks of lines. By far the biggest was the Dominion, stretching far beyond their current view, with the Telestry's rough sphere and other smaller territories off to the sides.

"It was expensive," Shawna said self-consciously, "but it was the only one that would plug into Adamant's system." She grimaced. "It had to be source-accessible for Adamant to read it."

"Where is the Dominion's home world?" Laura asked, frowning at the huge orange pincushion that showed Dominion space.

Keevan laughed mirthlessly, and Shawna did something with her controls, zooming the map out... and out... and out... Finally, an icon appeared, labeled 'Panoptica.'

Shannon said quietly, "It would take months to get there at our best speed." Tye whistled and shook his head. Most of the others made some noise of awe. Only Nate looked on impassively, his mind as far away as Panoptica itself.

After a moment, Keevan cleared his throat and held up a small electronic device containing the marks they'd received for their salvage. "So, ehh, who's gonna hang on'ta this?" He looked around.

No one answered until Nate stared him straight in the eye and said, "You keep it for us. I trust you."

Keevan nodded happily, but when Nate glanced back at him, he looked vaguely troubled, as if Nate's trust disturbed him somehow.

They spent several weeks in port at Bounty City, with Nate visiting the conclave every day to speak to the people. First, he taught them history—about The Betrayal, The Escape, and the enemy that was still relentlessly searching for a way to reach them, even in Aurora. Later, he began to show the people how the Telestry had misled the galaxy about Energematrice6, making power their aim instead of serving the people. Twice, after particularly draining days at the conclave, Nate visited Jack, Hannah, and Tasia.

At the same time, he started regular sessions that were half experimentation and half teaching, allowing his friends to teach each other what they knew of the fields and teaching them what he could.

During the very first such session, it quickly became apparent that Nate's ability with Energematrice6 was different from his friends'. When he started to demonstrate how he'd created air, Andrew cleared his throat loudly, eyeing Nate's hand, which was on the wall behind him. Nate blinked in surprise and a little embarrassment, then went to get the tungsten cube from his stateroom. The blasted thing was practically fifty pounds. It was impossible to carry around easily.

Cube in hand, Nate demonstrated three times how he used the fields to create air for himself in the vacuum before Shannon actually threw up her hands in dismay.

"You're doing so much at once! And how do you handle the gray that way?" She sounded so frustrated that Nate stopped what he was doing and blinked at her in surprise. From the other side of Adamant's bridge, the only space in the ship large enough to hold them all, Tye chuckled.

"You realize," Tye said, "even the master Telestics would struggle with something like that. I was a quick study and I was years short of doing what you're doing without even trying!"

"How're ya' even doing this?" Jesse asked, frowning. His attention was focused on his weaves, but exasperation still came through. "I was only able ta' hold air in my bubble because yeh helped. I took most of mine from the station and a lot of it leaked away. Is this just instinct?"

Nate had to stop and think for a long moment, then he shook his head slowly. "Not...not exactly. Some of it is the Schemic. Can't you feel it?" He looked around at his friends.

Most of them just looked at him blankly, but Jesse nodded. "Most of it isn't. I've tuned ta' the Schemic practically my whole life. What you do is... Something else." He stared at Nate, as if he were a puzzle to solve.

Nate grinned ruefully. "Seems like I'm going to have to figure out what I'm actually doing before I can teach any of you how to do it, then."

Tye snorted. "First, you're going to have to learn how we were taught to use E6 in the first place. There are some things I can do mostly on instinct. A few. Others..." He shook his head. "Mostly, I can't imagine how to approach the fields without thinking the way they taught me at the Telestry. One strand at a time."

From across the bridge, Rachel said, "We were never taught. I think we do things more the way Nate does, but making air??" She looked at Nate and shook her own head, almost disbelievingly. "Do you have any idea how complicated that is? You're not even just making oxygen. You're making AIR. It's a gas mix with a lot of nitrogen in it too. I can see it, and most people can't even see that much."

Nate grinned at her crookedly. "We all have a lot to teach each other, it sounds like. I'll put some thought into it."

He raised his hand from the cube in his lap, noting the faint hand print he'd already left in the dense metal. "Extropy." Nate threw up his hands, then pointed at Andrew, still grinning. "You realize that's not even a word, right?"

Teaching and exploring the fields also finally gave Nate the opportunity, starting in the very first session, to help Andrew with his Energematrice6 problems. They started with simply accessing it, but even looking at the fields left Andrew sweating.

Shawna came over to him and laid a hand on his shoulder, then asked, "You sure you want to force yourself to try this, Andy?"

Andrew shook his head doggedly. "I have to. I HAVE to figure out how to beat this. I can't stay this way."

Nate smiled compassionately. "This is going to take time. You may have to force yourself to face it, but you can't force yourself through it. Take the time you need."

On Andrew's fourth day of practice, he made his first attempt at actually using Energematrice6.

"Supreme Dirtnap!" Andrew was gasping for breath, but Tye snorted at his obviously heartfelt invective.

"What kind of swearing is THAT?" Tye asked.

Andrew laughed darkly. "That's what Dad always called Lastis. It sort of turned into a joke, I guess. It made Dad smile anyway, and that was hard to do by the end."

Tye nodded, but his puzzled frown just got deeper. "But where did something like that even come from?"

Andrew shrugged. "Before he became an Energematrist, Lastis was the Supreme Director of the Wise Earth Force. Bright Future all wanted to kill Lastis more than just about anything, so somebody called him Supreme Dirtnap. It turned into something between a joke and an obscenity."

Tye nodded again, this time in understanding. "Got it." He shook his head and looked over at Nate. "So if it's not the Dominion, is it Lastis you're after?"

Nate sighed. "Not...exactly." He paused, then asked, "What's the difference between Lastis and the Dominion? Or Lastis and the Telestry? They're all just interested in power, right?"

Tye looked puzzled, as if he hadn't thought about it in those terms, but he said, "Yeah, but the Dominion misuses their power way more than the Telestry. Sounds like Lastis is even worse... He's really evil, right?"

Nate's return gaze was thoughtful. "He is... but is he any worse than anybody else would be with that much power? And do you think the Telestry would really be any better than the Dominion if they were in charge?"

"But we're ethical and the Dominion isn't... The Telestry, I mean," Tye objected.

Nate shrugged. "And everybody running the Telestry is still human. Power corrupts, Tye. Do you really think they won't find some excuse to set aside their ethics?"

Andrew frowned at Nate. "It sounds like you're saying there's no hope, that we're always going to be under some kind of evil dictator."

Nate grimaced. "Well, in the long term the only hope is to either put somebody with perfect morals in charge or set up a system that keeps power spread out. E6 makes it harder, though. It makes power easier to get a hold of." He paused again, then smiled wryly. "It's not as if we don't have enough to deal with right now, anyway, is it? The Dominion and the Telestry are at each other's throats, and I obviously haven't done anything to improve that, have I? Then there's the Shades. If they get through from the Milky Way now, we're in really serious trouble. Then there's all the others..." Nate shook his head and sighed.

"Others?" Tye asked. "Like who? Are you talking about the Regency? They're a long way from here."

Nate snorted. "Tye, for every group you know about, there are ten in the universe you don't. Some of them aren't even human. Some can't be reasoned with at all. What we really need is a different way to think about it."

For the rest of their stay, Andrew's ability to grasp the fields slowly improved. Practicing every day exhausted him, but after two weeks he was able to manipulate small amounts of Energematrice6 without losing his concentration or being overwhelmed. It was obvious that his recovery would be a long road, but none of them doubted his dogged determination.

For Nate's part, even after a few days of comparative rest, he found himself tired at a level that was unusual for him. He brought it up with the others and Jon snorted. "Entropic shock doesn't just instantly go away, Nate. Don't push yourself too hard. It's like you told Andrew. It'll take whatever time it takes."

After a full month in Bounty City, Nate's dreams changed. The dream he'd had before, of the boy who was himself, forlorn and in pain, which was still terrible but had become familiar, disappeared. A new nightmare came upon him. The first time, he actually woke up screaming. In the dream his body was wracked by entropic shock so severe he thought he was dying; then something terrible fell on his head and drove him into darkness. By the time he awakened fully, the sensation had faded. All Nate was left with was a single word—Solas.

When Nate mentioned the dream to Shawna, she looked a bit startled. "I've been having nightmares too. That thing in the black gem…" she shook her head.

Nate laughed grimly. "This is the first new dream I've had since we left Lighthouse Station. It was more than a bit strange, though." His gaze turned inward for a long moment, then he shook himself and asked, "Can you look up Solas on the map?"

She readily agreed and they found that there was a system with that name only a day's travel away, along the perimeter of the Abyss. It was then he decided that must be their next destination.

Chapter 12

When they left port, they were in for a surprise. As they got out of the atmosphere and set their course for Solas, Andrew was eyeing his plot nervously.

He looked back to Nate and said, "Twenty-seven other ships launched from the Bounty City Spaceport within a few minutes of us. They're not approaching, but they're generally following us."

Nate frowned in response. "Any indications what they're doing? Any communication?"

Andrew shook his head grimly. "None."

Nate looked over to Jesse and Keevan. "Any ideas?" Keevan immediately shook his own head, looking just as grim as Andrew.

Jesse, on the other hand, was frowning thoughtfully. "Nate, yer a celebrity now. While you've been at the conclave every day, I was in the cantinas and walking the streets talking ta' the people. You've been trying to get 'em all to listen. It's working. I think some of 'em are following us because they wanna stay near you."

"Or because they want to hurt him," Shannon added grimly from her station.

Jesse nodded, but then he shrugged. "Yeah, but they can't all be out ta' get us, and that's a LOT of witnesses."

Nate thought for a long moment, then shrugged as well. "I agree. In fact, Andrew, let's reduce our speed to half of max on the trip. I don't want to leave them behind."

Andrew looked at him incredulously, then shook his head. "You're the boss."

Twenty-three of the twenty-seven ships followed them all the way to Solas. Two of the launches had been coincidental, and their efforts to get away from Nate's unintentional flotilla were almost comical. Two others had actually messaged Adamant en-route to signal that they were turning back, but were not in distress.

When they reached Solas, the situation was similar to the one they'd found at Bounty. An industrial space station circled the planet while commercial and tourism traffic were directed to the spaceport in Solasborough, the planet's largest city. The Solasborough flight controller seemed harried—no surprise with thirty vessels to coordinate at once—but he directed them to a berth on the outskirts of the spaceport.

Unlike Bounty, Solas was a full member of the Telestry. Shortly after they landed, Adamant received a call from the special assistant to the Adjutant, the Telestry's planetary governor, welcoming them and asking how long they intended to stay.

After a conversation that lasted far too long for the simple information the man wanted, most of which Andrew didn't even have, he closed the connection and grunted sourly. "He sure thinks a lot of himself."

Keevan grinned at him, pointing with his UPT. "A high muckety-muck under-functionary with little tin god syndrome, eh? We're movin' up in the universe! They're not ignorin' us anymore!"

Gazing out the bridge window on the spaceport, now bustling with activity from the travelers who had followed them to Solas, Shannon snorted. "We're a bit hard to ignore." She eyed Nate speculatively. "You know they've been getting rebroadcasts from Bounty's conclave, don't you? There's no way they don't know who you are by now."

Nate shrugged. "It had to happen. I'm just glad people get to see it."

The same day they landed, Nate went to the conclave in Solasborough to speak, again accompanied by three of his friends—Rachel, Tye, and Jon this time. As soon as he entered the structure, built above ground and with a permanent roof, likely because of the nearly constant rain in Solasborough, Nate could feel the difference in the atmosphere of the crowd.

There were actually more people here, but the crowd was subdued. A Telestic who was obviously tasked with keeping order in the conclave sat attentively near the podium. He was a gray-haired gentleman, with a weathered face and a dignified air. When he caught sight of Nate, his eyes went wide and he looked as if he might object when Nate stepped forward to speak, but instead he simply sat there, his jaw clenched.

Again, Nate surveyed the crowd before he said anything. They talked among themselves and there were shouts here and there, but the boisterous joviality of Bounty was missing.

Nate started slowly again, to gather their attention, "Most of you...most of you probably think entropy is a problem for Energematrists."

He looked around slowly, frowning. "For generations, the Telestry has taught that Energematrice6 is only available to a select few. They send Telestics to test you, and only a few are chosen for their abilities." He paused again.

The crowd was mostly silent now, and with his next words the rest quieted instantly. "Every single one of you has the ability to grasp and use Energematrice6, though you don't know how."

Nate waited a long time before he spoke again, scanning their faces. Finally, he said, "In one sense, the Telestry was right to keep this secret. Most Telestics are never even told. They believe just as you do that the use of the fields is reserved to the select few who can become the most powerful, and there is good reason. The Telestry has been forbidden to admit or teach anyone whose ability does not rise to a certain level. The early Telestics taught everyone, and because they did, those with only a little ability in the fields burned out from entropic shock. Hundreds of trainees were killed, and for most of you here today, if you tried to use Energematrice6 for even the smallest task, you would over-exert yourselves and die."

The Telestic in charge of the conclave, who might have been on the verge of stopping Nate before, was now sitting back in his chair, his expression conflicted. The crowd was buzzing, but Nate raised his voice and continued. "Have you ever known anyone who died for no reason at all? Have you seen a rainbow from the corner of your eye, but when you turned to look it was gone? This is why I must teach you about what we call entropy."

Nate waited for the audience to quiet again. The Telestic had a look somewhere between shock and guilt now, all signs of resistance gone. Nate looked over the crowd once more. Once there was quiet, he said, "Before The Escape and The Betrayal, entropy was only a rule. It said that whatever happens, some energy will always be lost. It wasn't until The Betrayal, when reality was twisted and any use of Energematrice6 drew a part of its energy from its user, that entropy came to mean death. The physical laws of the universe were corrupted by the Enemy who still pursues us."

Nate paused again. The elderly Telestic just sat there, his eyes now looking haunted. Nate put the man out of his mind.

After a moment, Nate said, "There will come a day when everyone uses Energematrice6. The universe must be set right."

Nate took questions, but there weren't many. Either the audience was too shocked, or they were too used to being told what to do and what to think.

A few glared darkly at Nate as he stepped down from the podium. Rachel stared around at the crowd and gave Nate a concerned look. "Maybe we'd better head back."

Part of Nate wanted to argue, but he didn't have any real reason to, so he nodded and they started back to Adamant. As they were leaving the Conclave, however, they encountered a small knot of excited, well-dressed people.

Upon seeing Nate, their excitement went from relatively muted to open jubilation. They were all talking at once, so it took Nate a few seconds to realize that their accents were slightly different from the rest of those he'd met on Solas. From there, he only required a few more seconds to piece together that these were some of the folks who had followed them from Bounty.

One man, even louder and more boisterous than the rest, managed to push his way forward to Nate and reach to shake his hand. "Name's Reggie! How d'ya do!" Nate didn't immediately respond, and Reggie plowed on. "You're Nate, right? It's great ta meet'ya! We can't wait ta join ya' movement! Aurora won't know what hit 'er!"

Nate blinked, then shook his head and asked, "What movement? What do you mean, Reggie?"

Reggie seemed genuinely shocked by the question. "Whadda'ya mean, what movement? What ya' been talkin' about in the Conclaves! We're goin' ta' change the galaxy! We got work ta' do!"

"Ah. I see." Nate nodded. "What do you propose to do, Reggie?"

"Whadda'ya mean, whadda we do? Yur tha' boss! You tell us what ta' do." Reggie's enthusiasm was slackening a bit with his obvious confusion, but the certainty in his purpose was absolute.

Behind him, one of the others from his crowd put in, "Oy told ya', Reg. We're gonna haf'ta set it up aselves! These visionary types got no ability ta' organize. It's up ta' us, I'm tellin yuh."

Nate's eyebrows shot up his forehead and he snorted at the absurdity of the assertion, but Reggie was not to be contradicted.

"Naw, Jorjie! Give 'im a tick ta' adjust. Ya can't jus' bowl 'im ova like that!" Reggie's lack of self-awareness was enough to take the situation from ridiculous to comical for Nate, but he saw their earnestness, and didn't smile.

Instead, he just nodded, raising his voice so the entire group could hear him. "I want to thank you all for coming. When I started speaking, I should have expected some of you to respond this way." He shook his head ruefully. "I never thought anyone would follow me from one port to another...and I wish this time you'd stayed home.

"I came to Solas because I expected trouble. I don't want you to get hurt because of me."

Nate stopped, frowning, and the group in front of him erupted in confused chatter. After a moment, Nate raised a hand for silence and shook his head. "The time will come when I may lead you more directly, but now isn't that time. You're welcome to stay and enjoy Solas, of course. I plan to be here for a while." He hesitated, then shrugged and added. "If you do stay...you might want to find a solid place to shelter." Nate glanced reflexively at the sky as a new explosion of talk broke out. Taking advantage of their excitement, Nate bid Reggie and Jorjie goodbye. Then, he turned to rejoin his friends, resuming his return journey to Adamant.

Solasborough was surprisingly scenic. It was obvious the settlers had built to some fondly-remembered architectural theme from Earth. Some of the structures were many hundreds of years old, but they held up amazingly well, with paneled wooden buildings overhanging cobbled stone walking streets. The ground was more uncomfortable to his feet than most of the walking streets he'd used, but the scenery's charm was enough that he didn't mind. When they reached the spaceport, the others had walked on ahead while Nate took the opportunity for some solitude. He entered the spaceport through the gateway that faced north toward the conclave, his friends well ahead of him, and began walking down the rows of berths toward Adamant. This spaceport didn't have one of the slidewalks he was used to, so progress was slow. They had, of course, dispensed with the cobbles for the benefits of advanced concrete.

It took Nate far longer than it should have to realize there was a girl walking beside and slightly behind him. Traffic was sparse and he couldn't remember when she had appeared there, but there she certainly was. She was small with brown hair, wearing what could only be described as rags. She looked almost mousy. The furtive glances she shot behind her every few seconds, made the impression even stronger.

She caught Nate's glance toward her and started to shrink back, but then she visibly straightened and asked, "You th'one they call Brightstar?"

Nate smiled and nodded. "I am."

The girl walked a little faster to catch up. "Oy... Oy need ya'help. O' ratha me mate does." Her startlingly green eyes darted back and forth as if she were ready to bolt, but there was a determination in the set of her small shoulders.

Nate stopped and turned directly to her then nodded again. "Alright, what can I do?"

Her head darted from one side to another as she stopped as well. "Not'ere. The'watchin. Somewher'else."

Nate shrugged. "Come with me to the ship then. We can talk there."

The girl hesitated, looking even more nervous than before, if that was possible, but after obviously thinking about it she nodded in return.

They started off again, together this time. The girl seemed at least a little relieved, though her head kept swiveling back and forth and it was obvious she was expecting trouble.

After they'd been walking for a minute or two, Nate looked over to her and asked, "What's your name?"

"Lissa," she said shortly, quickening her pace.

When they reached Adamant a few minutes later, Nate tried to usher Lissa up the ramp before him, but she stepped to one side and the nervous look she'd begun to lose came back full-force. He sighed and walked into the ship ahead of her, glancing back once to be sure she actually followed. Once they were inside, Nate's hand automatically went to the airlock controls to close it, but instead he turned to Lissa and raised his eyebrows. She actually blushed, but she nodded. Even so, when the airlock closed, she flinched.

Nate smiled at her lopsidedly. "You can leave any time you want. I promise."

Lissa nodded and gave him a weak smile in return. "Oy av'en got a choice any'ow. They gonna kill 'im."

Nate nodded back, but before he could reply, Jon asked from behind him, "Wait, who's getting killed?"

Nate turned to Jon. "This is Lissa." He turned back to Lissa and said, "Come to the bridge. I expect everyone will want to hear this sooner or later. May as well tell it once instead of two or three times."

A short walk and another set of introductions later, they were all crowded around Lissa and Nate asked, "Now who's killing who?"

Lissa nodded. Looking uncomfortable she said, "Tha Adjtant 'as me mate, Rawph. E's killin 'im... Suckin' the loife royt out of 'im. Usin' 'im up." There were tears in her eyes and she bowed her head. "Oy'm not strong enough to 'elp 'im. Ya gotta do somethin'. Oy've lost too many a'ready."

Nate frowned in thought as Jesse asked, almost hesitantly, "Ya said they're draining him. Are ya talking about emulging?"

Lissa sneered. "Yea. 'Ats what they call it. Whateva' fancy words they loyke. They killin 'im! Simple as 'at."

Nate shot a questioning look at Jesse while the others, all except Keevan and Tye, looked blank.

Jesse grimaced. "Emulging is... Just awful. It's how the Telestry killed Siever Radding, and he was a legend. The Telestry is supposed ta' be the 'good guys.' That means they can't ignore what's going on here, even if they try. They can't afford for people ta' think they're connected with this sorta thing."

He shook his head in disgust before he continued. "They forcibly drain E6 from a person. Sixers, especially untrained ones, give their E6 over to the flow by instinct, and once they start they can't stop. It's only partially voluntary. It takes a lot of training to resist it. Too much causes entropic shock and death, and the people doing the draining have no way to know how much is too much for any particular person. "

Tye cut in, frowning, "Old Professor Lourde told us emulging someone is like stealing their life force. The power is free to the one doing the stealing, whatever little they can get, but it's even worse than normal burnout for the poor guy getting drained. I'm pretty sure he wasn't supposed to talk about emulging, but somebody asked." Tye shrugged. "The Telestry only allows it as punishment for capital crimes, like murder."

Lissa snorted derisively. "Rawph didn' hoyt nobody."

Keevan eyed her skeptically. "Tye's right. That might'a been how they killed great granddad in the bad old days, but now? A Telestry official wouldn't allow that for just any offense. He must'a done somethin' pretty awful."

Lissa turned to Keevan with cold anger. "Oh Aye, 'e was takin' food 'at wasn't 'is. An' 'e only 'ad to 'cause the migh'y lord adjutant put 'im on the list in the fi'st place! Three stroiks, e's dead, and 'im only wantin' to feed 'is sistas!"

Nate laid a hand on her shoulder. "What list? And what did he do to be put on it?"

Lissa looked startled. "'Spose they don't 'ave the shame list whereva' you're from, eh? Sometoimes 'e adds you when you say somethin' 'e doesn't loike in conclave. Sometoimes it's 'cause you was blockin' 'is way or sommat loike that. Rawph got added 'cause 'e was 'makin' trouble.' You know 'ow 'e was makin' trouble?"

Lissa's sneer returned full-force. "'E wouldn' let one of the pervs near 'is sista. Punched the bugga roight in the mouf 'e did ...an well, once you're on the list, nobody will give ya' work. 'Fraid of makin the Adjtant angry, they are. What was 'e s'posed to do? Let 'is brothas an' sistas starve?"

Tye shook his head slowly, his expression sick. "If this is true, it's awful. When they test you at the Telestry, they make you use so much E6 that you go into entropic shock. Not enough to kill you, but I sure felt like I was dying. Emulging is so bad they wouldn't even talk about it. Entropic shock day after day until it kills you? On purpose?"

Jesse made a noise in his throat and Nate glanced up at him. Jesse looked uncomfortable, but he said, "Nate, where did ya find her? By her own admission, her friend is a violent thief. Are yeh sure..." He trailed off, but Nate could see the doubt and even a bit of disgust in his expression. Looking around at the others, Nate could see that at least half of them agreed with Jesse.

Lissa saw it too, and her eyes flashed dangerously. "Well, foine then. If that's 'ow it is."

She turned to go, but Nate said quietly, "Lissa..." She stopped and looked back, her eyes still flashing, and Nate continued. "It looked to me like it took all the courage you had just to talk to me. Is that about right?" Lissa blushed and her mouth opened to reply, but before she could say anything Nate addressed the others. "As much difficulty as she had coming to me, I can't repay her with a cold shoulder. You may have a point, but I have to know for sure...besides, I had a dream." Nate paused and shook his head. "I need to check into this."

Jesse nodded in acquiescence, and the others all followed suit. Jesse cleared his throat and asked, "How do ya want to do this, then?"

Nate looked back to Lissa. "Where are they keeping him?" Lissa brightened visibly, though her glance at the rest of Nate's party was anything but friendly.

She gestured in the general direction of the Conclave. "'E's at Bridewell." At Nate's questioning look, she made a face. "The Adj'tant's jail. I'll show ya."

Nate's friends all insisted on going along, and Andrew and his sisters wanted to take the time to lock Adamant down securely before they left.

During the exchange, Rachel had been watching Lissa thoughtfully. As everyone prepared to leave, she pulled Nate aside.

Nodding toward Lissa, Rachel said, "She's an Odd, Nate."

Nate raised an eyebrow at her. "How do you know?"

Rachel shrugged. "I'm not sure. I can see it...somehow."

Nate frowned thoughtfully, then nodded and turned to go, but Rachel stopped him. "Nate... I have to go find Dad. I have to... He's..." She stopped and shook her head helplessly.

Nate sighed. "Rach, I can't leave here yet, even if what Lissa's told us comes to nothing. I told you I had a dream about this place? At the end of it, something fell out of the sky and hit me in the head. Something more is going to happen here. I know it."

Rachel shrugged almost despondently and Nate squeezed her hand. "I know you want to see him again, but don't lose sight of what's in front of you, ok? What we're doing matters. You'll see."

It actually took them nearly a half hour to leave Adamant. By the time everyone was ready and the ship was fully shut down and locked, Lissa was practically dancing with impatience. As they walked away from Adamant, she scampered ahead before dropping back to walk with the group, obviously resenting their slow pace.

Their destination was about a half hour walk away, on the other side of the conclave. The walk was as pleasant as Nate's earlier walk to and from the conclave, and it would have been easy to forget their purpose as they exclaimed over the charm of the architecture and the age of the city, some of which dated back nearly to The Escape itself.

After their exposure to the crowds on Bounty, Shannon and Laura were at least somewhat prepared for the crush on Solasborough's streets, though they both kept a watchful eye on the people around them. Nate got the feeling that Laura was doing something with her psi talent, as their group always had a small, inexplicable bubble of space around it even in the most tightly-packed crowds.

Shawna had by far the most difficulty. She took one step out of the ship, gasped and closed her eyes. For the rest of their walk across the city, she kept her gaze fixed firmly on her feet, refusing to look up for any reason. Tye stuck close to her, even taking her by the hand at times, and Jon took up a position ahead of her without ever saying a word, leading the way so she didn't have to look up.

Andrew, on the other hand, was completely unaffected by either the crowds or the open space. If anything, some of the strain he'd built up over the past weeks of work with Energematrice6 seemed to clear once they were in the open air.

When they reached the imposing stone block building that Lissa had called Bridewell, Nate led the way through the main doors. The rest of his group followed him in, and with ten of them including himself, they made quite the crowd. The uniformed officer sitting behind the barred desk blinked in surprise at seeing Nate, then caught sight of Lissa behind him and the surprised look instantly became a smirk.

"This oughta' be good." The officer fixed Nate with a snide grin above his hand-held.

Nate decided politeness was his best strategy, despite the officer's attitude. "Uhh sir, do you have a prisoner here named Ralph?"

The smirk turned into an outright sneer. "It's Constable Bradford, and aye, I've got seven Rawphs. The one you wunt's in the special facility back 'ere. Docta Applebaum's usin' 'im as we speak. If ya listen real close, you might 'ear 'im screamin'."

It was Nate's turn to be surprised, but behind him Lissa let out a screech and started yelling incoherently at Bradford, who chuckled. "Careful, missy. Treatin' an officer of the government loike that's liable to get you thrown in 'ere with 'im. 'Course you're a bit young for all that." He leered at her and set his handheld down to lean back in his seat.

Nate felt his gut clench and what had been an attempt at politeness turned to cold anger. Lissa was still yelling, her accent so thick as to make her incomprehensible, and Nate held up a hand toward her. "Hush." She quieted and Nate turned back to Bradford. "Can you tell me, please, why he's in here?"

"Shore." It was obvious now that Bradford was enjoying himself. "'E was picked up for theivin'. Third stroike. 'E was a known troublemaker any'ow. Was on Adjutant Seledris's registry, 'e was." The guard leaned forward toward Nate and mock-whispered, "Rawph, e's a violent one ya' know. Smacked me mate Orrie a good one, 'e did. Knocked 'is front teef roight out of 'is head. 'Ats what got 'im put on the list."

Nate nodded slowly, then said, "Let me guess, Orrie was trying to get…'friendly' with Ralph's sister?"

Bradford snorted in derision and sneered at Nate. "They's common street trash. Good fa' nuffin. She's a pretty one, though. Sooner she learns what's good fer 'er…"

For a brief moment, Nate was beyond thought. He actually saw red. Bradford cut off mid sentence as he flew backward out of his chair and skidded across the floor. Instead of going for the barred door to his right that led behind Bradford's desk, Nate grasped the bars in front of him with one hand and lashed out with Energematrice6. The bars and desk disintegrated, sending shattered pieces of furniture and steel flying across the small room beyond, leaving shrapnel sticking into the stone walls and pelting Bradford with smaller fragments. At the last second, Nate threw up a partial shield around Bradford so none of the larger pieces hit him. Then, Nate was through the hole he'd made and standing above the officer. A kick to the ribs, with Nate reluctantly using only his physical strength, interrupted Bradford's own belated attempt to grasp the fields and knocked the wind out of him at once.

For what felt like a long time, Nate stared down at Bradford, his foot raised to kick again. Bradford was gasping for breath now, and as reason returned and his flash of anger cooled, Nate lowered his foot and said quietly, but with steel in his voice, "People, even the lowliest people, are not trash. How many people is the government here executing by emulging for crimes like theft?"

Bradford didn't answer, though his breathing had returned to normal. He simply stared up at Nate with fear in his eyes.

"Well?" Nate asked. "How many, and on whose authority are you doing it?"

"Oi'm, oi'm not doin anythin'. It's the Adjutant who authoroized it. E's always at the conclave this toime o' day. Go see 'im!" Bradford was obviously in shock and half-panicked.

Nate's eyes flashed. "How many, Bradford? How many people are being punished this way for non-capital crimes?"

Bradford flinched back. "Oi... Oi dunno. 'Dozens? 'Undreds?"

Nate nodded grimly. "Get up." Bradford looked at him, eyes wide, and Nate barked, "Get. Up." Bradford scrambled to his feet, then backed against the wall behind him.

Nate nodded again. "Now, go find the Adjutant and tell him I'm coming, and if you dare try to use E6 against me or my friends, I'll make sure you can never use it again."

Bradford hesitated, obviously expecting further violence, and Nate stepped to the side and pointed out the hole he'd left in the bars behind him. "Go!"

Without looking at Bradford again, Nate turned to the door that led further into the building and considered it, then looked through it using Energematrice6. Seeing no one directly on the other side, he shrugged and lashed out again. The door exploded inward, and he glanced back to see his friends staring after him, wide-eyed. Lissa had a look on her face like Christmas had come early. The others just looked stunned.

Nate smiled at her crookedly, but without much humor. "Sometimes a point has to be made."

Stepping forward into the hallway then pausing, Nate looked around. "Lissa, do you know where Ralph's cell is?"

Lissa bit her lip. "Oy... Oy think so. They only let me in to see 'im the once."

Nate frowned thoughtfully. "Anybody who wants to go see if they can find that 'special facility' he was talking about?" He looked at the rest of his group.

Jesse immediately stepped forward. "I'll go. Anybody else wanna come?" He too looked at the others questioningly. Jon and Rachel exchanged a glance and nodded, and Jesse nodded back. "Good enough."

The three split off, turning down the corridor to the right while Lissa directed Nate and the rest of the group to the left. They advanced into the building slowly, with Nate leading the way and simply blasting any door or wall that was in his way.

Once or twice he caught fleeting glimpses of people running from them as he checked behind walls or doors before he destroyed them, but by and large they found the front quarter of the Bridewell unoccupied. When they got to the cell blocks, Nate tried to blast the entry door and found he couldn't. Something inside him rebelled, stopping him.

Nate tried again and the same mental block made him stop again. It was exactly the same feeling he'd had on Lighthouse Station when the Schemic stopped him from using Energematrice6 on the crowd. He paused and looked at the steel door in front of him, puzzled. Then, using the fields, he scanned further ahead and found there were people in cages to either side of the hallway before him, some huddled at the backs of their cells, staring in his direction.

If he had used enough force to blow this door, the shrapnel would probably have killed some of those people outright. Changing his tactics, Nate grabbed the door with Energematrice6 and heaved, wrenching it out of its frame and tossing it to the side. The little group moved on, walking down the next hall and turning left again. As they passed by, many of the prisoners crowded up to the bars, begging to be released. Nate passed by them reluctantly, promising himself that he would see to finding them real justice once he'd left.

It took another few minutes, but they reached the cell Lissa had remembered from her previous visit. There was nobody inside at all.

"Well," Andrew said, looking into the tiny room, "I guess that means we're headed for 'the special facility.'" Nate nodded and they turned to retrace their steps.

When they reached the door Nate had wrenched from its hinges, they found Rachel coming toward them from the other direction.

"I think we found him!" she called, motioning back the way she'd come.

As soon as they reached her, passing back through the twisted wreck of the door frame, she said, "We're pretty sure we found the special facility, and there's an old man there."

"Rawph's not owd. 'E's on'y seventeen!" Lissa said, frowning.

Rachel shrugged. "Come see for yourself." They followed her down the hall, turning right twice, then left again before they finally stopped in front of another steel door, this one with the latch melted away.

Rachel smiled wryly. "We couldn't get it open. Jesse took care of it."

They passed through and found themselves in something halfway between a laboratory and a torture chamber.

Jon was bent over a slight, ancient-looking man strapped to an angled table, his arms in manacles to either side while Jesse stood by, watching. At first, Nate thought the man must be dead, but after a moment his chest moved slightly. All Nate's friends stopped as they came through the door behind. Then, Lissa caught sight of the man and let out a shocked cry, running to him in obvious distress.

"Rawph! Aww, Lightmaker. What'd they do?" Lissa's face was white as she reached out a trembling hand to touch him. She looked at Nate. "'E's on'y seventeen!"

Nate looked at the man again, and shook his head in disbelief. He crossed the room and Jon stepped aside while Nate laid his hands on Ralph's head, allowing Energematrice6 to flow out of him. What came back was such a sense of destruction and ruin that he actually cried out and pulled his hand away in shock.

Lissa was weeping openly as she cradled his face in her hands. "They've kiwed 'im. 'E's not dead yet, but they've kiwed 'im fu' shore."

Jesse reported. "There were a couple'a guards when we got here, but once I melted the door they took off through there." He pointed to another door in the back wall of the room then shook his head, half embarrassed and half aghast. "...Lissa was right, but I'm not sure what we can do for him."

Nate bowed his own head before once more laying a hand on Ralph's head and reaching out through the fields. Time seemed to stop as he extended his senses into Ralph's body and allowed the energy that underlay the universe to flood through him. An indefinable time later, Nate opened his eyes and sat down abruptly on the floor. The table Ralph was manacled to had a great crumpled, half-frozen handprint in it where Nate had been grasping it with his other hand, and the metal was flaking away in dry denatured hunks. Ralph, on the other hand, no longer looked like an old man. He didn't look seventeen, as Lissa had claimed, but he did look young again.

Nate had found so much damage in Ralph's body that he hadn't been able to heal all of it. Some was fresh, and that had responded readily to Nate's ministrations, the cells returning to a state that they obviously knew to be right. In the final examination, some of the damage had simply been too old. Ralph's body had accepted the damage, and while Nate could see how someone more skilled than he might attempt to re-teach it what health was, the task was beyond him. Still, he had managed to repair most of what the emulging had done, bringing Ralph back from near death into health and wholeness.

Nate's friends were all crowded around and after a moment, Jesse stepped forward. He drew on Energematrice6 and pulled apart the shackles that held Ralph to the table. There was a long silence as they all just stared—then Ralph moaned.

Tye said wonderingly, "You can't do that. Entropic shock can't be healed. It's like aging. It's impossible."

Nate looked at him, eyebrows raised, and Tye flushed a bit, then grinned. "For anybody but you, I guess?"

Jon stepped in close to put his own hands on Ralph, and green power raced up and down his body. He looked at Nate. "He's fully healed. There's a little damage left, but it's all old. How did you do it?"

Nate shrugged with a tired smile. "I'd love to know who decided it couldn't be healed in the first place. I'll see if I can figure out how I did it. Then maybe I can teach you."

At that, Nate pulled himself to his feet and smiled at Lissa. "Come see me at Adamant later, will you? For now, I think he's going to need your help."

She hesitated, then nodded. "Aight."

He turned to the others, his face grim. "For now, I think I'd better have a word with the Adjutant."

As they left the Bridewell a few minutes later, Shannon stared back up at the stone block structure with a frown. "Bridewell... Seems like a really strange name for a place like that."

Andrew laughed. "Probably something historical. There's a lot of that in Aurora."

Chapter 13

"The Lightmaker didn't make people to fill up the universe.
He made the universe for holding the people."
- The collected wisdom of Siever Radding

From the Bridewell, it was a short walk to the conclave. Nate was going on what Bradford had told him, hoping to find the Adjutant there.

Nate's initial flash of red-hot anger at Bradford's attitude toward the people of Solas had cooled as he blasted his way through the Bridewell, but seeing Ralph and the torture he'd been subjected to was enough to rekindle the flames. At the very least, the Adjutant was responsible for creating a culture that made torture an acceptable punishment for minor crimes. At worst, well, Nate had an ugly suspicion that what he'd seen was just scratching the surface.

As they entered the conclave, the booming voice of the speaker was audible even before they could see him.

"...and it is only proper that those with the gift of the fields follow the Tenets and concern themselves with the welfare of those less powerful than they. Indeed, I myself have always made the utmost effort to see that those under my care are properly treated."

The speaker, obviously the Adjutant by the elaborate robes of office he wore, turned to Nate's party and his eyes narrowed.

"Ahh, here comes the interloper now, a boy of no standing or stature…"

Meanwhile, behind Nate, Laura gasped and all of Nate's friends from the Milky Way stopped dead still, staring at the Adjutant.

"His eyes! Look at his eyes!" Laura was horrified.

Tye stood on tiptoe to see the Adjutant then shook his head in bewilderment. "He has Exsect eyes. What's wrong…?"

Andrew's grim voice cut clearly through the babble of the crowd to either side of them. "It's one of Them, Nate. He belongs to Them."

Nate glanced back at Andrew and nodded curtly, then turned back to the Adjutant, who was winding down his declamation, "…interfering in the justice of the Telestry and of Solas. What have you to say for yourself, child?"

Nate strode forward until he too stood at the podium, across from the Adjutant. His voice was low, but he made sure it was loud enough to carry across the conclave. "Adjutant Seledris, I've come from the Bridewell. I found a poor member of your population being tortured with Energematrice6 there. I was told his torture was the punishment for minor crimes."

The Adjutant's reply was louder than Nate, obviously intended to overwhelm him. "That man…that man was duly convicted of theft and sentenced. You have no right to question or interfere in Telestry justice."

Nate's voice was still low, but totally unwavering. "And what of your registry? Driving your citizens to crime because they cannot find legitimate employment is the worst kind of stewardship."

"Shame," the Adjutant replied, "is a fine motivator. It is only the most recalcitrant criminals who refuse to be corrected and go from the Registry to the Bridewell."

Nate stared the Adjutant down. "Public shaming may have its place, but denying people the ability to work because of their shame just guarantees they will have nowhere else to turn except to thieving. The Telestry uses emulging only in the case of capital crimes, yet you use it to punish simple theft. Is there any person here who would not steal to feed his family if he couldn't find employment because an unjust governor disallowed him from working?"

The Adjutant stared at him for a long moment. When he replied, it was obvious his contempt had gotten the better of him. "One of the many benefits of being Adjutant is that I do not have to explain myself to rabble like you."

Then, he lowered his voice, smirking at Nate. "Did you think you would escape so easily? I KNOW what you are!"

This time, the shock was familiar. Nate wasn't paralyzed as he had been when Rebus spoke, though the Adjutant's exsect eyes bored into him just as Rebus's had. At those words, Nate instinctively reached out to grasp the fields. This time, he could feel what the Adjutant was doing, the same thing Elder Rebus had done to him at Sanctuary. It was almost as if the adjutant's gaze and his knowledge of Nate's other reality were all it took to draw that world into this one. It transformed him from Nate Brightstar, long awaited hero and banisher of shades, into the broken thing he really was.

Nate wasn't ready for it. There was no way to be ready for such an assault, but this time he wasn't caught completely unaware. His attention didn't shatter as it had before Rebus, and he was able to seize Energematrice6, watching the enemy across from him grimly.

The adjutant sneered, then lashed out with Energematrice6. Though the attack took him somewhat by surprise, he had a firm hold on the fields and he saw the blow coming. It was a substantial attack, a great club of gray energy that sped straight at him from across the podium. Nate didn't try to dodge it. Instead, he absorbed the blow with a shield of his own power. Without the Sigil, the attack would have been significant, even difficult for him to handle, but with the Sigil's amplification bearing him up it was so trivial to dissipate that he doubted he was even dumping much extropy into the ground below, which was the only place it had to go presently...though his poor shoes might take a beating.

The adjutant smiled, then, and spoke again, for Nate's ears alone, "Witless." The word struck Nate like a body blow, shattering his hold on Energematrice6. He shuddered and his vision flashed back to that moment in that other life, before. His mind played back every nuance of Adrienne's tone as she'd turned to leave him collapsed on his bed, head aching.

It didn't take long for Nate's vision to clear, but he still felt utterly confused. Nate was staring at the Adjutant, fighting to regather himself, when the figure across from him collapsed like a puppet whose strings had been cut. Faintly, through his confusion, Nate sensed a retreating presence.

It was as if time itself stopped for a frozen heartbeat. In the crowd across from him and behind the Adjutant, he saw a flash of a face, its exsect eyes staring straight at him. It was only a glimpse, but it burned into his memory. Where had he seen that boy before? He was young, barely older than Nate himself. A flash of glittering crystal caught Nate's eye from the boy's neck. But there wasn't time. Nate was recalled to himself as the crowd's buzz cut off in a bare instant.

There were cheers here and there in the auditorium, but most of the crowd was too stunned to make any noise at all. Nate stared around, desperately struggling to gather himself. Before he could even begin to figure out what to say, though, the same Telestic who had been present to see Nate's address to the conclave earlier slowly rose to his feet.

He nodded to Nate, then bowed his head to think before speaking for the entire crowd to hear. "All of Solas owes you a debt. You see, I have here an order from the Telestry authorizing the removal of Adjutant Seledris. What I lacked was the ability to control him. He is to be returned to the Telestry to stand trial for his crimes. I believe there was even to be a team sent to retrieve him, but they have yet to present themselves, and the Adjutant was a powerful man. He was well beyond my own ability to overpower. Did you kill him? Perhaps as well for all of us if you did..."

Nate shook his head. "I didn't kill him. I don't know how long he'll be unconscious. I didn't even..."

Before he could finish, the Adjutant stirred and moaned, then struggled to his feet, head whipping around. A collective gasp rose in the conclave and Nate saw the other Telestic's eyes widening.

Then the Adjutant screamed, "It's GONE!" In the aftermath of that scream, the entire conclave was silent, and the Adjutant screamed again. "What have you DONE? The fields?? They're GONE!"

Nate frowned and, ignoring the Adjutant except to motion to him offhandedly, he said, "I don't know how long that will last, either. Are you taking charge of him?" The Telestic's eyes were wide and he nodded faintly, then motioned to two guards who had approached from their positions near the conclave's entrance. As they led the Adjutant away, Nate faced the Telestic who was apparently Solas's new leader.

The crowd was cheering now, yelling madly as the reality of the situation sank in. It lasted for a long time, but Nate eventually raised his hand for quiet. Slowly the crowd complied.

When the cheering had died down enough that he could be heard above it, Nate said, "As I told you, what just happened was not my doing. Regardless, I think for the time being you'd best suspend emulgings. The people of Solas have had enough of such torture. "This was followed by a renewed cheer from the crowd. Then it was the Telestic's turn to raise his own hand.

The Telestic nodded to Nate in return. "I believe some changes to the Adjutant's registry are in order as well." He looked around at the crowd. "You were right. Public shame may have its place, but Seledris used it as a means of oppression. Leadership should look to the future instead of shackling us to the past. Seledris will be returned to the Telestry, along with witnesses for his trial."

The Telestic eyed the crowd thoughtfully, then said, "Solas owes you a debt, young man. You are welcome here any time you wish."

The other man stepped forward to grasp Nate's hand. This signaled the end of the show, as far as the Telestic was concerned, and the crowd took to their feet cheering. Nate returned the handclasp and after a moment's hesitation followed the Telestic off the podium and back through the cluster of his friends, who were standing just off the podium on the entry walk.

When they were safely away from the podium, with crowd's cheering a dull roar behind them, the Telestic turned to Nate. "I am Tetsin Arsondus. I meant what I said about Solas owing you a debt. Whatever you have need of, we will be happy to assist you."

Nate smiled crookedly up at Arsondus. "I meant what I said also. Whatever you think I may have done to Adjutant Seledris, I didn't. I'm not sure who did, but it wasn't me. I'm not even sure what they did."

Arsondus looked startled. "That...hardly seems possible."

Nate snorted. "Well, I won't take credit for something that wasn't my doing. And on another note..." His crooked smile turned a bit sheepish. "You'll find I left the Bridewell...less than whole."

Arsondus's eyebrows rose in surprise. "Oh. Well..." He seemed at a loss for words. He simply stood there for long enough that Nate almost laughed. Then Arsondus laughed himself and shrugged. "I'm sure that will be part of the legend." His smile turned into something closer to a grin. "You know, whatever you might say about it, no one else who watched what happened in that conclave will believe it wasn't your doing."

Nate nodded ruefully and glanced back at his friends. "You're probably right. Except maybe them."

Arsondus nodded back. "How long are you planning on staying here? Seledris had powerful friends. I will try, but I doubt I can protect you from them." His own expression turned rueful and he added, "I'm going to have problems enough of my own, I suspect."

Nate smiled wryly. "You may at that. I'm not sure how long we'll be staying. I have a friend I promised to talk to, at least, and there's one other thing, too."

Arsondus raised an eyebrow. "Well, whatever your plans, I shall do my best to accommodate you. For now, though, I must bid you good day."

After returning Arsondus' goodbye, Nate made his way back to Adamant, his friends still trailing behind.

When they entered the spaceport, Keevan dropped back to walk beside him. "The Telestry's at it again, ay? Loriden can reach us even here!"

Nate sent Keevan an even stare, not denying what he said, but not confirming it either. Truth be told, he was still processing everything that had happened, and Keevan's insistent reminder of Loriden was just another piece of the puzzle that Nate was struggling to assemble.

Rachel, too, dropped back to walk beside them. "It might be Loriden, this time at least." She looked over at Nate thoughtfully. "He IS the head of the Telestry now."

Nate shrugged uncomfortably, remembering what Seledris had said. Nate remembered clearly his last meeting with Loriden, when his pupils elongated to become exsect, as if he were some other being entirely. Did Loriden know who Nate was? Did he know about Nate's life...before? It would explain a great deal, but for him to be responsible for everything...Nate just wasn't certain.

Jesse gave Keevan a dubious look and Keevan turned, obviously ready to argue the point. Nate dropped even further back, giving himself a little space. Rachel followed.

For a few minutes they walked quietly, side by side. Then, Rachel's lips twisted wryly. "I see it now," she said.

"Oh? See what?" Nate asked tiredly.

"You're the only one who could have set this place right," Rachel said. "You ARE here for a reason."

Nate nodded. "We're hardly started. There's so much that needs to change...so much to be done."

Rachel looked at him, her expression still troubled. "How do I live with it, Nate? He left, but he's not gone. I know he's out there somewhere."

Nate stopped walking and faced her directly. "Rach," he said, "There will come a time when I can give you an answer to that, but not yet. For now, trust me. I need you here. I need you all."

Rachel nodded slowly and gave him a brief hug, then turned to follow the rest of the group toward Adamant. As they were walking up the boarding ramp, Rachel grinned back over her shoulder mischievously at Nate.

"You know," she said, "You don't have to try to make up for a thousand years of boredom all at once."

It was a full two days before Lissa returned to Adamant. After the first day went by with no sign of her, Nate wasn't sure whether she would come at all. Especially knowing how difficult it had been for her in the first place, he began to doubt she'd show up, but when he left Adamant to go to the conclave on the second day, there she was. When he walked out of the ship, she was standing at the bottom of the ramp, looking uncertain.

Nate smiled when he saw her. "Lissa! I'm glad you came."

"Oy owe ya. Ain't neva welched on a debt." Lissa's voice was full of trepidation and she looked down after she spoke. "Ain't got nuffin to off'r in payment neitha'."

Nate looked at her thoughtfully, then said, "I came to Solas because I dreamed someone was doing to me what they did to your friend Ralph. You don't owe me anything, Lissa. I didn't ask you to come because I want repayment."

A look of surprise crossed Lissa's face and she scowled. "What then?"

Nate gazed at her intently. "How old are you?"

Lissa looked shocked now, as if Nate had guessed a secret, then grew suspicious. "Why you askin'?"

Nate barked a laugh. "You carry off the scared kid act pretty well, but I'm not blind. Every one of my friends on Adamant is an Odd."

Lissa's shocked look turned to profound discomfort. "Yea'. Why ya' think oy keep me 'ead down, ey? Gamin loike me... We come to bad ends if people foind out."

"Gamin?" Nate frowned. "You're not so different from me, you know." Nate was looking directly at her, his expression gentle. "So we're not normal. Every person is unique. We're just more different than most people are comfortable with."

It was Lissa's turn to snort. "Ya' right there fo' sho'."

"Do you have dreams about a world in chains?" Nate's expression when he asked was almost intense enough to make Lissa shy away, but she nodded slowly.

"Aye. That I do."

"And can you use E6?"

She snorted again. "Oh Oy've troied a few toimes. Maybe Oy could. Oi'm afraid Oi'd 'urt someone..." She shifted uncomfortably. "Oi did... Oi did 'urt someone." She looked pained, then the expression disappeared and she looked up at Nate, suspicious again. "Why you wanna know?"

"Because I want you to follow me," Nate said. "The Enemy is coming and there's not enough time to prepare."

Lissa laughed incredulously. "Me? Go out the' and foight what? The monstas in me dreams? On the terrible planet? Ye jokin'. Oi'm jus' a little street bird."

Nate smiled. "You care enough about your friends to come beg a total stranger for help saving them when you have nothing to offer in return. That's good enough for me."

Lissa actually looked thoughtful now, but after a moment she shook her head. "Too many rely'in on me. Oi 'elp people. If Oi leave, they'll doie, some of 'em."

Nate put his hand in his pocket, pulling out the remaining amulets. He took the soft purple one and held it out in one hand. Lissa looked at it, her eyes widening, then looked at the Sigil glowing where it hung around Nate's neck.

She asked, "Is'at... Is'at...?"

Nate nodded and Lissa's eyes widened further. She reached out to touch the purple stone and Nate smiled crookedly at her, then clasped her hand with his, the amulet between their palms. He could feel Energematrice6 flowing through the amulet into him, and though Lissa hadn't imprinted the Great Schemic she could obviously feel it too. She was staring wide-eyed.

Nate smiled at her. "What do you say?"

Lissa was silent. Then, withdrawing her hand from Nate's, she asked, "'Ow long do Oy 'ave to decoide?"

Nate shook his head. "I told you it was a dream that brought me here? There's one more thing that hasn't happened yet." He reflexively glanced at the sky, then smiled ruefully. "Not sure what it is, but it should be at least a few days."

Then, Nate frowned and asked, "Lissa, when you first came to me you said that you'd already lost too many friends. What did you mean?"

Lissa scowled and looked down. "People disappearin'... Friens Oy've 'ad fa' years, jus' gone. They..."

Lissa was cut off by a siren so loud that she and Nate both clamped their hands over their ears.

Part 3:
Invasion

Interval

He had beaten the odds for too long. He'd known something like this had to happen to him eventually, but not with the girl along. Lightmaker consume Them and all Their works, but especially this twisted situation.

He checked the scanners again, hoping he was wrong but knowing deep down that he wasn't, then looked outside at the streaks of light dogging his heels.

He had spent most of the life he could remember in the battle against Them. He'd visited Earth, the heart of their power, too many times to remember. Even after Lastis killed his father, he'd redoubled his efforts, rescuing the innocent from Them wherever he could.

He couldn't get to Earth now. It was ringed with sensor networks and defenses so thick it would take a miracle to get through alive. Getting through undetected was flat impossible. The billions who lived there were held captive, their lives barely better than those of animals. There was a chance he could make it to the moon or one of the other inner planets, but not a good one, and there would be no one there to greet him if he did. Whatever dregs of humanity remained free in the universe stayed as far away from Sol as they possibly could. Except him.

He'd known he was going to die someday, that his refusal to take to his heels and run away from the monsters would end him, and he'd tried it once or twice. He couldn't. It would have been a betrayal of all his father lived and died for, and now it was all he knew—hurting the enemy in any way possible, and freeing whoever he could from Their grasp.

What impulse had possessed him to bring the girl along on his wild crusade, he still wasn't quite sure. Utter hubris, probably. She was like his kid sister. He knew the comparison irked her, which was one reason he made it, if he was being honest with himself. He smiled and glanced over to where she sat, bent over and fiddling with something in her lap. She was always building some kind of gadget or experimenting with something new. It reminded him of his dad. He smiled again, as much a grimace as a smile, filled with pain.

Again he looked down at his scanners and shook his head. "There's no way out of this one," he said.

He could sense her trademark challenging glare on the back of his head. "Are you feeling all guilty again? I told you. It was MY choice. I do get to make my own choices, ya know?"

He just shook his head again in response, unable to meet her eyes. She asked, "Where we going?"

"Going to Sol. No choice. No other chance to evade. Not out here." His voice must have carried his defeat, but her tone never changed. She didn't even seem worried.

She nodded. "Well, when we get there I need your help."

He did look up and catch her eye then, surprised. "What?"

She smiled ferally, but with some real humor, and, he thought, maybe a bit of fondness. She held up the device she'd been tinkering with. "It's my turn to save your butt this time, but we have to get this closer to them than to us. And it'd help if we weren't moving so fast." She jerked her thumb in the general direction of their pursuers.

There was a glint in her eye then that he hadn't seen before as she said, "I'm glad I came along. I've been looking forward to this for a long time."

Chapter 14

Around them, the spaceport was suddenly in pandemonium. Any people they could see were running for cover. Nate looked at Lissa then pointed up the ramp into Adamant, clamping his hand back over his ear to run up the ramp, then smacking the airlock activation to open it.

As soon as they were inside and the airlock snapped shut behind them, the sound went from a deafening wail to a muffled, barely audible whine.

Nate headed for the bridge, calling over his shoulder, "Lissa, you'd better come strap in."

He found Shannon in the command chair, her eyes fixed on her screen.

"What's going on?" Nate asked.

"There's something…two things…coming down on us." She was obviously distracted, but she replied quickly enough.

"How close? Should we get in the air?" Nate was already heading for a seat. Everyone else on the bridge was seated, except Lissa who had come in behind him.

Shannon shook her head. "They're not going fast enough to actually destroy the city, and if we take off now, we'd better not plan on coming back. Flight control gets prickly about this stuff and we really could hit somebody. It looks like they'll be about five minutes apart, and I think they're both using Retton drive. Or they were? The second one is big." From off to one side where he stopped, Nate could see dread in her eyes and her scowl was unlike any she'd shown since he came aboard.

"What is it?" Nate asked.

"That looks like... It looks like a Changed destroyer."

Nate nodded grimly. "Well, that explains the dream. When I dreamed about Solas, something fell out of the sky and hit me on the head."

Shannon gave him a curious look, but all she said was, "The first one should be coming in...about a minute, and it's headed straight for us. It's about our size. Flight control just let us know there's been no communication. But I think they might be wrong." She did something on her panel then looked over at Nate with a half-smirk. "Thought so. They've been using a field communication system. It uses E6 for comms. I hadn't been listening because nobody here uses them."

Just then, a voice came over the bridge speakers, "I say again, this is Travis Retton on Earth's Revenge! Look out below! I dunno if anybody can hear us down there, but we're coming down whether we like it or not. Gona be a hard landing."

Nate nodded. "Somebody else from the Milky Way. Makes sense if that IS a Changed destroyer following him." A thought struck Nate and he added, "Shannon, can you signal him to land in the empty berth next to us? And relay that communication to flight control. We can at least do that much."

Shannon gave him a thumbs-up, then spoke, "Revenge, this is Adamant. Sending you a marker. It will bring you in near our position."

There was a fuzz of static, then Travis's voice came back over the comm, "Shannon? Is that...? Shannon??? Infested void, girl, it's good to hear your voice!"

Shannon grinned. "Yeah, that's Travis." Then she scowled reflexively, as if from long habit. She grumbled, "And he's bringing trouble. as usual."

From the hatch, Andrew said, "Travis? What? Here??"

Shannon snorted. "He's coming down on us, right about..." The entire bridge jumped, knocking Lissa off her feet and staggering Andrew even though he was holding on to the hatchway. The noise was painful, even through Adamant's hull.

Shannon winced. "Now."

Recovering his balance, Andrew shook his head. "Well, that probably didn't hurt us, but I'd hate to see what his landing zone looks like." After a moment, he added, "Not to mention Revenge."

Shannon was already trying to comm even as Andrew spoke, "Revenge come in, this is Adamant." No one answered, and Nate brushed past Andrew, heading for the outer airlock.

Outside, Nate ran down the ramp and peered around to see what the situation was. The siren was still blaring. No one else was in sight.

In the pad next to theirs, just over a hundred yards away, a vessel that very much resembled Adamant or Resolute stuck out up from a crater in the landing field. Earth's Revenge had a ragged, blackened scar down one side and the base was impacted into the crumbling concrete. Without stopping, Nate took off running straight for Revenge.

As he drew near the vessel, Nate felt the almost unbearable heat radiating from it and without slowing he hurriedly raised an Energematrice6 shield to protect himself. When he reached Revenge, Nate ran around it in a circle looking for the airlock. Halfway around the ship he found it, mostly buried in the concrete with only a hand's breadth sticking up above the ground.

Nate stopped and studied the situation, then shook his head. There was no time. Nate could see a way to unblock the door, but the collateral damage... He shrugged and reached into the fields, then reared back and punched the concrete next to where the airlock was buried, both pushing and pulling with the fields.

The concrete shattered. A great chunk of it came loose and blasted into the air, landing fifty feet away in the center of the walking lane. Wryly, fleetingly, he wondered what Tye would say if he could see. That push-pull with Energematrice6 was far from a simple maneuver.

It took three more great blows to open a hole big enough to access the airlock.

Breathing hard, Nate stepped closer, preparing to break it open, but before he could it slowly began to slide to one side. Inside, he could see a boy who looked about sixteen throwing his weight against a lever, pushing to manually force the airlock open. Behind him was a girl who looked ten or eleven.

Nate stepped to the door and, using Energematrice6, he pushed in the same direction as the boy, presumably Travis. The airlock slid open half way and Nate reached a hand down to help them both out. The boy, who was tall with blue eyes and brown hair, came first.

He winced at the heat radiating from the outside of the craft and the ground beneath until Nate pulled him inside his own shield. Next, he reached down for the girl—short and solidly built—extending his shield further to protect them both. The hole he'd opened wasn't large, but for the two of them it was more than enough.

Sirens still wailed all around, and Nate knew they wouldn't be able to hear him. Instead of speaking, he motioned toward Adamant and hesitated before laying a shield over the surface of the ground, allowing them both to follow with relative ease.

All three had to pick their way back through the crater and wreckage, both from the initial impact and his own efforts. As soon as he was clear of the worst of it, Nate started jogging.

When they reached Adamant, Jesse and Tye were waiting at the bottom of the ramp, watching him. Andrew, Lissa, and

Rachel all stood higher up on the ramp with their hands over their ears for the siren. It was so loud that Nate didn't even bother trying to say anything. He just led the way back up into Adamant. After they had all come back through the airlock, Andrew closed it behind them.

Nate nodded to the two newcomers, but instead of addressing them he looked back at Andrew. "How long do we have?"

Andrew shrugged. "Only a minute or two. It depends on how hard they decide to hit. We should probably strap in. This could be really bad."

Nate motioned to Travis and the girl. "We can get acquainted later. Whatever was following you is coming down even harder than you did." They both nodded, though the girl was holding her side and looking pained. It didn't stop her from following as they all headed for the bridge.

On the way, Nate asked Andrew, "Do we have any kind of shields that work on the ground?"

Andrew laughed grimly. "We could turn on the particle shield. Wouldn't help with anything much bigger than your head, though. Other than that, we've got nothing."

Nate paused at the hatch leading onto the bridge and looked back at Andrew. "Do it."

As they entered the bridge, Shannon looked up at them with a grimace. "Flight control says to batten down and strap in." She looked doubtful. "They seem to think this impact will be survivable." Outside the bridge window, they could all see a small, short-distance craft tucking in underneath the larger ship across from them.

Instead of proceeding to sit down in a seat and strap in like the others, Nate stooped down to pick up the tungsten cube from a compartment on the bottom of his seat. Then, he stepped to the wall of the bridge and laid his other hand on it and opened his senses to Energematrice6.

"Tell me when you have the shield on," He said. "I've told you the reason I wanted to come here was a dream? Well, at the end of the dream something fell out of the sky on my head. I've got a feeling we're going to need all the protection we can get."

"Okay, you've got it," Andrew said. "We have about thirty seconds left before whatever that is touches down...and it's moving WAY too fast. People are gonna get hurt."

Nate nodded and stretched out with Energematrice6, searching for the ship's defensive shield. When he found it, he reached out to the planet below them. He wasn't entirely certain how Paul had attached Hope One's particle screen to the nearby moon, but it gave him an idea. Nate reached out through the Sigil of the Mysteries and poured his power into the ship's shield, simultaneously bracing himself against the planet's mass.

Behind him, Andrew was counting down, "...Seven, Six, Five, Four, Three, Two, One..."

The impact made Revenge's landing seem positively tame by comparison. The ground leaped and bucked like a wild thing. Nate had anchored himself to the ship as he anchored the ship's shield to the planet itself. He felt the motion but didn't pay it much attention, too busy trying to fortify the ship's shield.

He did notice a moment later, though, when what felt like a mountain crashed down on the ship's shields from above, taking all the power he had infused into them in a bare instant. The shield held, and whatever it was skipped off. Then, the ship shuddered again from the secondary tremor when the object hit the ground nearby.

The aftermath was total stillness. Nate groaned and flopped down into a seat while Andrew stared out the front window of the ship at what might once have been a building, still clinging to a big hunk of the ground beneath it. The mass of wreckage, which was larger than Adamant itself, sat directly in front of them.

Everyone was on the bridge, Nate saw now, and they stared either at him or the massive twisted mess of metal and scattered rock and building materials. They were all a bit dazed, but whether it was the original impact or the piece of city that had come so close to turning them into pancakes, Nate couldn't tell.

Nate grinned weakly at them all. "Told you something fell on my head."

Characteristically, Andrew was the first to recover, and his eyes were already on his instruments. He remained silent, but there was something in the set of his shoulders that Nate noticed despite his exhaustion, heavy as it was. Obviously furious, Andrew rose from his chair and crossed the bridge so fast he seemed to teleport, right to where Travis had strapped himself into a seat beside Nate.

Eyes flashing, Andrew demanded, "What did you DO?"

Travis flinched, but he came back almost immediately, "It's not like I invited them."

"Not invited! There are DOZENS of them! Travis, they're coming!"

Travis shrugged, but he nodded grimly. "We'd better get out of here. There's no stopping them."

Nate was looking back and forth between the two and he held up a hand. "What? Stopping who?"

Andrew turned to him. "Nate there are dozens of those ships an hour or two out. The sensors can't even get a good count. The signatures are interpenetrated. The best estimate I got was forty."

Travis winced again. "Closer to fifty or sixty. The really big ones are a few hours behind."

Shannon snorted. "Travis, always bringing trouble."

"Look, I don't know about you," Travis said, "but I didn't exactly come here on purpose. I don't even know how it happened or where we are."

Laura cut in. "We can't leave. We don't know whether any of the monsters survived that crash. We can't leave these people to them."

Travis laughed incredulously. "What? Have you forgotten? We can't even kill one of them, much less a whole ship full. You've lost your mind!"

Laura pointed at Nate. "He can."

Travis eyed Nate with disbelief until Shawna chipped in, quietly, "He's Amasthena." Travis blinked in surprise and opened his mouth to reply.

Before he could, Nate raised a hand for quiet and looked to Andrew. "How long do we have?"

Andrew shook his head helplessly. "Half an hour? Forty minutes? They're already coming into orbit. It depends on how fast they want to be going when they land. If they come down as hard as the first one did, we could have fifty more ships dropping on us twenty minutes from now."

Nate looked to Travis. "Were they following you or coming to Solas themselves?"

Travis shrugged. "Until we came here they were following us. Now...I don't know."

Nate frowned. "We can't bring sixty of these ships down on Solas. One is bad enough. We've got to try to lead them out of here."

Lissa started to unstrap herself. "Oy 'ave to go. Moy frens need me."

Nate looked over at her, his face grim. "There's no good option here. We can't stay."

Laura's head was down, but she asked, "What about the people?" She looked up at Nate, her eyes haunted. "We can't abandon the people here. The Changed are monsters. What they did to my family..."

Nate shook his head. "We can't be everywhere. There are way more of them coming. We have to go."

Lissa had finished unstrapping and she stood up, facing Nate directly. She was resolved, but her tone was apologetic. "Oy 'ave to stay. They need moy 'elp."

Laura looked over to Lissa. "I'll stay with her." Lissa's face blanked in astonishment as Laura began unstrapping herself as well.

Nate looked pained. "If you stay here, I can't protect you."

Laura shrugged in response. "My choice. I can't leave them to face this alone."

There was silence for a long moment, then Jesse spoke up, "I'll stay too. I'll look out for 'em."

Nate's frown deepened, but he nodded. "It IS your choice, and there's no time to debate." He paused, then added, "If you stay, keep your focus on helping the people. We'll be back. We can deal with the Changed then."

Jesse nodded soberly back and began unstrapping as well.

Lissa stared at Laura as if she'd never seen her before. "Why? Why stay? Oy'm not askin' fer 'elp."

Laura's eyes were hot and she said tightly, "When the Changed took Resolute, Rex welded me into my compartment so the Changed couldn't get me. I couldn't see what happened to Mom or Da or Rex... except through E6. Do you know what the fields look like when a Changed rips someone apart? I watched!" She choked off, then a moment later, she grated, "I couldn't help them. I can't leave a whole planet to those things."

Nate nodded again, slowly, but he said, "I really wish you wouldn't do this. I can't see any good coming of it."

Laura looked briefly conflicted, but she shook her head and trailed Lissa off the bridge. Jesse stopped to clasp Nate's hand before he, too, followed the girls out.

Nate and the others still on the bridge watched in silence as the three walked quickly away from Adamant. Then, when they were beyond the line that signified a safe takeoff, Nate said, "We'd better get in the air. Time isn't on our side."

Keevan, who had been staring out the window, took the opportunity to ask, almost plaintively, "What are the chances Loriden's behind this, d'ya think?"

Everyone else on the bridge stared at him. Rachel snorted. "You're still stuck on that? This invasion came from another *galaxy*, Keevan!"

Keevan shrugged and mumbled something, while Andrew craned his head back around his chair to look Nate directly in the eye. "You realize, we're going to have to get past all those ships before we can actually run away, right? We can't even face one or two of them unless you have some plan...?"

Nate grinned at him, the grimness of his humor making his smile something closer to a rictus. "That's the rub, isn't it? I'll do what I can to shore up the shields. Plot the best path through them you can." With that, Nate leaned back in his seat and wrapped his hands around his tungsten cube. As Nate prepared himself mentally for what he knew was coming, he stretched out his senses through Energematrice6 further than he ever had before.

He could 'see' the entire ship around him and the rapidly-thinning atmosphere beyond. The incomprehensible mass of Energematrice6 behind him was certainly the planet itself, and far above, so far he had to refocus to 'see' them, was the enemy fleet. He could actually sense their evil intent somehow, though he couldn't have said how. The beings aboard those monstrous vessels were driven by wills and purposes not their own, the humans under their thrall almost snuffed out beneath the weight of their oppressors.

In the rear of their formation, Nate "saw" a presence so strong he shied back mentally. If the enemy fleet was alight with malice, this creature was a beacon of it—a piercing blaze of malevolence, its intent focused solely on the frail bubble of life that was Adamant.

A creeping horror began to take root in Nate's gut as that presence's attention fell on him directly. It called forcibly to his mind the encounter he'd had with the Changed in the belly of the Behemoth. It was the same horror, attenuated by distance, but Nate didn't have time to pay it any special mind.

The vessel that had crashed into Solas had been big, about three or four times the size of Adamant. Despite that, of the entire fleet arrayed above them it was the smallest, a hound that was built for speed. Each member of the fleet's vanguard was at least ten times Adamant's size, while some of the monsters behind them were an order of magnitude larger. The sheer mass of that fleet was overwhelming, and the power they could bring to bear was just as impressive.

Nate could sense the Energematrice6 charges already building up in the huge ships' weapon batteries. They were brute force weapons, with no finesse or control over their output. Still, the amount of raw energy those ships could throw was monumental. For a moment, he quailed at the thought of facing that firepower. He had never used even a fraction of the Energematrice6 required to turn back such a tide...but there was no choice. It was time to face it or die under its onslaught. Nate focused his attention fully on the fields and on the Sigil of the Mysteries with its lensing effect. Now the question was how much power he could actually handle.

"Nate?" Andrew asked.

Then again after a pause, "Nate??"

There was no response for what felt like a very long time. The seconds ticked by as Andrew watched the enemy loom closer and closer on the plot in front of him. Slowly, the tremendous force of their thrust subsided and their Retton drive began to come online, bringing artificial gravity and its inertial sump along with it. When gravity had returned to normal enough for him to move, Andrew turned in his chair to look back at Nate.

Nate was completely checked out, evidently deep in concentration. Whatever the case, it left Andrew with no doubt he was on his own, and he muttered, "Abyssal Void!" From the corner of his eye, Andrew saw Shannon eyeing him with concern and he turned to her. "I have to decide whether to take a path directly past them, which is the shortest route out and gives them the least time to shoot at us, or to go oblique, which means they're going to have a harder time hitting us, but it'll take longer to get clear."

Andrew jerked his head sideways. "And he's not going to be much help."

Shannon shook her head. "Cmon, Drew. You got hurt when we were running from them, but you can't let that stop you. You're leaning on him too much. I understand why, but you've been making decisions like this ever since Dad died. Nate trusted you with this." Andrew closed his eyes for what felt like a long time—longer than they could really afford—then nodded sharply and began inputting a course into the computer.

The first blast of raw power that impacted Adamant's shields didn't come as a surprise, exactly, but Nate's attention had been on testing his limits. As he felt the Energematrice6 battering at the shields, trying to overwhelm them and sweep through the ship, he focused on drawing power out of himself and the world around him, through the Sigil and into the shields. If even a fraction of the attack got through, it would vaporize them instantly.

The raw power it took was tremendous, almost unimaginable to him even now, but he did it. In fact, he did it easily, without really straining himself. The amount of energy he could use with the Sigil was so vast he found that when he tried hard to draw raw power the difficulty was actually in restraining and controlling the flow rather than creating it.

The trouble was the extropy it created. As he pushed Energematrice6 into the shields, it gathered rapidly, like negative energy flowing out of his hands into the tungsten cube. He couldn't control the stuff, but he could see it if he concentrated properly. It was like thick, foul whorls of darkness reaching out of him and sucking the life energy out of the world. There was no stopping it. It simply happened. After a moment, he realized his tungsten cube was almost gone. All that was left was a pile of dust in his lap and a few fragments, still clutched in his hands.

Andrew wasn't going to be happy, but...Nate pulled his hands out of his lap and slapped them against the bulkhead behind him. Then the enemy assault intensified and Nate lost the ability to concentrate on anything beyond the next wave of power colliding with the shields and ripping at them, then reacting with the previous barrage to create unpredictable explosions or even, once or twice, huge chunks of matter—was that ice? He reached out and shattered them, blasting them outward and away as the ship would have crashed into them, leaving pieces, some the size of small buildings, to rain down on the planet behind them.

He couldn't spare them a thought. All his attention was required just to meet the next onslaught.

An ugly certainty that he'd made the wrong decision had taken hold of Andrew. This was taking too long. The wave of power that crashed into them, sleeting off the shields and into the void, definitely came closer to overwhelming them than the last one. Nate had held out for almost thirty unbelievable minutes under conditions Andrew could never have imagined until he saw those incredible waves of energy...and they were only halfway through. The range was slowly opening up, but he'd taken them on the long route. It would be another thirty or forty minutes before they were far enough away that the last enemy could no longer effectively hit them.

Another wave of power sliced in and their shields were completely shattered for a gut-wrenching few seconds before Nate managed to restore them. The strain on Adamant's systems was showing too. Their shields were a simple system, but the secondary capacitors were at their thermal limit, and it was all Andrew could do to force himself to maintain his focus, knowing that now, when it mattered, he was blowing it. In panic, he almost reached out to Energematrice6 to lend his own strength to Nate, but he couldn't; whether from fear or simple prudence he couldn't tell. Andrew sat there for what felt like a very long time but could only have been seconds, his senses focused on the titanic struggle going on around him, feeling like a coward, then finally he forced himself to stop and adjust their course once again, jinking to keep their heading as unpredictable as possible.

"Help him!" Andrew cried, trying desperately to gain any advantage he could over the maelstrom of power lashing them from every direction.

Nate was so focused, the fact that he was getting tired crept up on him unaware. His mind losing its quickness and a flagging in its ability to direct his energies hit him suddenly. The bulkhead behind him was losing its integrity as well. It was a good thing it backed up onto an interior corridor instead of space itself, he thought. A wave of power came in and nearly crushed him, his mind having wandered for just a moment. He knew then that he was losing it, and he struggled to gather himself to meet the next onslaught. As if the enemy had sensed Nate's weakness, the pause before the next attack was longer, and the next volley of power that blasted out of the enemy armada was by far the strongest yet. It must have required the full armament of every enemy vessel in range to create such a barrage of interpenetrated power.

All he could do was contract his shield closer around Adamant and hold on. To his surprise, his strength was enough, just barely, to bear up against the tide...until it wasn't.

The brunt of the blow had torn his shield to shreds, and the tail of the attack streaked on to strike them unopposed.

Then, as the energy reached Adamant's hull, another presence joined Nate, and a new shield formed, tight to Adamant's skin. Admant's new defense was flimsy and thin compared to Nate's, amplified by the Sigil, even as tired as he was, but it was just barely enough to deflect the last remnant of the Enemy's wave. Almost instantly, that presence was joined by a second with a cry of fear so primal he actually felt it through the energy fields themselves.

Then, Nate felt another joining him, Rachel's presence buoying him up as her own shield took the brunt of the following attack. His relief was beyond words, but he still couldn't spare the time for more than a brief burst of gratitude.

Jon joined them next. A moment later, he felt Tye, then Keevan, then Shannon and Shawna at once, all adding their own efforts to his.

There was no communication as such, but they followed his lead as he formed a shell to protect the vessel from a wash of gray, then deflected a gout of red around them. It was as if the enemy realized their defenses were strengthening and the opportunity to kill Adamant had passed. Either that or they had overloaded their weapons, because the enemy's fire slackened noticeably following that tremendous barrage. After that, Nate and his friends fended it off almost casually, Nate having recovered himself enough to actually move his hands away from the holes he'd just made in the wall behind him and onto metal that was beginning to crumble but still relatively intact.

As the fight wore on, his friends slowly lost their own edges and he could tell the entropic shock was hurting them all, but none wavered. Even the two comparatively much smaller presences that had joined him first, the ones he knew must be Travis and the girl, were hanging on. They had passed the worst of it and slowly began to out-distance the enemy, accelerating exponentially away as they got clear of the planet, then the star's gravity well.

To his elation, Nate saw distantly that the enemy was following. He wasn't sure if they would, but their meteoric run through the enemy's gauntlet had been enough to pull them away from Solas.

As the last blasts of energy fell away behind them, Nate finally opened his physical eyes and called to Andrew, "Keep them on our tail. ...Straight for the Abyss."

Then the darkness claimed him.

Chapter 15

Nate awoke slowly and painfully. His head hurt, and he felt like he'd been run through a wringer. He could hardly think. At least there'd been no nightmares.

A fleeting sense of gratitude for tiny favors gave way to urgency. The nascent memory of what had happened pushed him from a reclining position onto his feet, but he found himself unable to move, fighting against restraints. He thrashed, then opened his eyes and forced himself to calm. There was dust all around him and his skin felt gritty. A wave of deja-vu hit him, pulling him back to his first waking moments in this universe, and he groaned as mixed reality and memory crashed down on him too hard to bear.

A voice—Andrew's voice—brought him to focus. "Welcome back."

Nate blinked, reaching up to brush at dust-caked eyes. "What..." He cleared his throat. "What's our status?"

Andrew laughed mirthlessly. "Well, they're definitely following us. You told me to head for the Abyss, so that's where we're going." He shrugged. "I had to reduce acceleration to half our max after we passed their stragglers just so we're not pulling too far ahead."

Nate nodded groggily and fumbled with his restraints. "How's everyone else? Did everybody make it through okay?"

Andrew didn't answer and Nate saw he was looking at the girl who had come with Travis, sitting several chairs over from Nate. Nate struggled to his feet and brushed more dust and metal flakes from his clothes. He glanced back at the wall behind his seat and stopped in shock. His extropy had left it a ruin, with great holes centered on the places where he'd put his hands and giant spiderweb cracks running in all directions. The surface had disintegrated and was flaking away. Bits of dust and slivers of metal fell even as he watched. Stepping forward, he realized he was walking through a layer of metal dust. The piles of shavings on the floor against the wall were ankle-high.

Ignoring the mess, Nate walked over to where the girl lay in her own acceleration chair, her breathing shallow. She seemed to be in bad shape. Her freckled face was too pale and her skin looked papery. Nate took a quick glance around the bridge. Several of the others lay reclining in their own couches, blinking at him and looking none too good themselves.

Nate reached down to lay a hand on the girl's head and probed gently with Energematrice6. She really was near death, and Nate thought back to the insanity of the battle they'd just barely survived thanks to her. "I don't even know her name. She had less to give than any of us, but she gave all of it—everything she had." He shook his head bitterly. "She shouldn't have to pay for my mistakes."

Beside her, Travis's eyes opened. He said, "Amy... She's a fighter. No half measures. If anybody can live through it, she can."

Nate nodded. "I can help with that, at least." He laid one hand on the already-damaged wall and another on Amy's forehead. Repeating what he'd done for Ralph on Solas was far from trivial with his head hurting and his focus so abysmally poor. As he prepared himself, a ghost of memory reached out grasping hands to pull him into the struggle he had felt when trying to accomplish simple tasks in that other world. No matter. However difficult it was, Nate owed it to her. As he reached into the fields and forced a complex weave of power into her body, Nate heard Travis gasp next to him. Amy's damage was actually less entrenched than Ralph's had been. Ralph had been drained again and again over the course of days and weeks, left near death every time, while Amy had used herself too hard only once. After less than a minute, Nate was done. The transformation was remarkable. Amy's face was flushed and healthy, her brown hair curling around her ears instead of hanging limp. He reached out to Travis next, raising his eyebrows in question. Travis hesitated, then nodded his permission.

As Nate finished healing Travis, Jon caught his eye. "Can I help?"

Nate eyed him up and down and barked a laugh. "Hah. You look almost as bad as he did." He motioned to Travis. "Here," Nate stepped over to Jon and repeated the same healing for him. It got a little easier every time he did it, as the pattern burned itself into his brain, and when he finished he looked up to see Jon watching him closely.

"If you think you can manage it..." Nate shrugged. Jon nodded and stood, stiff motions attesting to lingering pain.

He watched closely as Nate put his hands on Rachel's shoulders and did the same for her as he'd done for Jon himself. After that, Nate spent the next ten minutes walking around the bridge healing everyone else. After watching Nate's increasingly deft work on several of the others, Jon attempted the same with Keevan. He was still trying when Nate had completed his work on the others and as Nate came over to him he shook his head helplessly.

Nate laid a hand on his shoulder and smiled. "It's ok. I've got him." By the time Nate finished, he felt ready to collapse again. His head was swimming and it was all he could do to stay upright.

Nate flopped into an empty seat that wasn't covered in metal dust and flakes, then looked around again at his friends. They were all silent for a time, each recovering from the trauma of their desperate battle. As he sat resting, Nate felt the grim reality of the situation settle like a mountain on his shoulders. His friends were relying on him. He was supposed to be leading them against a universe in which even the rest of humanity hated them, simply because of what they were, and they didn't even know what he really was. He had been so slow and useless at the end. If he wasn't on the edge of being sucked into that "witless" other self, would he have come so close to getting them killed?

Only Amy's intervention had saved them, and Nate's insufficiency had almost cost her life. He wasn't sure if Rebus or the Adjutant had done something to him, but he thought he could feel his own clumsiness seeping through from that other version of himself to dull his mind. The trouble he faced now, even just finding a way to deal with this monstrous fleet of Changed, seemed impossible. The larger situation was simply too much for him to face.

Eventually Tye said, "So I think maybe... Just maybe they were trying to kill us."

Groans and chuckles circled the bridge and Shannon grinned at him. "Nah. Pretty sure it was just you."

Tye nodded mock-seriously. "I'm definitely the scariest." The groans were universal this time, and Tye asked more soberly, "So... What now?"

Nate stared at him, trying to think. His brain fog was slowly clearing, but 'slowly' was the operative term. Still, there was something at the back of his mind, something that had occurred to him in the thick of the fight that he hadn't been able to give attention to at the time. After the silence had dragged out for long enough that Tye looked ready to speak again, Nate turned to regard Andrew, Shannon, and Shawna.

Frowning as he thought his idea through, Nate asked, "How many of Them were following you three when you came through from the Milky Way?"

Shawna shivered in memory. "About a dozen. Only Resolute could get close, though."

Nate nodded acknowledgment, then asked Travis, "How about you? You said there are at least fifty of them out there?" He jerked his thumb toward the rear of the vessel.

Travis frowned in turn, thinking, but Amy cut in before he could answer. "Oh it wasn't fifty at first, and by the time they came up on us there were at least a hundred of them."

Nate raised his eyebrows questioningly. "So they waited for you?"

Amy was obviously thinking as she spoke, "They spent a long time herding us around before they actually tried to box us in. The only reason I can think of for them to do that would be to make sure there were enough of them...but that's silly. Even one of those monsters could have shot us to rags."

Nate said ironically, "Those differences in numbers are quite a coincidence."

"So... they knew?" Travis spoke slowly, still catching up with Nate's thoughts. "They knew we'd come here? How?"

Nate shook his head. "How they knew isn't as important as the fact that they did know." He looked to Keevan. "Keevan, the Keeper said the Abyss was dangerous. Why?"

Keevan grimaced, clenching his hands around his UPT. "That place has a lotta' really bad attention on it. I dunno who's watchin', but it's easy to feel, even if you don't go all the way ta' the center."

"It's the Watcher," Rachel said. "Jon and I spent a thousand years with that awful voidspawn's attention on us. It's in the whole Abyss, though we were pretty close to the edge. It may be stronger further in."

"It feels like... Like the shard of the black gem." Shawna's gaze still carried shame when she looked at Nate, but he just nodded. She was right. The feeling was very much the same.

"So," Nate said thoughtfully, "people keep coming through from the Milky Way in the Abyss, and there's a presence here that can actually be felt. Another coincidence?" He finished with an ironic twist to his lips.

Looking around the bridge, he saw that everyone had caught up and there wasn't a single face that didn't have an expression as grim as his.

"So what can we do about it?" Shannon's question was almost despairing.

Nate looked at her thoughtfully. "Do you feel normal?"

Shannon blinked. "No, of course not. We just fought..." She stopped abruptly and stared at him, obviously noticing something else.

"You feel it too, then? Like somebody staring at you out of the dark?" Nate turned to look at everyone else on the bridge. "And the rest of you?" They all nodded except Andrew, with Keevan even looking around nervously.

Nate turned back to Shannon. "We keep going, that's what we do. As to what's after that... You'll have to trust me for now."

Shannon nodded slowly, her face troubled, then again, sharply. "I do trust you." Several of the others hurried to agree.

Meanwhile, Andrew had been staring straight ahead, obviously not paying attention to the rest of their conversation. He blurted out, "I... was a coward."

"What?" Nate stared at him, dumbfounded. "You were flying the ship. What more could you have done?"

"I... I should have... Amy almost died." Andrew shook his head. "I could have done something!"

Nate snorted, echoed by several of the others around the bridge. "Andrew, you're not allowed to call yourself a coward. You have less to prove than any of us." Nate paused, then asked, "Nothing I can say will change your mind. Will it?"

Andrew shrugged uncomfortably and Nate sighed. "If it's any help, I promise you'll have plenty of opportunity to use E6 against Them. For now, I'm just glad you were there to fly the ship."

Rachel spoke up quietly, "None of us helped Nate soon enough. None of us even realized we could until you said so, Andrew. Even then, we were almost too late. If anything, you saved us. We should all have thought of it sooner."

Nate looked around at all of them. None met his gaze and he sighed, then said, "Look, we all need to give each other grace sometimes. Accepting grace for yourself matters just as much." He bit his lip as his own words struck him deeper than he expected. Nate sighed again and shook his head tiredly.

Andrew nodded. "Thanks."

Nate nodded in return. "For now, stay just far enough ahead that they haven't got a chance of hitting us even if they try. Keep heading for the center of the Abyss."

Over the next few days, the sensation of being watched intensified more and more as they streaked into the emptiness of the Abyss.

It might have been Nate's imagination, but as they proceeded he could have sworn there were fewer and fewer stars visible from the bridge. Then again, that might have just been an artifact of the mental and emotional strain. He couldn't have said where the feeling of oppression and darkness came from exactly, but after they entered the Abyss proper it became undeniable.

It was like having the great eye of some evil being fixed on them through a telescope. Though they saw nothing different around them, the sensation of being watched plagued them all, and there was no reprieve, even when they slept. The feelings of apprehension and stress got to be so strong that Jon began regularly asking the rest of the group if they wanted him to help put them to sleep using Energematrice6. Tye, Shawna, and even Shannon agreed to it. The others just soldiered on in silence, or in Jon and Rachel's cases, with something approaching the grim amusement of gallows humor.

As Rachel said to Nate on the second day, "We lived with the Watcher for so long when we were imprisoned, it hardly registers now." Her obvious discomfort made it clear that she was putting a bolder face on things than was justified, but they did cope better than any of the others.

Shawna still tended the plants growing in Adamant's primary corridor and Shannon still grimly went about her normal work checking the ship's mechanical systems, but no one visited the rec room or spent any time going through the ship's library. Entertainment and exercise were beyond all of them.

For Nate's part, when he was able to sleep at all, his dreams were even more disturbing than usual. Waking up was downright terrifying. The feeling of being watched by something utterly malevolent was excruciating when his mental defenses were down from sleep. The feeling that he, the weak link, had no business leading became almost inescapable after the third night of awaking from the same nightmare—staring helplessly at himself beating his head against a wall in pain and despair. Insufficiency and self-loathing impressed themselves into his consciousness so firmly, Nate could hardly function any longer. Grim determination was all that kept him moving.

It was three days after they crossed into the Abyss proper that Nate found Shawna crying uncontrollably in the passage outside the bridge. She was sitting against the wall, her arms wrapped around herself, shoulders hunched against the presence that haunted them.

When Nate bent over her, she looked up into his face. "I... I can't... It's always there..." Nate hugged her gently, racking his brain for anything he could do to help, feeling the weight of that unspeakable attention pressing down on him more terribly than ever.

Behind him, the hatch to the bridge opened and he heard Shannon's voice. "Sis...?" A moment later, Shannon was beside him, holding her sister in her arms.

Shannon looked up at him, her face grim. "I should have known. She's always been so sensitive..." She shook her head. "I don't know how to help her. I'm having a hard enough time of it myself."

Nate nodded, then said slowly, "I have a thought." He turned and entered the bridge, then moved to the acceleration chair he'd used during their wild escape. They'd done their best to clean up the mess he'd made of the bridge, sweeping the floors and washing the dust from the couches. Andrew had even gone so far as to try to clean the flaking surface of the wall, shooting Nate exasperated looks all the while. His efforts were to no avail. It took at most an hour or two for a fresh coat of dust to break loose and fall free to coat everything nearby.

Under the circumstances, Nate decided, there was no reason to cause damage to some other part of the ship, and who knew how much extropy this particular brainstorm would create? He sat down in the seat and set his hands against what remained of the wall behind him, then reached out once again and grasped Energematrice6. He couldn't exactly see the malevolent presence that haunted them, but he could feel it even more acutely with his senses attuned to the fields.

Again using instinct to guide him, he reached out to Resolute's shields and set to work. Other than restoring Ralph or the others from their entropic shock, this was the most detailed task he had ever attempted. In a sense, what he did now was even more difficult, because in the former case their bodies wanted to return to health, and that had helped to guide him. Here he had only his wits to work with, but once he had a pattern started he had a much easier time completing it. It was almost like some bizarre, cosmic version of knitting, he thought, looking over the weaves.

Almost an hour later, as he was finishing tying the weave together on the opposite side of the disruption field he'd created, he heard sharp intakes of breath all around the bridge. He completed his weave enough that all he had to do was hold it steady and opened his eyes, looking around. Everyone on the bridge was staring at him in disbelief, their relief almost palpable. Nate grinned at them, wanly, only then realizing how much the work had taken out of him.

After a minute or two there was a cry from the hatchway and Shawna was throwing her arms around him. Nate stopped in shock, then returned her hug gingerly.

After a moment, Shawna stepped back looking abashed, but she said, "Thank you. I just couldn't take it." She stopped to look at what Nate was doing with Energematrice6, then whistled softly. "How long can you keep that up?"

Nate shrugged. "Dunno. A while at least. Long enough for you all to have a breather." He looked around, noting that only Keevan and Amy were absent, and said, "So...we still can't talk freely, but we should at least try to go over what's next. Andrew, how far are we from the center of the Abyss?"

Andrew shrugged from his place at his console. "Roughly a day, but what exactly constitutes the center of this hole...? I really couldn't tell you."

Nate nodded thoughtfully. "What I have in mind won't take precision. We will have to cut the engines, though. How long can we coast before they catch us?"

Andrew looked thoughtful, then asked, "Can I pull ahead of them? Right now, you'd have maybe two or three minutes before they could range on us. I can open that up without too much trouble, though."

Nate nodded again. "Yeah. Give us an hour's leeway. I don't want to take chances. And along those lines..." He looked over at Travis. "Can you go find Amy? I have a question for you two."

It didn't take long for Travis to return to the bridge with Amy in tow, and Nate stared at them both for long enough that Travis actually started to fidget. Nate snorted. "You both joined us in defense of Adamant, even though it almost killed you." He gestured toward Amy.

"I have a question for you before we wind up in really serious trouble again," Nate said, the increasing effort of holding his disruption field in place making his voice hoarse. "Travis Retton and Amy Miles, will you follow me?"

Amy nodded without hesitation. "I will."

Travis took longer to consider, but he nodded as well. "You've had more success against those monsters in less than a week than I've ever seen from anyone else in my whole life. If you can really kill them..." He shook his head as if he couldn't truly believe it. "I'm in."

Nate raised an eyebrow. "Is that an 'if'? Or a 'yes'?"

Travis grinned. "Yeah. I'm with you."

Nate nodded back, then turned his head to look at Jon and Rachel. "Would you two see to the Schemic?" During the few minutes he'd been talking, Nate's disruption field had begun to warp. He could feel it slipping away from him, and he turned his attention from Travis and Amy to focus on the failing weaves, straining to bring his work back into alignment. Part of it was so distorted that he decided his best bet was to actually rebuild it. Whatever force was watching them had managed to actively twist his work into a near teardrop shape despite his use of Adamant's shield to anchor it in place. Nate vaguely sensed the use of Energematrice6 near him as Travis and Amy both accepted the Schemic. His mind was focused, though, as he fought to restore the field, feeling the gaze of whatever it was leaking through like water through a sieve anywhere the weave had warped.

By the time he'd finished, Nate had little doubt that if he wanted his construct to continue working he'd have to focus his whole attention on keeping it in place. Whatever was fighting him had figured out very quickly how to affect his hold on the fields, something he hadn't known was possible. Now, his work didn't stay in place without constant adjustment.

Nate turned his attention back to Travis and Amy, then fished in his pocket and pulled out the remaining amulets. He held them out, allowing Amy to pick first, taking the brown one, followed by Travis, who chose the turquoise.

As Amy took her pendant from him and it began to glow, her eyes widened. "So THAT's how you're doing it!" Immediately her eyes narrowed again and she looked outward. Nate could feel what almost seemed like gentle fingers probing his weaves, and he grunted.

"Andrew," Nate said, "If I'm asleep when we're an hour from what you think is the center of this hole, wake me up. I get the feeling this is going to take all my concentration." With that he turned his attention back to what had become a real battle to keep the weave steady. The sensation of someone touching his weaves continued. It was Amy. He knew it was. Then, she was pushing on his weaves where they were weak, trying to help hold them in place.

Nate's instincts took over again and he gave her access to his working. Next to him, Amy gasped.

Nate vaguely heard Travis murmur, "Impossible…"

Then Amy's furious efforts to help maintain his field redoubled. Giving her access had made changing his own construct harder than before, but only a little harder, and with two of them they were able to keep up with the interference. Then he felt Rachel next to him, her hand on his arm, and he shared control with her as well.

Over the next few hours, Nate was able to keep his field active with the help of his friends. They took turns coming in to help, ducking out when they started to get tired. Every single one of them took a turn. Controlling the construct took a huge amount of willpower, and left Nate progressively more and more exhausted. Once created, though, it required almost no new use of Energematrice6 to maintain. After what felt like days of constant effort but could only have been a few hours, Nate was so tired he had to try to sleep, so he passed control of his construct to Rachel. Sleep took him within seconds.

Nate awoke to Andrew shaking him gently. He felt groggy, but he still had no sensation of being watched, which meant…what?

Nate looked around the bridge to find Shawna, Jon, and Keevan all in couches with their eyes closed, concentrating. Nate raised an eyebrow at Andrew. "Still at it?"

Andrew grimaced. "We're all tired from keeping the field up, but it's better than…before. I wish we had Laura here. A psi talent would be particularly good for this."

Nate nodded and opened his senses to Energematrice6, noting the disruption field was still in place. He tracked across it, looking for signs of strain. They were there, but the field corrected as quickly as it warped.

Shannon turned from her own console to give him a grim but self-satisfied smile. "It got really bad for a while, but I guess whoever it is decided he couldn't break it. Since then, it's been easier. It's more like he's just poking at us now."

Nate smiled back. "Good work. This is better than I'd hoped." He turned to Andrew, who was still standing beside him. "How close are we? Did I sleep long?"

Andrew shook his head sourly. "We're close enough. It's like I said, this thing doesn't have a center. It's just a bigger empty spot than the space around it. Now or an hour from now is about the same, really."

Nate nodded slowly, thinking. "No time like the present, then. We'll have to shut down the Retton drive and coast, but I need to get to the airlock first."

Andrew looked at him with narrowed eyes. "Can you tell us now? What are you planning?"

Nate twisted his lips sourly. "Better not. I'll comm you intra-ship when I'm ready." He paused, then shrugged. "If you've guessed, that's fine, but I'm not giving that...thing...out there any clues if it can see through the field."

With that, Nate rose from his seat and headed for his cabin. Once there, he unstrapped the Globe of the Vale from its place in his acceleration couch and started for the airlock. Nate had been making too many assumptions for his own peace of mind during their trip into the Abyss.

First, he'd assumed the presence watching them was somehow commanding the ships in pursuit. He had no way of knowing who or what was watching them. It could have been Lastis Ralond himself from the Milky Way or one of the Shades from within the Twilight, or even some unknown third party.

Second, he'd assumed whatever it was wouldn't know what the Globe of the Vale was—or if they could see it was an artifact, they at least wouldn't know what it was for. If Paul had used the Great Schemic in his construction of the Globe, that was a fairly safe bet, but it wasn't a certainty, even now.

Finally, he'd assumed he drew the right conclusions from his all-too-brief examination of the Globe when he originally shut it off. He needed to be able to activate it again without trouble, unleashing a Vale that was far larger than it had been before.

Taken together, that was far too many gambles for his liking. Something was sure to go wrong. He could even feel something tickling the back of his consciousness, something he'd missed. It didn't matter. It was the best idea he could come up with. Anything else that had occurred to him was an even bigger gamble. The only other idea he'd briefly considered trying was to outright destroy the enemy by himself. He might have the power for it, but controlling that much Energematrice6 at once would almost certainly consume him or burn him out or something equally horrible. He'd had no chance to experiment with such forces, and now was definitely not the time.

When he reached the airlock, Nate tried to open it. Whoever had built Adamant had apparently thought entering the airlock while under Retton drive was a bad idea. All told, he had to override four different warnings, but within a minute it was open and he stepped inside. Then he pushed the call button on the intercom set inside the lock and said, "Andrew, I'm ready. Go ahead and shut off the drive."

"Roger," Andrew said a moment later.

Weightlessness wasn't quite instant, but it came quickly enough. Clutching the Globe in one arm, Nate grasped Energematrice6 and drew a bubble of air around himself, then cycled the airlock.

It took some time, holding the air bubble and concentrating on the Globe, to find and fumble open the channels he'd seen closed, hopefully increasing the size of the Vale when it activated. It took far too long for him to figure out how to nudge the first one just right to change its state. Once he'd figured it out, though, the rest came much more quickly. With every channel open, Nate held the Globe out in front of him and tried to activate it.

There was a momentary flicker inside, then nothing. Nate got the distinct impression of floating free, unsecured. It was enough to give him vertigo. Strange. Being in microgravity had never done that to him before. He shook his head, which actually did start him floating slightly so he had to grab the globe to his chest and reach out to steady himself with a handhold.

When he was sure his spin was under control, he reached out again with Energematrice6 and tried again to turn the Globe on. This time, the impression of floating free was so strong the vertigo made him retch. That answered that question. His subconscious had been telling him the Globe needed an anchor. That had been the itch at the back of his mind, but hindsight wasn't going to help him with the enemy less than an hour behind. If he'd known sooner he might have done something different, but wishing wasn't going to help him either.

The question was, now what?

Chapter 16

Still holding his air bubble and clutching the globe with one arm, Nate awkwardly twisted himself back into the airlock, making sure his air bubble covered the comm, and smacked the activation key. "Andrew, I have to anchor to something. Is there a gravity well that's detectable out here? Anything at all?"

The answer was a long time coming.

When Andrew spoke his voice was hesitant. "Nate... The only thing that's strong enough to register here is the galaxy's center of gravity."

Nate barked a laugh, then keyed the comm again. "What's our comparative motion? I need to get stationary relative to it."

The pause this time was even longer, and Nate's gut felt the bad news coming even before Andrew spoke. "It'd take about fifteen minutes at max Retton drive to do that, but Nate... That puts us right in the middle of them."

It was what Nate had feared and suspected deep down was coming, but hadn't wanted to acknowledge with his conscious mind. They would have to go back through the enemy armada, whether they liked it or not. That meant he would have to rely on

213

his friends to hold the enemy off. It put them in terrible danger, both from the enemy themselves and from entropic shock. It left him afraid for them. Somehow, knowing what the enemy was capable of and deciding to turn back into their teeth was even worse than choosing to face them the first time, especially since he was needed to activate the Globe. The situation was not one he would have chosen, but he couldn't see a better option.

Nate hit the comm again, but didn't speak immediately. His sigh must have come through though because Andrew asked, "I'm guessing there's not much choice? This is probably suicide. You realize that?"

"Put me on speaker, Andrew."

A moment later, Andrew came back, "Okay, you're on." Nate was silent, trying to put something into words that he barely understood himself.

Eventually, he sighed. "Andrew just said this is probably suicide. He may be right, guys. I'd say I'm sorry, but this had to be done. We were the only ones who could do it. I need you to hold the shield like we did when we ran the gauntlet the first time. Whatever it costs, hold it."

Rachel's voice cut through the comm. "Nate, we can't hold this disruption field and the shield at the same time. How important is the field?"

Nate nodded, even though they couldn't see it. "I can hold the disruption field until it's time to let it go. You guys have to handle the shield, though. I've got nothing to sink extropy into out here."

Nate paused again, searching for words, but he couldn't find any. Finally, he said, "Thank you all."

Nate's attention turned to what was about to happen and after another moment he asked, "Uhh, Andrew, is it going to be a problem if I have the airlock open for all this?"

Andrew's laugh, complete with some measure of actual humor, came back to him. Andrew half-grumbled, "Why not? Going to be some serious field fluctuations when I start the drive though. Be ready."

"Roger." Nate's voice was as steady as he could make it. Nate tried to prepare himself, but almost instantly the Retton drive's rainbow flared to life around him. There was no sensation, no indication anything had even changed other than his Energematrice6 sense being nearly swamped by the tide rolling across the airlock. Slowly, gravity came back and Nate reached out to the disruption field, taking control of it back from his friends and turning his attention to keeping it from distorting.

Whatever else their stop and now reversal had done, it certainly put the force trying to interfere with the field back into high gear. It was all Nate could do to keep the thing anchored and in approximately the right shape. Through the rainbow blur of the Retton drive, Nate could see his friends preparing the ship's shield to take fire from the enemy, feeding as much of their strength into it as they could.

It didn't take long after that for the enemy's fire to start streaking in on them, in dribs and drabs at first, then in a continuous wave that was, if anything, even fiercer than what they faced before.

Then, it was all Nate could do to keep the distortion field in place alongside the shield his friends were somehow holding fast. Over and over, stronger and stronger, the Watcher's will beat at his shield. Over and over, he restored it to its proper shape. It was amazing how fast the effort sapped his mental energy, and he could only imagine his friends holding their own against the titanic wash of power constantly sleeting in on them. Once or twice, Nate caught glimpses of ice or other physical substances being snapped apart by waves of force that must have been Rachel's, and once actual plasma streaked out to envelop something Nate hadn't seen clearly, consuming it completely.

Again, as the enemy armada closed, Nate felt the same creeping dread he'd felt before when he faced the Changed. It was still relatively faint, but whatever it was seemed to emanate directly from the twisted horrors aboard those huge vessels. Nate could only hope his friends would be able to hold their concentration with that extra interference.

What played the biggest part in saving them was a stealth ability that must have come from Keevan... or was it Tye? Whoever was responsible, the enemy's sensors were obviously confused, and fully half their attacks missed Adamant outright, costing them nothing.

It felt like an eternity that they fought their separate battles, him keeping the Watcher's influence off them, his friends somehow deflecting, dodging or absorbing the unimaginable waves of Energematrice6 slamming into them. Somehow, they were holding on, though he shuddered to think what it must be costing them.

With sudden finality, gravity disappeared and Nate's attention snapped to the Globe. He checked, as quickly as he could, that all the channels were still open. Then, holding it out in front of him, he tried once more to trigger its activation. This time, the sensation he got was one of searching.

Just as suddenly, Nate's disruption field failed completely and the full weight of the Watcher's attention crashed down on him.

There was no comparison to what he had experienced before he created the disruption field. This wasn't a sensation of eyes from the dark drilling through the back of his head. This was the undiluted attention of accusation incarnate, scouring his soul and laying his secrets bare. Whatever this creature was, it made any human enemy seem laughable. The reality of its presence made Keevan's speculations about whether Loriden might be behind their many woes laughable. Drake Loriden was like a gnat compared to the whirlwind of this creature's attention.

"*I *Know* What You Are.*"

The invasion of his consciousness was more than speech. It was as if a mockery of his own thoughts had been amplified and fed back to him at a mental volume that left no room for anything else, and this time Nate's other reality didn't rise to haunt him. It didn't leave him with a feeling of duality, fighting to separate his two selves. It simply pulled him under. All that was left was the broken, pitiful thing he had always been.

Nate shuddered, eyes squeezing shut as the reality of his own wretchedness came home to him fully. He was the boy from his own dreams, helpless and in pain, beating his head against the wall to distract himself from his defectiveness. A flood of helpless tears poured from his eyes to drift around his face in the microgravity.

He had forgotten the Watcher, his focus completely absorbed in himself, when the litany of his failures washed over him. One after another, he saw every way in which he had fallen short since he came to this reality. The Ochroleucum was an empty husk in his tortured imagination, the ghosts of its students crying out for mercy from a pitiless Dominion. Without a pause, Loriden smirked at him, hand held out in an offer of alliance that Nate had refused. Then he was paralyzed as the crowd carried him bodily through Lighthouse Station, Elder Rebus's sneer just visible over their heads. Adjutant Seledris's laugh boomed out across the conclave, mocking him. Beyond it all, he could see Lissa and Laura and Jesse, the three he'd left behind, watching him with judgmental eyes.

Vaguely, beyond himself, he could still feel the enemy lashing them with unimaginable torrents of energy, his friends barely holding on, and he was crippled, unable even to move. The paralysis that gripped him was the same one that defined him in that other world, now so far away, and rendered him worthless. The darkness that reached out and smothered Nate might have lasted an instant or a lifetime. Time lost its meaning for him, much as it had during his entry into this world, and the agony stretched and stretched until he couldn't bear it.

The Globe of the Vale's activation was as abrupt as the Watcher's intrusion had been. It flared to life and Nate went instantly blind, darkness engulfing him. The suddenness of it pulled him out of his paralysis, and he thrashed wildly. It took a frantic moment for him to realize he was seeing the inside of a dust cloud that was even thicker than the one he'd jumped into on the bridge of Hope One.

Then Nate was moving. Somehow, miraculously, his bubble of air was still in place around him. He had never lost his grip on the fields despite the mental onslaught that still had him disoriented. Every second was critical now. There was no time to recover.

He smacked the airlock's cycle button from memory and grabbed for a handhold, leaving the Globe to float in space outside Adamant's airlock. As the airlock cycled, Nate fumbled for the com switch and yelled, "Go! GO!"—his voice sounding clumsy, almost drunk.

Whether from the Vale's activation or something else, the Watcher's assault had completely disappeared, and Nate was as capable as he'd ever been.

Then, he was through the airlock and inside the bridge passage, looking frantically outward through his Energematrice6 sense. He was barely in time. Adamant's shield was finally failing. He stopped in the passage and smacked both palms against the wall, bracing his feet, then reached out through the Sigil of the Mysteries and flooded as much power as he could safely control into his friends' shield.

The problem they faced was completely different from his own. Nate could access almost unlimited power. He had to be careful because any use of Energematrice6 on his part pushed entropic anti-energy—extropy as Andrew had called it—out of him into his surroundings, but that wasn't really what limited him. Provided he was willing to destroy whatever he was touching, his limit was the willpower and attention he could devote to his task.

His friends had far more attention than he did. There were nine of them and only one of him, but their ability to draw power was strictly limited to the entropy they could absorb before it burned them out or killed them outright.

Nate's tsunami of energy reinforced Adamant's shield instantly and he felt his friends retreating in exhaustion and pain. He hadn't felt nine of them. He'd only sensed five.

That realization was enough to unbalance Nate again, as an echo of the Watcher's presence reverberated in his head.

Only five. He'd been too late. Nate's guts twisted and he howled aloud, momentarily losing control of the flow of energy he had been directing into the shields.

The results were unlike anything he'd imagined possible. Where before Adamant had been a globe of condensed light, its shield flickering in his senses, he was now surrounded by the noonday sun. The entirety of Nate's current access to Energematrice6, a flow of a magnitude that dwarfed anything he could actually control, blasted outward like a supernova.

There was no time to understand it. One moment the enemy ships were all there. The next, half of them were hemorrhaging wrecks, barely shielding their brethren from the same fate. Then, the Vale expanded and covered everything in its muddy darkness.

Internally, Nate was struggling to regain control of the power he had unleashed. The flow ravaged through him, still somehow following his mental pathway into the ship's shields before roaring out across space in all directions in an unstoppable torrent. The Rechemacula on his neck and shoulder was white-hot fire, but he barely felt it. Under Nate's hands the wall simply disintegrated and he fell bodily into it, hitting the other side of the hollow space, then losing contact with any solid surface as that disintegrated as well.

In panic, Nate felt the extropy starting to build up inside him, creating an inevitable backlash. There was simply too much of it. Still howling, he clamped down with all his might on the terrible fountain of power he had become. The universe went dark.

Conclusion:
Streaks of Light

Interval

Again, he fought through the slough of his own consciousness, desperately trying to escape the morass. Again, with sustained effort, he managed to fight free.

This dream was different from the others. It HURT. The pain was all around him, drilling into his skull, swamping all other sensation except the cold... It was so cold. It was the same darkness he found himself in any other time he slept, but this time was different.

When he saw the boy against the wall there was none of the normal confusion or familiarity. Instead he simply knew. It was himself. It had always been him. He had always been this. There was nothing but this, inside him where the pain lived. He was the little boy, cowering by the wall, unable to face the world, unable to function, wretched and broken, driven so hard by the clamor and judgment constantly leveled at him that he was left with no recourse other than to hurt himself to drown it out.

No one could see him now, but the shame still burned. No one could hear, but he could hear himself, feel himself crying out for help. What help was there for one such as him, who could not help himself? His cry echoed out into the terrible nothingness that was himself... And there was an answer.

He didn't open his eyes, but he could see. Or he thought he could see. There was light, shining from everything and nothing. He knew who he was, could remember what had happened—everything that had happened—the book, the room, Adrienne and his aching head. He remembered coming to Aurora, meeting each of his friends, one by one. He relived it all, felt the emotions, experienced the friendships so rapidly that when he was done he felt as if he were spinning. Then came his final failure. Even in Aurora, where he wasn't a helpless child, he had failed the friends who followed him.

Was this what it was like to die?

He stood on a sheet of sheer crystal, so bedazzled by the light that came from all around now that he couldn't see anything beyond that floor beneath him. There was no world, only the light and the crystal beneath his feet and the perfect awareness of the wretchedness that was himself. The grinding weight of his failures and his unbearable weakness... his worthlessness.

Then, the light, or whatever unfathomable majesty must be the source of such a light, spoke.

"I made you."

He didn't answer, couldn't answer, but seeing his broken life, he could feel, and what he felt was bewilderment and rejection. He was twelve years old and he couldn't tie his shoe, or use the toilet properly. He couldn't feed himself or even talk...not really. Even in Aurora, where he was whole, he failed. The Watcher was right. Its accusations struck him to the core. What reason could there be for such as him?

The speaker must have known his incredulity, because he spoke again, his voice so deep it would have shaken the world to pieces, if there had been a world to shake. "Seek nothing from a liar but lies. I MADE you. Your value is mine to set."

Confusion and anguish filled him, but there was a quality to this voice that he couldn't disbelieve. It was certainty and authority incarnate. Still, he knew that accepting this reality was his choice. He could just as easily turn away and return to all he'd ever known.

Nate remembered Lissa, then. When he offered her the amulet she hadn't believed he would make such an offer. The same hunger he'd seen in her eyes filled him now, to overflowing. But what was Aurora? Was it a dream? What of his failure?

"Failure is how you LEARN. I set your light before the worlds. I know your purpose." The voice was not hostile, but there was a terrible weight to it, pressing into him with its certainty.

The darkness that gripped him began to loosen as he accepted what he heard. That quickly, he saw the lies that had clung to him for what they were. They had been impressed upon him from the outside, ingrained in him with each lash he had taken upon his soul, from a time before he even had memory. Accepting those lies—making them the core of his identity—had cost him so much...

There was no question in his mind as to whether he was dreaming now. This voice was real. Its authority was unquestionable. This place was real... Aurora? His friends? His failures? Were they real? What about home? Dad? Adrienne? Were they real? Was HE real?

The voice was gentler this time. "Even this is but a shadow of what you will see, one day."

Doubt was beyond him in that moment. Lightmaker... What now?

"Now?" The voice carried a smile. "Now, wake up, and save them."

Epilogue

Nate did wake up, driven by the knowledge that his friends might—must—be dying. He dragged himself out of a crater in the floor and stumbled onto the bridge, then checked each of them in turn. Somehow, they were all alive. Jon and Shawna were even still conscious. Jon was kneeling next to Amy, who had driven herself to the ragged edge of death yet again. Jon was struggling to heal her despite being half dead himself, obviously unable to focus, tears running down his face in desperation. Nate gently nudged Jon aside and dug deep in himself to find the reserves he needed. Then he healed both Amy and Jon in turn, restoring their bodies and leaving them with nothing more than simple fatigue. After Nate had finished with him, Jon slumped next to Amy, watching helplessly as Nate proceeded to heal the others.

Andrew and Rachel had pushed themselves almost as hard—hard enough that at first, Nate thought Andrew really was dead. Like Ralph, Nate found damage in Andrew's cells that was too old to heal, obviously from his first bout of entropic shock. The vast majority, however, was current, and Andrew's body still recognized what it meant to be whole. As he finished healing him, Nate poked Andrew, who was stirring a bit, and grumbled, "I don't want to hear anything more about you being a coward. You got it?" Andrew grinned sheepishly and nodded, then fell instantly asleep.

Shawna was the only one other than Jon who was awake enough to be coherent. She looked exhausted and ready to cry, but she was still at her console, peering blearily into the dust ahead of them.

When Nate finally reached her, Shawna gave him a brief, grateful look. Taking his hands away, Nate smiled at her and said, "Thank you, Shawna." She returned his smile with a weary one of her own but she was as focused on her task as he was on his. Somehow, he managed to restore each of the others, one by one. Tye was the last, and when he had finished, Nate collapsed against the wall, his hand still resting on Tye's shoulder. Sleep took him while he stood there, leaning against the wall, and he slumped to the floor and once more into darkness.

It took a full month to escape the Abyss, newly covered by the Vale of Mysteries. The Vale was even thicker than it had been before, and they had to reduce their speed even further than when they first visited Sanctuary to compensate. Andrew, Shannon and Shawna collectively decided that two seconds was their minimum safety margin if they were to approach anything with significant gravity, and that meant reducing their speed to a tiny fraction of the power they had available.

From the beginning, Keevan questioned whether they'd ever make it out, to the point where he finally drove Shannon to pull her amulet off her neck and hang it from her hand. It "fell" toward the ceiling, as did all the others when tested, confirming that they still had a means to find the center of the Vale, even now. Shannon re-created her navigation system, using a point on the back wall as a target—what was left of it after Nate had crashed through from the passage beyond when he turned himself into a human power conduit.

The navigation aid was necessary. Gravity twisted and warped so strongly that Nate was certain without it they never would have escaped from the dust at all.

The horrible presence that had watched them as they entered the Abyss was barely noticeable with the Vale in place, and after the first three days it faded away entirely, whether because it was searching blindly for them in the murk or simply losing interest, they had no way to tell. Unsurprisingly, they never encountered another one of the Enemy's vessels either. Space was vast, and when you couldn't see your hand in front of your proverbial face... Suffice to say, none of them were sorry to miss out on such an encounter. As far as any of the friends were concerned, any Changed Nate hadn't barbequed when he lost control of his power could wander the newly-restored Vale forever or fall into a gravity well, and they wouldn't shed a tear.

Two hours before they actually broke out, Shawna excitedly told them via ship-wide comm that particle density was down to half what it had been for the last few weeks. They all gathered then, watching as the dust ahead gradually thinned from a muddy, impenetrable soup to a point where they could vaguely see the bright spots that marked the stars beyond its edge.

Tye grinned at Nate as the stars grew brighter. "So, what we gonna do first when we get out?"

Nate's mouth quirked and he said, "We're going to go get Laura and Jesse... and Lissa. You know that."

"Yeah. I know." Tye's grin was completely unapologetic. "I'm just glad to be out of here." His grin widened and he gave Nate a mischievous look. "And, I'm looking forward to seeing Nate blast some Changed."

Rachel frowned. "You know, before we left Earth there weren't many Changed. We only ever saw one or two. That was terrifying enough. How can there be so many now?" She shook her head, then after a moment, as if to preserve the lighthearted mood, flashed a grin of her own at Tye. "I can't wait to be back on a planet again either, even if we do have Changed to worry about."

"Same," Keevan said, with a twirl of his UPT. "I'm just glad we didn't meet any 'a those void eating ships in the middle of this soup. Though after what Nate did, it'd be a miracle if any of em survived." He shot a glare Nate's way. "You could'a done that before, ya know? Maybe saved us all some pain?"

Nate snorted. "You wanted me to turn us into the biggest light bulb in the history of the universe on purpose?"

Keevan's eyebrows climbed his forehead. "Hey, it worked, didn' it?"

Amy smirked from her place by the hatch, her fingers twisting around the cylindrical stack of disks they'd found on Hope One, her eyes probing for its secrets.

Shawna must have increased their speed then, because they burst from the Vale all at once, finally, into the vast black expanse of the space beyond. There was a collective intake of breath across the bridge as the heavens opened and they were free once more.

It was Travis who let out the first imprecation, but Andrew was right behind him.

Nate looked questioningly at them, his eyebrows raised, and Travis merely pointed mutely to a spot almost beyond the edge of Adamant's main window, where a dozen streaks of light like shooting stars blasted away from the Vale into the free space of the Aurora galaxy.

Character Roster

Alastor Railin [Al-as-tohr Rey-lin]: Nate's father.

History - From our world.

Alden Rebus [Al-den Ree-bus]: (Title—Elder) A council member at Lighthouse Station, Sanctuary system.

History - System of birth, unknown. Aurora galaxy, alternate universe.

Alina Starsown [A-lee-nuh Stahr-zown]: A resident of Lighthouse Station, Sanctuary system.

History - From Lighthouse Station, Sanctuary, Aurora galaxy, alternate universe.

Amy Miles [Ey-mee Maylz]: One of Nate's companions, holder of the brown Amulet. Thought to be an Odd.

History - From the Milky Way galaxy, alternate universe. Daughter of Kevin Miles.

Energematrice6 Specialization - Geotic;

Talent - Mechanical Manipulation.

Anastasia 'Tasia' Amadea [Ah-nuh-stey-shuh 'Tey-shuh' Ah-muh-dey-uh]: Girl who befriends Nate on the planet Bounty.

History - From Bounty, Aurora galaxy, alternate universe.

Andrew Logan [An-droo Loh-guhn]: One of Nate's companions, holder of the yellow Amulet. Thought to be an Odd.

History - From the Milky Way galaxy, alternate universe. Son of Jim Logan. Co-owner of Adamant.

Energematrice6 Specialization - Nephelic;
Talent - Unknown.

Argos, Merich [Mer-ik Ahr-gos]: (Title—Professor) Telestic and educator at the Ochroleucum.

History - From Panoptica, Aurora galaxy, alternate universe. Political exile from the Dominion.

Adrienne Anders [Ey-dree-en An-derz]: Nate's caretaker. Has a history of thoughtlessness and even cruelty.

History - From our world.

Arsondus, Tetsin [Ar-sohn-duhs Tet-sihn]: (Rank—Telestic) Telestry official on the planet Solas.

History - System of birth, unknown. Aurora galaxy, alternate universe.

Bettina Strong [Bet-teen-uh Strawng]: (Title—Elder) A council member at Lighthouse Station, Sanctuary system.

History - From the planet of Sanctuary, Aurora galaxy, alternate universe.

Bradford, Cassian [Cas-see-an Brad-ferd]: (Rank—Constable) Telestry official on the planet Solas.

History - From the planet of Solas, Aurora galaxy, alternate universe. Known ties to the Brotherhood.

Brightstar [Bryht-stahr]: (First Name—Nate) An autistic boy who has been transported to a different (presumably future) universe.

History - From our world.

Energematrice6 Specialization - Unknown;

Talent - Unknown.

Bundy Stedrix [Buhn-dee Sted-riks]: A student at the Telestry's Ochroleucum.

History - Unknown.

Energematrice6 Specialization - Pyric;

Talent - Thermal Form.

Douma Asher [Doo-mah Ash-er]: A student at the Telestry's Ochroleucum.

History - From Aterria, Aurora galaxy, alternate universe. Born to a family that has ties to the Brotherhood.

Energematrice6 Specialization - Nephilic;

Talent - Stealth.

Drake Loriden [Dreyk Loh-rhy-den]: (Rank—Telestic) Telestry operative whose vessel, Ocharist, found Nate. Known to be an Odd.

History - From Aurora galaxy, alternate universe. Known to have been a Telestic for at least 100 years NST (300 Earth Years). Known to be involved in the Telestry's capitulation to the Dominion.

Energematrice6 Specialization - Nephilic;

Talent - Unknown.

Duramen, Pontifus [Pohn-ty-fus Doo-rah-mehn]: (Rank—Telestic) Founder of the Telestry proper. A feared warrior who presided over the beginning of the Telestry's golden age, before the secession of Sanctuary and activation of the Vale of Mysteries.

History - From Aterria, Aurora galaxy, alternate universe. Disciple of Paul Casisia. Last chief councilor of the Society of Telestics.

Energematrice6 Specialization - Ionic;

Talent - Unknown.

Carl Winton [Kahrl Win-tyn]: Partner to, then enemy of
Lastis Ralond during the Betrayal and the Escape.
Founder of Bright Future.

History - From Earth, the Milky Way galaxy, alternate
universe.

Eldruin, Tedros [El-droo-en Ted-rohs]: (Rank—Captain)
The captain of Ocharist, a Telestry vessel.

History - From Aterria, Aurora galaxy, alternate universe.
Generational Telestic servicemember.

Elesinth Castigan [El-e-synth Kas-ty-guhn]: A student at
the Telestry's Ochroleucum.

History - From Aterria, Aurora galaxy, alternate universe.

Hannah Amadea [Han-uh Ah-muh-dey-uh]: The mother
of a girl who befriends Nate on the planet Bounty.

History - From Solas, Aurora galaxy, alternate universe.

Ilvin Shanes [Yl-vyn Shaynz]: A resident of Lighthouse
Station, Sanctuary system.

History - From Lighthouse Station, Sanctuary, Aurora
galaxy, alternate universe.

Jack Amadea [Jak Ah-muh-dey-uh]: The father of a girl
who befriends Nate on the planet Bounty.

History - From Bounty, Aurora galaxy, alternate universe.

Jesse Galton [Jes-ee Gawl-tun]: One of Nate's companions,
holder of the dark red Amulet. Known to be an Odd.

History - From Sanctuary, Aurora galaxy, alternate
universe. Son of Teron Galton, the "Keeper of the
Mysteries," and Kass Lera.

Energematrice6 Specialization - Pyric;

Talent - Heat, Fire, Plasma.

Jim Logan [Jim Loh-guhn]: Paul Casisia's best friend during the Betrayal and the Escape. Father to Andrew, Shannon and Shawna Logan.

History - From Earth, the Milky Way galaxy, alternate universe.

Energematrice6 Specialization - Geotic;

Talent - Unknown.

Jon Casisia [Jon Kas-is-ee-uh]: One of Nate's companions, holder of the green Amulet. Known to be an Odd.

History - From the Milky Way galaxy, alternate universe. Paul Casisia's son.

Energematrice6 Specialization - Anima;

Talent - Healing.

Keeper of the Mysteries: See Teron Galton

Keevan Raddink [Kee-vuhn Ra-dink]: One of Nate's companions, holder of the gray Amulet. Known to be an Odd.

History - From Lighthouse Station, Sanctuary, Aurora galaxy, alternate universe. Grandson of Siever Radding, "The Wild Man." Exiled from Lighthouse Station for sabotage.

Energematrice6 Specialization - Nephelic;

Talent Stealth.

Kelland, Stavros [Ke-lund Stav-rohs]: (Title—Professor) Telestic and educator at the Ochroleucum.

History - From Reticula, Aurora galaxy, alternate universe.

Larifer Malleus [La-ri-fur Ma-lee-us]: (Title—First Councilor of the Telestry) "The Lightmaker's Hammer." Re-founded and restored the Telestry after the assault of the Regalians.

History - From Sanctuary, Aurora galaxy, alternate universe.

Lastis Ralond [Las-tis Ra-lund]: Architect of the Betrayal. Mastermind of the events that led to Energematrice6 being used by humanity and originator of the destruction that introduced Entropy into the use of all Energematrice6.

History - Unknown

Energematrice6 Specialization - Nephelic;

Talent - Command.

Lana Trent [Lay-nuh Trent]: Close associate of Lastis Ralond, destroyer of Paul Casisia's fleet during the Escape.

History - Unknown

Energematrice6 Specialization - Pyric;

Talent - Heat, Fire, Plasma.

Laura Gilvers [Lah-rah Gil-vurs]: One of Nate's companions, holder of the dark blue Amulet. Thought to be an Odd.

History - From the Milky Way galaxy, alternate universe. "Abandoned" and traumatized after her family was killed on the vessel Resolute. Daughter of Hal Gilvers, the "Hero of Bright Future."

Energematrice6 Specialization - Aqueous;

Talent - Psionics.

Lissa Grona [Lis-uh Grown-uh]: One of Nate's companions. Apparent heir to the purple Amulet. Known to be an Odd. Fiercely loyal to her friends.

History - From Solas, Aurora galaxy, alternate universe. Grew up on the streets of Solasborough.

Energematrice6 Specialization - Geotic;

Talent - Unknown.

Lourde, Alfons [Al-fawn-z Loord]: (Title—Professor) Telestic and educator at the Ochroleucum. Generational aristocracy of Aterria.

History - From Aterria, Aurora galaxy, alternate universe. Ancestors served as aides and confidants to both Duramen and Malleus.

Malleus, Larifer: See Larifer Malleus

Melindra Malleus: See Proctor, The

Nate: See Brightstar

Neil Eden [Neel Ee-dun]: (Title—Elder) A council member at Lighthouse Station, Sanctuary system.

History - From Lighthouse Station, Sanctuary, Aurora galaxy, alternate universe. Great grandson of Siever Radding, "The Wild Man."

Orrigen 'Orrie' Transital [Or-i-jen 'Or-ree' Tran-zi-tahl]: (Rank—Constable) Telestry official on the planet Solas.

History - From the planet of Solas, Aurora galaxy, alternate universe. Known ties to the Brotherhood.

Paul Casisia [Pawl Kas-is-ee-uh]: Architect of the Escape from Earth. During the Betrayal, partner to Carl Winton. In Aurora Galaxy, founder of the Society of Telestics, creator of the Mysteries. Chief adversary of the forces of darkness in Aurora Galaxy. Father of Jon and Rachel Casisia.

History - From Earth, the Milky Way galaxy, alternate universe.

Energematrice6 Specialization - Ionic;

Talent - Unknown.

Proctor, The: See Melindra Malleus

Raskowick, Raul [Ra-ool Ras-ko-wick]: (Rank—Captain) The captain of Chandri, a merchant vessel in the service of the Regency.

History - From New America, Aurora galaxy, alternate universe.

Rachel Casisia [Ray-chel Kas-is-ee-uh]: One of Nate's companions, holder of the blue Amulet. Known to be an Odd.

History - From the Milky Way galaxy, alternate universe. Paul Casisia's son.

Energematrice6 Specialization - Aqueous; Telekinesis, force projection.

Railin, Alastor: See Alastor Railin.

Ralph Trebeska [Ralf Tre-bes-ka]: Friend to Lissa Grona. Incarcerated for stealing food.

History - From Solas, Aurora galaxy, alternate universe. Grew up on the streets.

Rectis, Genghis [Jeng-gis Rek-dis]: (Rank—Stratograve) Dominion enforcer and investigator.

History - From Regalia, Aurora galaxy, alternate universe.

Regen Sorell [Ree-jen Saw-rehl]: (Title—Elder) A council member at Lighthouse Station, Sanctuary system.

History - From Lighthouse Station, Sanctuary, Aurora galaxy, alternate universe.

Reggie Oglive [Rej-ee O-glyve]: Citizen of Bounty whose party followed Nate to Solas.

History - From Bounty City, Bounty, Aurora galaxy, alternate universe.

Rex Gilvers [Reks Gil-vurs]: Deceased. Brother to Laura Gilvers.

History - From the Milky Way galaxy, alternate universe. Son of Hal Gilvers, the "Hero of Bright Future."

Roderick Jaben [Rod-rik Jay-bun]: (Title—Elder) A council member at Lighthouse Station, Sanctuary system.

History - From Aterria, Aurora galaxy, alternate universe.

Royne, Hobbes [Hobs Royn]: (Title—Professor) Telestic and educator at the Ochroleucum.

History - From Iltovar, Aurora galaxy, alternate universe.

Richlant, Kalista [Ka-lis-ta Rich-lunt]: (Title—Master) Telestic and educator at the Ochroleucum.

History - From Stelastipol, Aurora galaxy, alternate universe.

Rundican, Gorbal [Gor-bul Run-di-cun]: (Title—Master) Telestic and educator at the Ochroleucum.

History - From Aterria, Aurora galaxy, alternate universe. Seventy-third degree, Grand Society of Telestics.

Seledris, Alvinor [Al-vi-nor Se-led-rys]: (Rank—Adjutant) Telestry governor of the planet Solas.

History - From Colecanth, Aurora galaxy, alternate universe. Twenty-second degree, Grand Society of Telestics. Suspected ties to the Brotherhood.

Shannon Logan [Shan-uhn Loh-guhn]: One of Nate's companions, holder of the pink Amulet. Thought to be an Odd.

History - From the Milky Way galaxy, alternate universe. Daughter of Jim Logan. Co-owner of Adamant.

Energematrice6 Specialization - Pyric;

Talent - Unknown.

Shawna Logan [Shaw-nuh Loh-guhn]: One of Nate's companions, holder of the deep green Amulet. Thought to be an Odd.

History - From the Milky Way galaxy, alternate universe. Daughter of Jim Logan. Co-owner of Adamant.

Energematrice6 Specialization - Anima;

Talent - Flora and growing things.

Sheskin, Albadora [Al-ba-doh-ruh Shes-kyn]: (Title—Professor) Telestic and educator at the Ochroleucum.

History - From Restomere, Aurora galaxy, alternate universe.

Siever 'The Wildman' Radding [See-vur Ra-ding]: (Rank—Telestic, Excommunicated): Famous/Infamous prophet, wanderer, and ne'er-do-well. Excommunicated from the Telestry three times and eventually murdered. Known to be an Odd.

History - From Earth, the Milky Way galaxy, alternate universe. Passenger on Hope One with Paul Casisia during the Escape.

Energematrice6 Specialization - Aqueous;

Talent - Unknown.

Stratograve Rectis: See Rectis, Genghis

Tasia Amadea: See Anastasia 'Tasia' Amadea

Teron Galton [Teh-rawn Gawl-tun]: Paul Casisia's closest protege and confidant after his children's imprisonment. Later, the "Keeper of the Mysteries," Jon and Rachel's adopted brother. Known to be an Odd.

History - From Earth, the Milky Way galaxy, alternate universe. Passenger on Hope One with Paul Casisia during the Escape.

Energematrice6 Specialization - Pyric;

Talent - Unknown.

Travis Retton [Trah-vys Ret-tuhn]: One of Nate's companions, holder of the turquoise Amulet. Thought to be an Odd.

History - From the Milky Way galaxy, alternate universe. Son of George Retton, inventor of the Retton drive.

Energematrice6 Specialization - Ionic;

Talent - Unknown.

Tyler 'Tye' Wrighten [Tye-luhr 'Tye' Rye-tun]: One of Nate's companions, holder of the light blue Amulet. Known to be an Odd.

History - Unknown. Grew up on the streets of Aterria, Aurora galaxy. May have been a victim of piracy.

Energematrice6 Specialization - Ionic;
Talent - Electrical Manipulation.

Wildman: See Siever 'The Wildman' Radding

Yelena Seiver [Yuh-lay-nuh See-vur]: (Title—Elder) A council member at Lighthouse Station, Sanctuary system.

History - Born to the Gyps, Aurora galaxy, alternate universe.

Yimakh [Yee-mack]: A powerful Shade who manipulated Lastis Ralond and Carl Winton into creating the chain of events that led to the entropic decay being entangled with the human use of Energematrice6.

Glossary

Abyss [Uh-bis]: An unusually starless region of space in which Brightstar is found. Also home to the presence known as the Watcher.

Adamant [Ad-uh-mant]: A vessel belonging to the Logans. Originated in the Milky Way galaxy.

Amasthena [Ah-moss-they-nuh]: "The light in the darkness." The subject of a prophecy made in the Milky Way galaxy that appears to refer to the same person as the prophecies of the Brightstar.

Amulet [Am-you-let]: An artifact, usually worn around the neck, that changes the way Energematrice6 is wielded, usually by amplification. Most artifacts in the Aurora galaxy and all artifacts considered Amulets proper were created by Paul Casisia.

Anima: See Energematrice6

Aqueous: See Energematrice6

Artifact [Ar-tuh-fakt]: An object that has been entangled with Energematrice6 in such a way that it has specialized effects on the world around it or on the energy fields themselves.

Aterria [Uh-ter-ree-uh]: The planet on which the settlers in Aurora galaxy first landed after the Escape. Now home to Casisia City and the center of power of the Telestry.

Aurora [Uh-row-ruh]: The galaxy refugees fled to in the distant past after the Escape from Earth.

Behemoth [Buh-hee-moth]: The largest wreckage in orbit around Aterria; the remains of a world ship from the Dominion War.

Betrayal [Bee-tray-yul]: The time during human history when Lastis Ralond attempted to harness the power of Energematrice6 to dominate the human race and unintentionally caused it to be entangled with thermodynamic decay.

Bounty [Bown-tee]: A neutral system (with a planet of the same name) in the Aurora galaxy.

Bridewell [Bryd-wehl]: A prison, primarily for those not gifted with Energematrice6 ability, on Solas.

Casisia City [Kas-is-ee-uh Si-tee]: The city that is both the capital of Aterria, humanity's oldest world in the Aurora galaxy, and the seat of power for the Telestry.

Changed [Cheynjd]: A being that has been overtaken by a Shade and physically altered in a monstrous fashion.

Diaspora [Dahy-as-pohr-uh]: A time when Humanity spread out from the Aurora galaxy to colonize other galaxies.

Dominion [Doh-min-yun]: The primary power in the Aurora galaxy. Capital: Panoptica.

Earth's Revenge [Urthz Ree-venj]: A vessel belonging to Travis Retton. Originated in the Milky way.

Energematrice6 [En-er-gem-uh-tris Six]: The power that was used to create the universe to which Nate is transported. Energematrice6 underlies and can be used to manipulate both matter and space. It is broken into six hexaparts, each of which affects a different aspect of the universe and reality. Energematrice6 can be manipulated directly by humans because of the chain of events recorded in the Betrayal and the Plague.

Anima [A-ni-muh]: The hexapart of Energematrice6 that affects living things. Uses include healing and enhancing plant growth. *(Often appears green.)*

Aqueous [Ah-kwee-us]: The hexapart of Energematrice6 that affects fluid dynamics and physics as well as thoughts and mental faculty. Uses include telekinesis, alteration of physics, and psionics—the ability to manipulate humans mentally. *(Often appears blue.)*

Geotic [Gee-ah-tik]: The hexapart of Energematrice6 that deals directly with matter, particularly solid matter. Uses include mechanical manipulation and physical defense. *(Often Appears brown.)*

Ionic [Eye-on-ik]: The hexapart of Energematrice6 that affects electricity and atomic bonding forces. Uses include manipulation of electrical systems and electromagnetic interference. *(Often appears white or blue-white.)*

Nephelic [Ne-fil-ik]: The hexapart of Energematrice6 that affects connections and chaotic systems. Uses include stealth and command. *(Often appears gray.)*

Pyric [Pi-rik]: The hexapart of Energematrice6 that deals directly with energy in its purest forms. Uses include introducing or directly manipulating the energy in a system. *(Often appears red)*

Emulging [E-muhl-jing]: Causing a person to use Energematrice6 against their will, pushing them into entropic shock and killing them, usually slowly.

Energematrist [En-er-gem-uh-trist]: A person who is able to directly manipulate Energematrice6.

Entropy [En-truh-pee]: Originally a thermodynamic term denoting energy loss. Later appropriated to denote the negative energy created by human use of Energematrice6.

Escape [Es-kayp]: The period in human history when Paul Casisia and his expedition fled earth to escape Lastis Ralond and the control of the Shades.

Exsect [Ex-sekt]: Split-pupiled eyes. Thought by many at the Telestry to denote great potential power.

Extropy [Ex-truh-pee]: Slang. Externalized negative energy.

Flerovium [Fluh-row-vee-um]: The element with the atomic number 114. Highly unstable. Used for fuel by some vessels from the Milky Way.

Gamin [Ga-min]: A homeless child; pathetic urchin

Geotic: See Energematrice6

Great Schemic [Grayt Ske-mik]: A special schemic, used by Paul Casisia, and Teron Galton. See Schemic for more information.

Hexapart [Hex-uh-pahrt]: See Energematrice6

Ionic: See Energematrice6

Lighthouse Station [Lyte-hows Stay-shun]: The space station in orbit around the planet Sanctuary. The only known space station with artificial gravity.

Malak [Mah-lahk]: The vessel used by Teron Galton, Keeper of the Mysteries.

Milky Way [Mill-kee Way]: The galaxy of humanity's birth. Home to the planet Earth, both in Nate's home universe and the one he is transported to.

Navetta [Naw-ve-tuh]: A crystal that contains a record of the life of the person who left it behind—the mortal remains of a human from the universe to which Nate is transported.

Nephelic: See Energematrice6

Nosufer [No-soo-fur]: A non-human being, presumably originating in the Milky Way galaxy. Nosufers' bodies are composed of a crystalline matrix that gives them the ability to control Energematrice6, which they drain from the world around them instead of creating internally.

Ocharist [Aw-kuh-rist]: A Telestry vessel used by Drake Loriden; the vessel that discovered Nate.

Ochroleucum [Aw-kruh-loo-kum]: The Telestry's academy for Energematrice6 at Aterria.

Odd [Awd]: A person who ages at an extremely slow rate in the Aurora galaxy. Also normally characterized by high Energematrice6 ability.

Panoptica [Pan-awp-ti-cuh]: Capital and seat of power for the Dominion.

Plague [Playgh]: An event during the Betrayal that bestowed humanity with the ability to use Energematrice6 directly instead of through machine intermediaries.

Polestar [Pohl-Stahr]: Dominion space station in orbit around Aterria. Seat of governance.

Pyric: See Energematrice6

Rechemacula [Rek-eh-mok-you-luh]: A tattoo-like skin

modification that is intended to reduce the likelihood of Entropic shock. Originally introduced by Paul Casisia.

Regalians [Reh-gall-ee-uns]: A polity that was once at war with the Telestry. Now defunct.

Regency [Ree-gen-cee]: A known polity in the Aurora galaxy.

Resolute [Re-zo-loot]: A vessel from the Milky Way, owned by Laura Gilvers and her family, then taken by the Changed.

Retton Drive [Ret-tuhn Drive]: The method of projecting Energematrice6 that allows vessels from the Milky Way to move through interstellar space very rapidly. Also provides an inertial damping effect.

Sanctuary [Sank-choo-er-ee]: A star system surrounded by the Vale of Mysteries (or its major planet).

Schemic [Skee-mik]: A pattern that both controls and aids in the use of Energematrice6.

Shade [Shayd]: An inhabitant of the Twilight; may refer to a being that has overcome a human in order to exert control and create a Changed.

Sixer [Sick-ser]: Slang term. *See Energematrist.*

Sol [Sawl]: The star of humanity's home solar system; The Sun.

Solas [Sah-luhs]: A planet in the Aurora galaxy whose star system shares the same name.

Society of Telestics [Sow-sigh-i-tee of Teh-less-tiks]: An organization started by Paul Casisia to regulate the ethical use of Energematrice6. Precursor to the Telestry.

Telestic [Te-les-tik]: A full member and agent of the Telestry. Only those deemed the most powerful Energematrists are eligible for this status.

Telestry [Te-les-tree]: An organization of Energematrists, based on Aterria, originally dedicated to the ethical use of Energematrice6.

Tenets [Teh-nets]: Rules or laws instituted and passed down by Paul Casisia. Held as sacred by the Telestry.

The Order [The Or-dur]: An organization dedicated to the extirpation of Energematrice6 ability and the removal of humanity's influence from Energematrice6.

Twilight [Twy-lyt]: An alternate realm or dimension, inhabited by the Shades.

Vale of Mysteries [Vayl of Mis-ter-eez]: A strange, almost unimaginably large and nearly impenetrable cloud of dust surrounding the Sanctuary system and likely many others.

Vampyr [Vam-pyr]: See Nosufer

Watcher [Wah-chur]: A being or force that has focused its attention on the Abyss and those that enter it.

Against the Odds
The Epimyth - Book 3

Adamant charged like a mother grizzly to the rescue of her captured cubs. They broke atmosphere at a speed that had Andrew and Shannon Logan literally white-knuckling the arms of their control stations. Their sister Shawna, at the helm, was all focus, her gaze locked on her instruments as they streaked toward the ground so fast that a simple surrender to gravity would have been a relief.

Behind them, Nate--whom many called Brightstar--only had a tiny sliver of his attention on the ground ahead and below. Mostly, his focus was in an entirely different realm--the energy fields that underlay the world. If he registered their terrible speed and the seemingly inevitable collision with the planet below, he trusted his friends implicitly, and Shawna was the best of them at the helm. His responsibility was to defend against the possibility of an Energematrice6 attack coming for them at light speed from the planet's surface.

When the Changed destroyer awaiting them on the surface of Solas below had crashed nearly a month before, Adamant only survived the debris thrown up by its impact due to the same sort of Energematrice6 shield Nate was currently maintaining around them. Now what he was concerned about was that the destroyer might still have functional weapon systems, or that the enemy might have gained control of the planet's native defenses, whatever they were. Once Adamant was on the ground, space defenses would be unable to fire on them, but until then Lightmaker only knew what might come up out of the gravity well and try to vaporize them.

Unlike the last time he held such a shield, most of Nate's friends were with him now, sharing the burden. Even if the enemy vessel still had the capability to strike at them, together they could hold a shield against many times the firepower a single destroyer could throw. They had done exactly that on their insane run through the enemy's entire armada a month before. Then, Nate had been alone, maintaining the shield on his own. Until their second battle with the enemy armada in the Abyss, sharing the shield in such a way was a feat none of them had known was possible. It was yet another lesson Nate had taught them by simply doing what seemed instinctively right to him, breaking all the bounds of traditional understanding. Now, however, as the seconds then minutes ticked by, no wave of energy reached up from the ground to smite them.

The curvature of the planet was starting to disappear beyond the edge of the bridge's great window and they could actually see the tiny dot of the city below when Rachel Casisia snorted aloud, "Well, so much for a hot landing. Do you think the Telestics were able to..."

She was cut off by a voice coming through the bridge speaker system, "Adamant? Is that Adamant?? What are you DOING? They'll SEE you."

They all looked at each other in surprise, their attention pulled partially away from the shield they were maintaining, and Nate saw Shawna doing something on her console that immediately started the ship rotating until the great bridge window was pointed toward the sky instead of the ground. It was a bit earlier than she had planned, Nate could tell, but he thought it was probably the right move.

After a moment, Andrew spoke, "Is this Solas control? We've come to help. Can you elaborate?"

The snort that came back to him was somewhere between exasperated and derisive, "You're a bit late for that. Best just get outta here while you can. We've had two other vessels sneak out in the last week. So far They've left us alone here... mostly. Now, though... There's no way they can miss you. That re-entry has'ta be visible to half the hemisphere."

Andrew looked around at Nate ruefully. "So what now?"

Nate frowned and shook his head, thinking. "Well, we're not leaving. That's for sure." He glanced over at Shawna, "You can probably ease up on the landing... as much as you can."

She grunted in response and the inertial dampening that came along with Adamant's deep space Retton drive finally cut out, deceleration pressing them all back into their seats as if with a giant hand, trying to crush them. Further speech was impossible, and they all simply endured the rest of the descent.

When the pressure finally eased and motion stopped, they breathed a collective sigh.

Flipping his Universal Positioning Tool back and forth in his fingers, Keevan Raddink grinned, "We made it down anyway."

Before any of them could reply, Solas control's voice came back over the bridge's comm system, "Adamant, you ought'ta know you're gonna have... guests. There are a lotta people tryin' to get off the planet any way they can..."

As if to illustrate the point, Andrew gestured toward the main window where they could already see people running toward them across the spaceport's reinforced concrete landing field. He frowned, "That doesn't seem good."

Nate smiled grimly, "It certainly tells us something about what's going on down here. I think maybe we'd better go meet them."

Andrew's sister Shannon gave him a sharp look, as did Rachel Casisia. Rachel said, "You really think that's safe?"

Amy Miles laughed from her seat next to Travis Retton, "Since Travis and I crash-landed, we've rocketed right through a Changed flotilla head first, spent a week leading them into the middle of the most dangerous hole in space anybody's ever seen, then run back into the middle of them, all while the Watcher who made that hole dangerous was trying to crawl into our heads. I mean, that almost makes flying through the middle of the densest cloud of dust ever seen in space to escape again seem pretty tame in comparison. You really think talking to a few scared groundies is going to stop him?"

Tyler "Tye" Wrighten snorted half in amusement and half in disgust, "At least they don't have an airlock to throw him out of down here. You should have seen what happened on Lighthouse Station." Tye smirked as Rachel's frown darkened and her brother Jon put a restraining hand on her arm.

"Exactly." Rachel gazed flatly at Nate.

Nate returned her glare with a crooked grin, "I'm not here to be safe. Surely that's obvious by now. Let's get moving." He suited words to action by unfastening the restraints that held him in his seat and rising to lead the way out of Adamant's bridge and down the corridor toward the airlock.

As usual when Adamant was landed, the vessel remained suspended on an invisible cushion of force. When Nate opened the airlock and started extending the ship's ramp to the ground, he found the crowd below practically ready to storm the ship, reaching to catch the ramp even before it hit the ground. A few eyed the hovering vessel with wonder or trepidation, but most seemed desperate to board, presumably to escape Solas.

As the ramp dropped, Nate stepped to the open outer door of the ship's airlock and stared out over the gathered throng. Except for those under the ramp and out of view, the crowd actually hesitated when they saw Nate's face. One of them called out, "Oy, in'at the Brightstar?"

Nate had known that his time spent speaking in the conclaves at Bounty City and later Solas had given him some measure of fame, especially after Adjutant Seledris was deposed, but these people had been frantic just a moment ago. Did he really have that much influence?

A moment later, the question became moot. Across from Adamant, between two other parked vessels, three grotesque, hulking figures appeared. In the daylight, at a distance, the Changed were somehow even more hideous and disfigured than Nate remembered from when he faced the one that attacked them before. Far worse than the sight of them was the sense of dread that rolled across the field like a physical shockwave. Nate actually watched the crowd shudder as it curled over them and pressed them down. When it reached him, he actually gasped aloud, echoed by his friends. Despair assaulted him, instantly recalling the most pressing darkness he had ever fought to the forefront of his consciousness.

When Nate first met Andrew, Shannon and Shawna Logan, they had found Adamant's sister ship, Resolute, crashed inside the Behemoth, the giant hulk of a world ship, long abandoned above the planet Aterria. At that time, he'd fought a Changed in the vacuum of space, deep in the bowels of the crashed Resolute. That fight had been eerie and dreadful, but it had never occurred to Nate at the time that his dread might have been caused directly by the Changed itself. Now, the psychological assault that blasted everyone in range as they moved into position was unmistakable.

One by one, Nate's encounters with the Enemy played back through his head, beginning at Resolute, snapping to Sanctuary, where he had seen Elder Rebus's eyes grow vertical slits and the Enemy had spoken to him, then moving to Adjutant Seledris here on Solas and finally playing back through the agonizing ordeal they had endured on their trip into the Abyss. Simultaneously, Nate felt his other world and his real, damaged self attempting to forcibly intrude on him once more.

IIe gritted his teeth as it pulled him under for a long moment and his consciousness drowned in horror. Then, through the darkness, he caught a hint of the light that he had encountered in that darkest moment when he thought he had failed his friends. It was only a memory, but it was enough. Grinding his teeth, Nate pulled himself into the present. Despair still pressed down on him so hard that all he could do was focus on what must be their next objective--the Changed still lurching toward Adamant.

In the atmosphere of a planet, without the intervening environment suit and the unreality of null-gravity, these Changed were somehow an even more obvious perversion of what a human should be. Their features were distorted and swollen, as if normal human beings had been inflated with compressed air until their features were twice as massive as they should have been, but not evenly or well. Bulbous noses and jowls hung from bloated heads stuck onto stumpy necks. Slit-pupiled eyes bugged from sockets that were too small to hold them, their whites blood red. The way each Changed had been deformed was different, as if whatever had filled up their bodies had simply been pumped in and allowed to derange their flesh however it would.

They were moving startlingly fast for such misshapen creatures, lumbering across the field toward the back of the now-silent crowd that had gathered around Adamant. A few of the people in their path glanced around, warned by some sound or sense. Their panic was instant, spreading rapidly as those around them realized something had caught their attention and turned to look themselves.

Nate let out a muffled imprecation under his breath and immediately reached for Energematrice6. It came almost instantaneously now, after the practice of the past few months. His senses opened to the fields and he "saw" the world around him in shocking color and detail. Bands of energy flowed around every material object he could sense. The colors were vivid in ways he had never experienced before, and he always thought he could see colors that had no place in the visual spectrum, though his brain didn't seem to want to interpret them properly. Even in circumstances like this, it never failed to amaze him how much information he could gather on the world all at once through the fields.

He could tell exactly how fast the Changed were moving and how quickly they would reach the back of the crowd, now flowing away to spill around Adamant, fleeing from the horrors that threatened them. Nate caught a flash of a Changed reaching out to grasp one of the slower members of the crowd and fling him to the ground, but no. The monsters were still at least a few seconds away. Was he imagining things now? He shook his head and focused, forming a shield like the one he'd used to protect

Adamant from the energy discharges of the Changed fleet and the strange chunks of matter they created. Nate pushed the shield outward and back to surround his friends, anchoring it to himself, even though it was centered behind him.

"Stay behind me." Nate called over his shoulder.

Turning back to the crowd, Nate saw the Changed finally reach its rearmost rank and the scene he'd caught what he thought was an imaginary glimpse of a moment before, of the Changed reaching out to slam a man to the ground, played itself out in reality.

The act was brutal enough to be shocking, but the real shock was the fact that he'd seen it before it happened. Had that been precognition? Nothing like it had ever happened to him before. He'd had occasional moments when his uncooperative, inaccessible memory crystallized and he saw his situation and his future with startling clarity before everything went fuzzy, leaving him wondering what he'd ever been so certain about. This was different...but there was no time to ponder it.

One member of the crowd rebounded off Nate's shield, having tried to rush the ramp, obviously thinking his momentum and size would be enough to force him past what were, after all, only children. Then Nate was pushing forward bodily through the crowd, using his shield to make a path through the press as the Changed grabbed two more screaming people, hurling them brutally across the concrete.

Most of Nate's friends followed him, though he saw Shawna hanging back at Adamant's ramp, already fending off one attempted boarder with her own version of his Energematrice6 shield and a truly ferocious scowl. It was just as well she'd stayed behind. Her agoraphobia wouldn't do her any favors here.

As they moved through the crowd, Nate's friends began to spread out, moving out from under his shield. A single glance back showed him that they were all surrounded by their own mostly-transparent bubbles of force and he relaxed, withdrawing his shield until it rested close around him. The larger it was, the more mental focus it took for him to maintain it, and withdrawing it until it surrounded only his body allowed him to give that much more attention to the monsters before him.

The crowd had managed to clear the way between Nate's party and the Changed, fleeing to either side and around Adamant, most never looking back. As Nate watched, the middle Changed, the only one of the three that had an arm ending in a giant weapon, smashed the end of its "gun" into a woman's head, dropping her to the pavement. The field was littered with the mostly-still forms of those too slow or unlucky to dodge the monsters, scattered behind them in gruesome trails.

The creatures themselves had spread out somewhat as they pursued the fleeing crowd and were now facing Nate and the others, their twisted forms still.

"Who arrrrrhhe hhyyou?" The voice was gutteral and deep, as if echoing from inside some strange cavern instead of coming from a living creature's throat. Of the three monsters, it was the middle one that had spoken, its gaze fixed on Nate through eyes that were unable to quite focus because of its bloated face.

Nate cocked his head, surprised. The other monster he faced never tried to speak, though now that he thought about it, the vacuum had made that impossible even if it wanted to do so.

"I'm Nate." He turned his gaze to each of the monstrosities in turn, then glanced to either side at his friends. Most of them seemed tense but calm, and their shields were solid. When he first grasped Energematrice6, habit had led him to instinctively reach through the Sigil of Mysteries, the Amulet given to him by Teron Galton, the Keeper of the Mysteries. The Sigil amplified any Energematrice6 use that flowed through it, as did the Amulets held by Nate's friends. Their amulets had been found on Hope One, the vessel that originally brought humanity to the Aurora galaxy, later used by Paul Casisia as a headquarters and repository when he began creating Energematrice6 artifacts.

Nate could tell his friends were using their Amulets as well. They were all glowing from their places around his friends' necks. He imagined his own was just as bright.

"Hhnnnnayte. Hhyyou shhhould not hhhhave come hhyyeere." The monster's gloating certainty made Nate grit his teeth. Either the creatures had sized Nate and his friends up to their satisfaction or the words had acted as some kind of signal, because two of the three creatures charged while the third raised the weapon that made up the end of its arm.

Then the weapon was belching a stream of red energy that must have had both an Energematrice6 and a mundane component. Still striding purposefully forward, Nate caught a glimpse of the shimmering air around the plume of plasma, then the energy impacted his shield.

The effect was nothing like he expected. When Nate and the others had fought their way through the enemy armada, both leaving Solas and in the Abyss itself, the power of the enemy's attacks depleted his shield at a rate that left him scrambling to re-energize or even, at times, completely rebuild them. Compared to those tremendous blows, this attack was like being hit with a feather. The shield he had prepared to receive the attack was so much more powerful than the force the enemy exerted against it, he didn't even register the hit, except as a physical blow that literally knocked him onto his butt, leaving him blinking in surprise.

Nate started to stand up, but then the secondary effects of the hit reached him. It was as if the air had caught fire, and Nate realized he hadn't thought to protect his air supply at all. Muttering a curse under his breath, Nate reached back down to put his hand against the concrete and concentrated, creating a blast of fresh air around him while adding an air-retention layer to his shield.

As he picked up his hand, he felt the prickling of the Rechemacula on his neck and shoulder, telling him that it was trying to protect him from overusing Energematrice6. Unlike his friends and other Energematrists, any time Nate drew on that power, he externalized the resulting negative entropic energy his efforts generated. For most, that energy simply escaped into their bodies. His body rejected the energy, pushing it into the environment around him instead. Rising again, Nate noted the telltale handprint in the concrete left behind by his "extropy," but it was only a passing glimpse.

Nate pushed himself back to a standing position, watching the smirk slide from the face of the monster in front of him as it realized how badly its attack had failed. Another massive blast of plasma and raw power followed almost instantly, but Nate was ready this time and the comparatively small kinetic portion of the blast, which had knocked him down before, was redirected around him with the rest of the blast wave.

Nate started to step forward, but looking down he realized that the concrete in front of him was so hot it was actually glowing. Nate snorted. Dealing with this kind of energy on a planet's surface was way more complicated than fighting in space.

From his left, Nate heard Andrew call, "Hey Nate, what should we do with this thing?" Nate glanced over toward Andrew to see Travis hunched over in front of the monster, his hands on his head as it pummeled his shield from above as if it were trying to drive him into the ground like a human fence post while Andrew blasted its shield with gray energy. Keevan, Tye and Amy were spaced around the creature in a half circle, each doing something different with Energematrice6, presumably attempting to overcome it.

"For starters, try not to get killed," Nate called back, glancing to his right to see Jon flying across the parking lot to land in a heap while Rachel and Shannon lashed out at the creature on that side with their own blasts of energy. "Just keep them busy."

A tremendous wave of heat and electricity washed over them, and Nate looked back up to see one of the space vessels behind the Changed engulfed in flames, toppling away from them as Tye stared at it, his mouth gaping.

The others had stopped to stare at Tye and Nate called out, "And try not to destroy anything important." Lightmaker knew that between them all the amount of energy they had to draw on was so vast they could easily rip the city apart.

"D'yeh want us to kill it?" The question came from Keevan this time, but Nate's gaze was again fixed on the creature in front of him, and he was too busy preparing an attack of his own to answer.

A moment later, Shannon's holler alleviated his need to do so. "What if the Shade escapes? We need Nate."

There was some sort of response, but Nate was finally ready and he unleashed a blast of his own toward the target in front of him. As before, the energy sparkled off some sort of shield surrounding the creature for a long moment, but Nate had been prepared and with the aid of his Amulet, the effort required to sustain the burst was minor. Then, the monster screeched its torment as the power eroded its shield and pulsed into its body, making it writhe in uncontrollable agony.

Nate's instinct was to do exactly as he'd done aboard Resolute and destroy the creatures one by one, but as he raised his hand in preparation for letting loose another blast of power, the creature turned its head up from the ground toward him. Nate wasn't exactly sure what clue he caught, whether it was something in the creature's eyes or its body language, but it made him hesitate. He muttered an imprecation and looked down at the ground in front of him, which was doubtless still far too hot to walk on. After a moment's thought, he blanketed the ground in a thin layer of power, some strange combination of blue and gray that he knew would work for the purpose.

Then he was walking forward toward the monster that still lay a hundred feet in front of him. A deep, low moan emanated from it, and as Nate drew near, the creature turned weakly half on its side to look up and sideways at him.

Those eyes were full of pain, but without a trace of the rage or hatred they'd held barely a moment before. "Khill meeeee," it rasped in a voice that, unlike its previous incarnation, could almost have been human. Surprised, Nate inhaled sharply, realizing what he was actually looking at. He had disrupted the shade's hold on the body. That was a human being talking to him.

Then the creature roared and whatever Nate had seen in its eyes was gone as fast as it had appeared. The massive body flipped over, swinging its gun arm in a huge arc to smack into Nate's head.

If Nate hadn't incorporated a small amount of blue Energematrice6 into his shield to damp kinetic effects, the blow would have crushed him to paste. As it was, his body shuddered with the impact, but a sympathetic wave of power blasted out of Nate's shield and back up the creature's arm to send it rolling across the concrete.

Nate followed, wondering how he could kill the monster in good conscience if there was a person still alive inside it. Could there be some other way?

Nate stared down at the creature once more. Now, it was struggling to untangle its limbs while simultaneously trying to rise once again. There were times when Nate wished he had more actual training and experience using Energematrice6. Often, his natural understanding of patterns led him to do things that most Energematrists would have said were impossible. His use of Energematrice6 was based on an instinctive understanding of how the energy field worked. It was as if the autism he battled in that other world, a world which now felt more like a nightmare than reality, supercharged his abilities here. There were times like this one, though, when he would have given almost anything to have spent the same years of study and experimentation that some of his friends had in learning to use their own power.

About the Author

Jared N. Michaud is a devoted fiction writer driven by a passion for writing that began before he reached age seven. Influenced by literary giants like C.S. Lewis and Orson Scott Card, he discovered the power of storytelling, and at twelve he began crafting his first novel.

Today, Jared writes from a little house in a little town in Wyoming, where he lives with his wife and seven children. As a Christian with a deep love for the truth and appreciation for the values that underlie Western civilization, he endeavors to create myths that will inspire future generations.

© 2023 - Rachel Collins Photography LLC